Sheri Shields

Venin

Abyss

ISBN: 978-1-7333373-0-4 (Paperback)
ISBN: 978-1-7333373-1-1 (Hardcover)

Any references to historical events, real people, or real places are used fictitiously. Names, characters, and places are products of the author's imagination.

Front cover image by Sherika Shields
Book design by Sherika Shields
Edited by Stephanie Cohen

First printing edition 2019

www.VeninAbyss.com

ACKNOWLEDGMENTS

Blake Shields- Thank you for pushing me and encouraging me in this process. You've helped me focus in many ways, including sitting back and taking the time to really think before making important decisions!

Sylvester Williams- Dad, you have been a fan since day one before I entered into the endeavor of adapting my story into a novel. Thanks for raising me, for all of your support and for the willing phone calls about the storyline.

Josephine Nybo Ploug Hassø- Thank you for helping me become a better writer. You have helped me tremendously in your zeal and support. You have given advice that ultimately catapulted me into writing this story in its completion. I appreciate your critique and guidance!

SPECIAL THANKS

Venin Abyss started off as a YouTube machinima series I began making when I was only a teenager. I am extremely grateful for the following people: Øystein Schiefloe Kanestrøm, Ross Workman, Kyra Tiffany W., Alex Lew, Matthew, Demi Dunn, Christian Sekhanan, Kayla Derocher, Valentina Pătrună, Jose Arturo Palos, Nicolas Bill, Corinne Mene and many others. These people are wonderful, talented voice actors who helped make my characters truly come alive in the series. Their gift inspired my writing and influenced how the story developed. I could not thank you enough for sharing your talent.

Table of Contents

Prologue

*M*y eyes were locked on the horizon, observing the glory of the beautiful warm colors through my bedroom window. I tried to fully take in this moment. The heavens turned into a wonderful canvas as the warm hues swelled across the sky, just before the darkness came. Soon this composition would dissolve forever, as no two sunsets were exactly the same.

The ancient Egyptians deemed the west to be a symbol of death, and it was the reason most of their burial grounds were located west of the Nile River. They believed that the sun would be born on the eastern side of the horizon every morning, then it would die each night when it set to the west. I understood this symbolism as I continued to watch. The colors slowly started to lose their vibrancy, merging, as the day finally ended.

The darkness swiftly poured into my room and began to swallow me whole; it crawled over my bare feet, up my legs, ascending my chest and finally engulfing my face. I would have liked to believe I was not afraid of the dark, but whenever night fell, I felt an uncontrollable chill slither down my spine; it seemed to be a message, a warning. I discerned a feeling that the darkness was not just the absence of light, but an entire, unseen entity within itself. My hopes were set on the light that would inevitably, and soon, return.

I was sitting alone in my house, waiting for my company for the evening; they were about half an hour late. I sighed and impatiently checked the clock resting on my carefully crafted end table, made of the rarest African blackwood. I struggled to make out the time, as my eyes still hadn't adjusted to the change. Being alone in the silent darkness made me start to think about my life—my fortunate situation that came from an unfortunate past I barely remembered.

Anxiety brewed inside of me, and a sharp pain traveled through my chest. Following this pain was a heaviness that seemed to sink me further down into my chair. It was a burden too big for me, a yoke I could not bear. My legs grew numb, so I rose from the chair and leaned against the open window, looking out to my private beach. As the clouds swiftly moved across the sky, the glow of the moon and stars were revealed, giving me just an ounce of what I thought was peace.

I listened to the familiar sound of the waves crashing

onto the shore and felt the warm summer night breeze flow through my hair. Taking in a few deep breaths, I inhaled the refreshing seawater air. My breathing began to slow to match the rhythm of the waves as I shut my eyes. This routine calmed my nerves, and the painful weight on my chest started to wear off. Though I was feeling better, the uncomfortable feeling was still there. I began to reflect on what I had been so desperately trying to avoid, the mystery of the man who rendered me an orphaned boy: my father.

His name was Gabriel. The night he passed away was one I would never forget. The night of his death was etched in my mind and yet, I could not even recall his face. Was there a reason why—of all people—my father had to be the subject of this inconvenient gap in my memory? The dissolution of his countenance had eaten at my core ever since. My father, like I, did not like to take pictures. As impossible as it seemed, I wasn't even able to find a single photograph of him. It was as if he had never existed.

That night, the woman who was babysitting me while my father was away answered a knock at the door. A few hours later, I distinctly remembered strangers storming into our home and taking me away. I was not sure where I was going, but I was terrified.

As a lost and confused three-year-old boy, I grew up in foster group homes, mainly trying to discover pieces of my past that would help me put a face to the only family member I'd ever known—my mother had passed away during my birth. On the subject of the cause of my father's death, what I found left much to the imagination. He had suffered an undetermined trauma, but they said it was a heart attack that actually killed him. Vague information is all I managed to rummage up. My life quickly cascaded into a stranger-consumed existence that provided little to no information about my father. In consequence, I felt like my identity was incomplete, shattered like a broken vase that I could never truly mend.

As a kid, I suffered greatly from insomnia and paranoia that stemmed from nightmares I started to experience frequently. The others called me crazy when I would tell them what I would see in these dark visions. I soon learned to keep all of those stories to myself.

Growing out of my awkward phase, the others in the group home began to deem me the pretty boy, but I was still very much an outcast—mainly by my own choice, I suppose. Our priorities were vastly different; I wanted to better myself, while most of them, unfortunately, led troublemaker lifestyles. I spent my days working myself to the bone, at one point juggling three jobs. I wanted to make sure that when my time was up, I was ready to take on the world.

I was never adopted, so I eventually aged out of the foster care system at the age of eighteen. It was then that I received an extremely generous amount of money—seven figures— claiming to be my inheritance. No one could give me answers as to where the money had come from, seeing as my father and I had lived in relatively mediocre conditions before his passing. I was skeptical of the news of this sudden wealth, but sure enough, it was specified for me: Adrien Seth Reed, of the same birth date as my own, born in the same hospital and the same city. There was no denying that it was mine.

Using the money that I had already saved up on my own, I donated half of it to the foster care system and then the other half to local homeless shelters. Choosing to spend my time volunteering at the shelters, I was able to help many of the guys I grew up with that had unfortunately ended up there. I quit all of my jobs and invested chunks of my inheritance money into local businesses, so I could spend even more time volunteering while I continued to grow my wealth.

Wanting a permanent place to call home, I purchased a brand-new house in Wellfleet, Massachusetts, located off the shore of Cape Cod. The location on the beach was somewhat of a safe haven for me, but I was still vexed with insomnia that had plagued me for as long as I could remember. The comforts of my new home weren't suitable enough to put a stop to my nightmares as I had, for some reason, thought they would.

A man with extremely pale skin, red eyes, white hair and a face slightly obstructed by a black woolen scarf was always the primary subject of my nightmares. My first nightmare of this strange man occurred the night of my father's death, just moments before I was taken away. The man seemed to be an illusion; he disappeared without a trace before the others arrived.

The nightmares came almost every night and displayed no sign of ending. I would sometimes spend hours sketching images of this mystery man. The drawings would gather in my nightstand, never to see the light of day again, as the finished images absolutely terrified me. I didn't know whether he was a figment of my imagination or something entirely different. Every time I woke from my sleep, the presence of this man was nurtured, as he seemed to become even more intertwined within my real world.

There was only one thing that came close to overcoming my troubles: Jenna McBrayer. The love I had for her helped with my worries, insomnia, fears and anxiety when I was with her. For those moments, I mostly forgot about the mysterious, white-haired man and the twinge of the mystery my father left behind. It was only when I was with her that I felt I could temporarily overlook my obsession with the past and create an overlaying existence with ease. However, there was still a hole that needed to be filled, something that was missing.

Chapter 1

"You are the light of the world. A town built on a hill cannot be hidden."

Matthew 5:14

*A*drien struggled to focus on the picture consuming the television screen before him. His mind fought against him, not wanting to direct his attention to something mundane while someone truly breathtaking sat next to him. He shifted his weight slightly and let his gaze finally slip away from the television and onto her. Jenna was intently focused on the screen and recited the entire dialogue word for word under her breath to her favorite movie. They were watching an old 1940s film that they sat and viewed together every few months as tradition.

Any other time, Adrien would be completely enjoying the film with her, but that night was different. His mind was focused on one thing: why he was in love with this woman. He mulled over her beauty and studied her features discreetly. Her beautiful, blonde, wavy hair let off a brilliant whiff of mango-pineapple fragrance. Her bright blue-green eyes held an intensity that he'd never seen before. Her face was a striking feminine sculpture, her skin imperfect and at the same time, utterly perfect. She had one dark freckle on her skin above the left of her upper lip, and her face was softly decorated with faint freckles here and there. Her seemingly flawless appearance was one thing, but when he discovered the little details of imperfection that tarnished that flawlessness, he found them far more enticing than the former. He continued to look at her and her eyes flickered over to him; his stare was no longer a secret.

Adrien was an extremely handsome man just over six feet tall, with an unlikely set of features. He had red hair that couldn't stay fully curly or fully straight, and rather was a mixture of textures. It was a medium-length cut that was less of an orange color and more of an auburn-maroon. Since he was very active, he had a toned athletic build. His olive skin—tanned from his regular time out in the sun—was complemented by his green-hazel eyes, light freckles on his cheeks and a very small birthmark under his right eye. He did not have any tattoos, but he did have snake bite piercings; two gunmetal rings were on each side of his bottom lip.

"Adrien...I could probably hear you breathing even if I was across the room. What are you thinking about?" she asked as she turned to face him.

He quickly snapped out of his trance. "Nothing. I was just...looking." He gently bit his bottom lip.

"Looking? At me?" She became curious and sat up straight. "Is there something on my face?"

He flashed his white teeth at her, unable to help but smile from the genuine concern in her voice. Suddenly, a bolt of lightning brightened the sky and thunder crackled in the distance. Adrien caught a glimpse of something outside that was illuminated from the corner of his eye. He jerked his head in the direction of the window that overlooked his backyard.

It started to rain and the tiny droplets lightly tapped on the glass pane. In his vision beyond the pane, there was nothing but the silhouettes of trees as they swayed in the wind. However, what he saw aside from just the lightning was brighter. It couldn't have been the trees—nor the rain—what was it?

"What are you doing?" Jenna asked, even more concerned than she was a few moments before.

He jumped out of the seat and walked up closer to the window, slightly pressing his face to the cold, hard glass. His eyes jumped around frantically, searching for the object he swore he had just seen within the darkness. After he scanned the trees and everything in sight, he saw nothing out of the ordinary.

"Adrien! What is it?!"

He unfocused his vision on the backyard and swapped to the window's reflection of Jenna, who was standing by the couch and waiting for an explanation.

"Oh, um," he said as he scratched his head. "I thought I saw..."

"Adrien," she said as she came up close behind him and placed her hands on each of his shoulders. "I'm sure there isn't anything outside to worry about." She gently rotated him to face her and patted him on the chest. "You can't just keep letting this fear in all the time."

He nodded, and they both made their way back to the couch.

"I...I'm sorry," he apologized.

"It's okay. Maybe you should revisi—"

"I've seen doctors and psychiatrists, babe, they all say the same thing. Everything about me is normal. I'm not mentally or physically ill, so what if this guy really is..." He turned his head towards the window, and Jenna did the same. "Out there?"

Her eyes grew wide for a fraction of a second, then she shook her head as if to rid her mind of the thought. "Okay, say it is true. Why has this man been stalking you? You have no idea who he might be, and you say he hasn't aged a day since you started seeing him when you were three...it's been *nineteen* years now. It has to be all in your head. That's the only explanation that makes sense."

"I'm telling you, there is no way my imagination can create something so vivid. I can *feel* his presence, Jenna." Adrien saw the fear in her eyes from his statement, and this time her fear was solely for his sanity.

"Adrien, I really think you underestimate yourself. You have a very powerful mind. I wouldn't put it past just being your imagination. Regardless, all that matters is that I am here for you," she said with a trace of depression in her voice.

"Ha, wow...how did a guy like me get a girl like you? I bet any other girl would drop me in a second after hearing some of the things I've told you," he said gratefully.

He thought back to the day they first met nearly two years prior. Jenna was only eighteen years old at the time. Adrien was reluctant to approach her, but she made it easier on him by being the first to introduce herself. They hit it off that night, finding out that they had something significant in common. Both of them lacked a family to go home to, and they instantly bonded due to this fact. Shortly after that night, he fell in love with her. He couldn't help but grin ear to ear at the thought of it all, and she noticed.

She chuckled while resting her right cheek on his shoulder. "I never get why you say things like that. Not only are you hilarious and extremely handsome, but you are intelligent, generous, deep and the sweetest guy I have ever met," she expressed with sincerity.

Jenna had told Adrien this multiple times before, but he felt a rush of heat as his face turned red at the sound of her affection towards him. He hadn't gotten over the way she made him feel, the fresh feeling of a new love, though his love for her was anything but new.

"I love you...so much," he whispered.

"I...love you, too," she said so quietly that it was barely audible. Her eyes slowly started to pool up with tears.

They stared into each other's eyes with the noise of the

heavy rain around them as it attacked the surface of the roof.

"Are you okay?" Adrien asked.

She continued to stare, her eyes darted around his face in concern, then she bit her lip and looked back towards the television screen. "I'm good..."

"Jenna. I'm here for you, just as much as you are for me."

She was still looking forward at the TV, slightly sad. He wondered: what's going on in her head? He reached over and began to tickle her.

"Ahh! Adrien!" she giggled profusely and squirmed around, not able to control her laughter.

After losing their balance, they both rolled over the edge of the couch and crashed to the floor. Adrien broke her fall but she rolled off him and onto the plush carpet, landing in it face-first, her giggles muffled by the long fibers in the rug. She lifted her head to look at him, and they erupted in laughter from their clumsiness.

Jenna rotated her body and sat up with her elbow supporting her as she continued to giggle. "I really needed that!"

A faint and rhythmic hum interrupted the moment, as her pocket vibrated roughly against Adrien's leg. Jumping up, she pulled her phone out of her pocket to read what was displayed on the screen. She looked annoyed.

"Is everything good?"

"Just...a text from my boss. I have to go. I have to work tomorrow. Early."

He looked at her in confusion, then strained his neck to view the clock up on the end table. Fueling his confusion, the time read one o'clock in the morning. That was a very odd time for her boss to message her.

"Wow, I didn't even realize it was this late. Let me take you. I don't want you to drive home this late by yourself," he said while lifting himself off the floor.

"Well, I will need my car for tomorrow morning to get to work, anyway."

"Yeah, good point. I guess I will see you later tonight, then?"

"What time?" She bent down to grab her shoes off the floor and then her purse from the coffee table.

"I will pick you up at seven." He tried his hardest to make his voice sound as normal as possible, but his voice cracked as the result of the secret only he knew.

Her eyebrows creased in confusion to the sudden change in his voice. "Can we make it 7:30? I will meet you there, don't worry about picking me up. Where do you want me to meet you?"

"You know...not once since we have been dating have you ever let me pick you up at your place. I don't even know where you live...why not let me get you this time? Just tell me where to go," he said without taking his eyes off hers.

Her eyes flickered. "No, really, it's fine. If you really want to drive me, I guess I'll just come over here as usual, okay?"

"Yeah sure, I guess..."

"I can't wait to see where you are taking me, you've been so secretive about it." She started to giggle. "You're not planning to kill me, are you?"

"Darn, how'd you know?!" Adrien joked while he caressed her cheek and chuckled. "You're silly. We will leave here at 7:30, then."

She leaned in, kissed him and headed towards the door to peek out. "Perfect. Looks like the rain has stopped already." She turned around to look back at him and winked. "Goodnight, babe."

Adrien lurched forward, choosing to not take the time to put on his shoes before leading the way out of the door. He held the door open for her as she exited. Jenna began to walk towards the hill, then she was startled when Adrien came from behind and swept her up into his arms. She softly squealed, but then laughed after locking eyes with his.

"You know I can't let my girl get her new shoes wet," Adrien joked as he secured her in his arms.

Having felt comfortable in his embrace, she leaned her head into the side of his neck, sighing in contentment. They reached the bottom of the hill and began to climb up.

Adrien's estate was divided into two separate buildings, one of which was located on top of a steep hill while the other was at sea level, located at the bottom of the hill. The building right off the beach comprised of his bedroom, a kitchen, a dining room, two extra bedrooms and an entertainment game room. It was arranged in a U shape around a pool that was installed shortly after he moved in. The one building on the top of the hill had a living room, a personal gym off to the right of the living room and a grand, elaborate balcony.

They made it to the top of the hill and then he playfully ran to the car with her bouncing around in his arms. She laughed hysterically as she held onto dear life, but she knew confidently that he would not let her go, she was safe with him. He strained as he shifted her weight in order to open the car door for her. Then he gently kissed her as he set her down on her feet.

"Goodnight, Jenna." He grinned at her as she fixed her hair.

"You are wonderful," she said to him as she sat down in the driver's seat. She started the engine and shut the door, blowing a kiss through the tinted glass window before she started to pull off.

Adrien blushed; he still found himself in awe of her beauty. After her car was out of sight, he trekked over to the front door of the living room and turned the knob to enter. A slight blue glow showed through the back wall of windows from the pool down below. He wiped his bare feet on the entrance rug and quickly flipped the light switch. This was his favorite room: the white stucco walls, the back wall composed of only glass that overlooked the rooftops of the rest of the estate and the elevated view of the beach. Compared to the rest of the house, this room was the brightest—he liked to call it his lighthouse. Having a nice bedroom seemed to be in vain, as he always slept on the couch in this room, across the room from his collection of instruments. It was the spot where he tended to find himself most comfortable.

Adrien walked over to the couch and sat down. He leaned into the backrest and kicked his feet up onto the glass coffee table just in front of him. A cool draft breezed across him and he sighed, tossing his head backward in annoyance. Leaning forward, he pivoted in his seat as he searched around him. He got off the couch, dropped to his knees and pressed his face to the floor to look under the furniture. The blanket he liked to keep in the room had been misplaced for a few days; he kept forgetting to search for it elsewhere in his estate before he retreated there for the night. There was still no blanket in sight. Adrien stood back up and huffed. As he rolled his eyes, he caught a glimpse of his cello in the distance.

It practically beckoned him. He trekked across the room to his cello and ran his fingertips gently over the familiar fingerboard. After he plopped down on the chair behind it, he took his bow and began to play a piece fully committed to memory. In one of the group homes he had lived in, they received an anonymous donation from a local man that was kind enough to provide the institution with old, used instruments. All of the other children fought over the mini guitars and drum sets, while Adrien was the only one who took a liking to the run-down cello in the corner. He taught himself how to play throughout the years.

Adrien was able to take the old cello as he aged out of the foster care system since it was such an unwanted instrument amongst the others. Though Adrien purchased his own new cello as soon as he had the means to, there was something about his original one that kept drawing him back to it.

Playing with those strings for hours each day, he had become so acquainted with them that—aside from Jenna—they were his closest form of family. Part of the reason Adrien had grown so keen on this instrument was the fact that every time he played it, he envisioned the last memory he had of his father, Gabriel: the moment he left the house the night he died. In that memory, though, his father's back was turned to him. Adrien kept replaying the thought while plucking the strings. He hoped that more of the memory would come back to him and that he would remember the moments before his father had turned around to leave him. Lost in the music, he played the piece until his arm started to cramp and his eyelids grew heavy.

***

Adrien jolted up in shock. He found himself covered with a blanket—the blanket that had been misplaced for a while—and laid out on the couch. He did not remember how or when he got there. The light in the room was also turned off. He looked around, confused and disoriented.

Feeling like he had been asleep for ages, he looked at the clock. It was only 2 a.m. He sighed exasperatedly and fell back roughly onto the soft pillows on the couch, a powerful gust of air escaping from under them. He began to think he really was losing his mind.

"Ahhh, when will this ever end?!"

Frustrated, he rubbed his hand through his hair and over his face. He paused when his fingers covered his eyes. Time seemed to stand still as the silence in the room somehow grew deafening. He felt a sudden uneasiness, and he slightly parted his fingers to peek through them. His heart leapt in his chest.

A pair of eyes were staring back at him curiously from above. The eyes reflected a striking bright red as if they belonged to a nocturnal animal. Shortly thereafter, the pale white-haired man appeared completely from the shadows, adding a face to match the glowing eyes. In such a state of shock, Adrien was unable to move, scream or breathe. As the man drew closer, his eyes lost their glow and revealed their true color. Not only were his irises actually red, but his pupils were abnormal as well: they were vertical slits, similar to that of a snake. When the man drew even closer, his eyes morphed, yet again, to a vibrant green.

Adrien jolted awake once more. He realized he had still been dreaming; he sighed out of relief. However, his sigh was cut short when he noticed what was on him: the blanket. What he saw of the white-haired man had been strictly within his dream, but somehow the blanket remained a reality. An overwhelming feeling of doubt and confusion washed over him. This blanket had been misplaced for days, yet somehow it was now in his possession and keeping him warm.

Adrien held his breath and listened to the faint sound of waves crashing to the shore in the distance, and the crickets chirping. His neck remained stiff as his eyes jumped across the room suspiciously. The pressure in his chest was too overwhelming. He exhaled slowly, allowing himself to breathe again. There was no sign of anyone else nearby.

He started to think back to the vivid details of his dream that especially captivated him: the unusual eyes of the man. His eyes seemed so animalistic and somehow very human; deadly, and yet completely harmless. There was something about the eyes of the man he saw...they didn't seem threatening. The piercing eyes looked concerned, as if they were watching—waiting for something to happen.

Chapter 2

"Moreover, no one knows when their hour will come: as fish are caught in a cruel net, or birds are taken in a snare, so people are trapped by evil times that fall unexpectedly upon them."

Ecclesiastes 9:12

The heat from the sun spilled into the foyer and woke Adrien from a deep sleep. It was seven in the morning. Rising up, he swung his legs over the edge of the couch, cracked his ankles and had a satisfying stretch. He felt revitalized from five straight hours of sleep, a very rare occurrence for him. Adrien took this as a good sign, that today was going to be a great day.

He exited the living room with a pep in his step and hummed a tune while heading to his kitchen. Entering through the large French doors, he made his way over to the fridge. He tugged at the stainless-steel handle and took the last swig of orange juice from the carton, then tossed it into the trashcan on the opposite side of the room. He closed the fridge, his eyes meeting the calendar that was held up by a magnet on the door. It was the same day that he and Jenna met for the first time two years prior: July 24th.

After rummaging around in the drawer next to the fridge, he grabbed a key to a metal container under the sink and took it from its hiding spot. After unlocking the container, he tilted and jiggled the metal until a fancy velvet box landed in the palm of his hand. He then flipped the velvet lid, eagerly peeking at what was inside.

"This is it. Tonight's the night," he said to himself.

Anticipation and excitement bubbled up inside of him to the point where he felt like he couldn't contain it. He quickly set the box back down and ran through the kitchen door that faced the outdoor pool, ripped off his clothes and cannonballed into it. The cold water against his skin was exhilarating, and it increased his excitement even more. Adrien's head broke through the surface of the water after he emerged from his jump. The water flying off his hair created a festive dance of droplets around him, and they sparkled, having caught rays of sunshine.

"Tonight's the night!" he belted out loudly, his voice echoing throughout his estate.

***

After Adrien finished his morning swim, he had quite a few hours to waste before his date with Jenna. Whenever the weather was nice, he made a point of being outdoors as much as possible. When he was not volunteering for the shelter, he spent most of his free time either surfing out from his backyard, swimming, playing his cello or finding something to study or sketch.

Contemplating how to pass the time, he decided to venture out to the local park. Having a family of his own had been a dream of his for as long as he could remember, so usually, he avoided the park: he tended to become consumed by a poisonous resentment towards the families he saw all around him.

This day, though, he made an exception. Adrien and Jenna had countless conversations about how they were going to do the family thing right, making sure that their kids wouldn't experience the lack of love that they did while growing up. He came to catch a glimpse of a future that seemed more attainable to him now.

He plopped down on a wooden park bench under a large pine tree for shade. After settling in, he whipped out his sketchpad, took out his charcoal pencil and searched around for a subject to draw. He saw children playing on the playground, a toddler that was being chased by her mother, a family that was enjoying a picnic together, a grandfather that was fishing on the small lake with his grandson and another family kicking around a soccer ball. Everyone looked so content.

Suddenly, to Adrien's left, a little boy began to cry. Adrien directed his attention to the child and watched as the tears streamed down his little red face. The boy looked lost, for no one was with him. His cries were now all Adrien could hear;

the laughter, the birds chirping, the creaking chains from the swings, cars driving by on the road behind him—all of that fell mute as he focused on this little lost boy.

Adrien remembered when he was three years old and fresh in government care: he cried for months on end, feeling lost and confused, waiting for his father to return. It was quite some time before he had realized that his father was not coming for him.

Adrien got up, feeling the need to help the child, but simultaneously the boy's mother and father ran up to him and swept him into their arms. Adrien stopped and stared with a bittersweet ache in his heart: what he saw was foreign to him, but it was something that was immensely desired.

"Hey, look out!" a teenage voice yelled.

A soccer ball came careening toward Adrien and hit him in the back of the head. He was startled, knocked back into reality. He quickly focused on the ball, his ears slightly ringing from the impact. A young man of about eighteen years old was running his way.

"You got me there, dude!" Adrien went to grab the ball and faced him. "I think this belongs to you," he said wryly as he held it out in his hand.

The boy took the ball from him, tossed it up in the air and caught it repeatedly. He stopped and scratched his head, then turned to look towards his family.

"Actually, that was my sister. She's pretty bad at this. I tried to tell her it wasn't a good idea for her to play," he snickered.

The boys' sister jogged up to them. "Are you okay?" she asked, embarrassed.

She was a bit older than Adrien, in her late twenties. With sterling grey eyes, delicate features and red hair a mix between red and strawberry blonde, she was quite pretty. Her hair was in a thick French braid off to the side. She had sweeping long eyelashes and a slim frame, but also looked very strong and mature. Adrien could tell by looking at her that she had seen a lot during her life: whether that was comprised of good or bad things, he was unsure. Regardless, there seemed to be a joy emanating from her that was contagious despite the slight throbbing of his head.

Adrien cleared his throat, then he laughed. "Yeah, I am fine...don't worry about it. I mean, it kind of comes with the territory here, right?"

"I'm sure you didn't sign up for a concussion when you came out here, though..." she responded quickly.

He smirked, then shrugged. She laughed and then punched him playfully on the shoulder. Adrien looked down at his shoulder then back at her, and raised his eyebrows, amused.

"Name's Michelle." She pointed her thumb in the direction of her brother. "This is my brother, Timothy. Never seen you around here..."

"I'm Adrien. I hate the park."

Michelle stiffened as her eyes widened. The boy laughed and elbowed his sister in the side, she grunted—caught off guard by the bony elbow that smacked her in the ribs. She raised her eyebrows in amusement this time.

"Huh. Well...I feel *honored* to help justify why you loathe this place," she scoffed, then rolled her eyes in embarrassment as her cheeks flushed a rosy shade of pink. She cleared her throat. "Enjoy the rest of your day. Hopefully, it will be a lot less painful."

Michelle and Timothy walked away, chuckling amongst themselves. Adrien watched as they playfully hit and tripped one another while walking back to meet up with the rest of the folks they were with. They were both greeted by two people who looked like their mother and father. He recognized their father from television; he was the chief of police for the Boston Police Department. They all laughed and played with the soccer ball again, the dad attempting to start a game of keep-away. The son tripped the dad, and they wrestled each other playfully to the ground.

"One day..." Adrien sighed and reassured himself.

He sat down on the bench and looked back over to the little boy, who was no longer crying. The boy found whom he was searching for. The little boy's eyes were gleaming in delight; he giggled while his parents showered him with affection. They kissed, hugged and lovingly warned him not to wander out of their sight again.

Adrien found the strength within him to crack a smile at their exchange. He twisted slightly in the bench seat and decided to do a quick sketch of the family before they got up and walked away. Adrien let out another sigh and continued to observe the people around the rest of the park. A few hours later, Adrien looked at his watch and realized that Jenna would be arriving at his house soon.

***

Adrien was dressed in dark jeans and a grey vest, with the white shirt he had on underneath rolled up to his elbows. He was also wearing Jenna's favorite cologne. It was 7:30 and Jenna just arrived at Adrien's home. His heart fluttered rapidly like the wings of a hummingbird as he saw her walk up.

She was in a light pink off-the-shoulder dress that came to just above her knees and was layered with a sheer fabric on top of silk. She was also wearing earrings that Adrien gifted her for her birthday a few months ago, and her hair was pinned half up in a romantic style. Her cheeks blushed softly as she saw how he was looking at her. He was captivated, and for a moment, at a loss for words.

"You look absolutely stunning," he expressed in awe after regaining his composure. He escorted her to a limo that was waiting for them.

She paused and looked at him endearingly as he held the door open. "Thank you...you look very handsome yourself."

"I've got to at least try to look as half as good as you. Otherwise, people might think I've bribed you to date me," Adrien said as he took one of her hands.

Jenna chuckled as he helped her into the limo. She took her seat, and he walked around to the other side. His nerves were shot, and he was unsure whether he would be able to successfully pull off his plan. He patted his pocket to ensure that the velvety box from under his kitchen counter was secure. He adjusted his collar and took a few deep breaths before he got in the limo along with her.

Adrien had made reservations at one of the most renowned restaurants in the city. This restaurant was known for how it mimicked the water streets in Venice, Italy and how it was lavishly adorned with soft romantic string lighting inside and out. Jenna had talked about visiting this place for months, but Adrien purposefully saved the trip for that night.

They arrived at their destination and took a seat at their reserved table outdoors, a slightly secluded table that was right along one of the many streams of water throughout the restaurant.

"So, you remembered that I've wanted to come here? Wow, this place is absolutely gorgeous!" she reveled at their surroundings.

Adrien grinned and stared at her eyes that were happily glistening. She looked over the railing next to her where koi were swimming up and down a channel and she spotted a very large fish. He followed her eyes and looked over as well.

"That one is huge!" she said as she pointed through the wrought iron bars in the railing.

"Yeah, pretty cool! Apparently, they can get very old. I think the oldest one was over 220 years old," Adrien explained.

"Wow. All these fish can do is swim around in circles with no purpose. To do that for over two centuries…that's depressing."

"Tell me about it," he responded.

"Can you imagine that, though?" she scoffed.

Adrien stared at the koi, temporarily captivated by them. His eyes widened as he looked through the iron bars in the railing that now seemed like a jail cell in light of their conversation.

Multiple servers walked up to the table with drinks and an array of appetizer dishes. This forced his attention from the fish, and his eyes dried, as he had forgotten to blink. When Adrien made the reservations, he chose all the courses from start to finish. He knew her tastes well, so the plates were brimming with all of her favorite foods.

"Whoa, Adrien this is—" Jenna was cut off by her cell phone ringing. She looked at her phone under the table and got up abruptly. "I have to take this...I'm sorry." She moved across to the other side of the restaurant and disappeared through the double doors.

While Jenna was away, Adrien quickly waved some of the workers over and talked to them about starting up the live music that was discussed during the reservation process. He started to get clammy from the nerves and exhaled loudly, realizing that he had been holding his breath since they sat down. *Get it together!* he berated himself.

After a few minutes went by, Jenna emerged from the building and made her way back to the table. She looked flustered, and her eyes and cheeks were slightly red. Adrien, mid-sip of his glass of water, quickly placed the glass down onto the table and leaned in toward her as she sluggishly took her seat.

"What happened?" he asked in concern.

Jenna took a deep breath and pressed her lips together. She sighed before she apprehensively began to speak, "There is something I've really needed to tell you," her words resonated with a shameful tone.

When she was about to continue, four musicians circled the table and began to play music for them.

Jenna mouthed to him from across the table, "*Never mind, tell you later.*"

Adrien looked at her confused and mouthed back, "*Are you sure?*"

She nodded.

Three violinists and one cellist were performing a song Adrien requested: "Ave Maria" by Giulio Caccini. This was the first song Adrien learned to play on the cello, but he didn't quite remember exactly why it became such an important piece of music for him before then. It was something he knew he had heard in his childhood; it made him happy, and it made him even happier to share it with her in this moment.

Jenna stared at him, but her eyes lost focus briefly into space before she turned her attention to the musicians. She closed her eyes as she enjoyed the music for a few moments, then peeked at Adrien sheepishly to smile, her mood flipped almost instantly.

He smiled, happy to see her enjoying the moment. He reached for the utensils and grabbed a fork. Starting with an appetizer of stuffed portobello mushrooms, he loaded the fork with a bite and lifted it to her lips. Jenna gently parted her lips and ate the food from it. They both then began digging in, feeding each other bites from the various appetizers. When they finished, the servers brought out their entrées. They continued to feed one another until only crumbs remained on their plates.

This was it—this was now the time he had planned to ask her. Adrien's temperature started to rise, and his heart rate increased again. He reached across the table and grabbed Jenna's left hand that was resting on the tablecloth. Jenna noticed that his hand was abnormally warm.

"I have something very important to ask." He stared longingly in her eyes, gulping as his mouth dried to sandpaper. He reached for the ring box with his other hand, his heart thumped madly in his chest. "I am unmistakably in love with you, Jenna. You are so loving, gorgeous and kind to me. You inspire me to become a better man, and I can't wait any longer to take this next step with you." He paused and took a deep breath, his eyes were fixated on hers intensely. "Jenna, will you marry me?"

He sat the box on the table next to her hand and flipped the lid, exposing a twenty-four karat white-gold engagement ring. It was covered in diamonds, had one large 4.9-carat alexandrite stone and was complete with intricate designs of filigree on the band. Jenna gasped and gravitated towards the ring.

"Oh, Adrien! Yes! Yes, I will!" She jumped up and reached across the table to grab him.

They both embraced and almost knocked the table full of plates and glass over. The other people in the restaurant took notice and started to clap and hoot for the happy couple. They sat back down, and he took the ring out of the box to slip onto her finger.

"This is much better than killing you, isn't it?" he asked jokingly while he kissed her hand multiple times, his heart racing from elation.

Jenna laughed. "I can't believe you remembered I said that! Adrien, I am just so excited! I was not expecting this!" she exclaimed while she gazed at her new, extravagant ring.

"Are you ready for this? An adventure of a lifetime—just you and me," he gushed while squeezing her hand.

She nodded excitedly and glanced at her lap, where her phone was sitting. Her expression changed to worry for a fraction of a second, then reverted to excitement. They finished their meal complete with a toast, fresh flowers he had delivered to the table and dessert.

"Let's get out of here." Adrien stood up and offered her his hand.

Jenna grabbed his hand, and they left the restaurant. Hand in hand, they started to walk down the street. She was carrying the bouquet of red roses and gardenias, they were exceptionally fragrant, so she occasionally rested her face in the flowers.

They decided to not end their night just yet. With the limo still waiting back at the restaurant, they took a walk down a secluded street. The summer night sky was filled with the glow of the moon and stars.

"So...Jenna?" he asked nonchalantly while they were walking, "What did you want to tell me at the restaurant?"

"Huh?" She was caught off guard. She diverted her attention from the sky and shifted her attention back to him.

"You said you would tell me later," Adrien prodded.

She looked at him confused, then her eyes widened as she remembered the exact moment he was speaking of. "Oh, that," she sighed. "It was nothing."

"Really? You said you've been meaning to tell me this. Does it have anything to do with your family? Jenna, you can tell me anything," he said, now starting to grow very concerned.

"Tonight has been a dream, Adrien. I don't want to take away from all of this," she said, stopping to face him.

She kissed him on the cheek and put her left hand back in his. Adrien felt a surge of excitement as he brushed against the engagement ring that was on her finger, as if what happened earlier had finally sunk in.

"Why wait? Let's get married tomorrow. What do you say?" he asked endearingly, and with a sense of urgency.

Off in the distance, a very disturbed, angry-looking man wearing a suit was staggering towards them. Jenna saw the man coming from the corner of her eye.

"Um, let's turn around and go back," she said frantically.

"What?" He was thrown off by her lack of response but

also saw the extreme discomfort in her eyes. He glanced and saw the man that was coming their way. "Okay, let's go."

They turned around and started to quickly walk back to where the limo was parked; a few more blocks and a right turn up the street.

"Hey!" the man that was coming their way shouted, picking up his pace to catch them quickly.

Adrien turned around to face the guy who was a little too close for comfort. A strong smell of alcohol was emanating from the man. He was obviously very drunk.

"Can I help you?" Adrien grumbled impatiently.

"No. *You* can't help me. But, this beautiful lady can," he mocked while moving even closer to them. His words were slightly slurred, "Jennnna."

"What? Jenna? You know who this guy is?" Adrien looked over to Jenna, who was standing with her back to the guy.

She turned around to face the drunk.

"Of course she does." The stranger reached out to caress her cheek with the back of his hand. "Isn't that right?"

Jenna slapped the man's hand away from her face, her eyes filling with tears.

"That's my fiancé! What's your problem, dude?!" Adrien shouted, getting in between them. "Who the hell are you?!"

The guy flared his nostrils and his eyes grew dark as he lunged for Adrien and grabbed him in a headlock. Adrien broke loose from the headlock, and they began fighting in the middle of the sidewalk. Jenna tried to stop them, with no success, and she was knocked down, her flowers crashing to the pavement along with her. She shuffled out of their way and into the grass, watching helplessly as they continued to brawl.

The drunk threw a few punches, but Adrien was quick enough to duck and dodge them all. With that, the man grew furious just before Adrien sunk a solid right hook to his face. The impact to his jaw forced him to stagger backward. The man grabbed onto his jaw, his eyes grew darker in anger. He lurched back at Adrien just as a vehicle came recklessly speeding around the corner. The man spotted the opportunity and shoved Adrien into the street, directly in front of the passing vehicle.

SCREEEEEECH!

The speeder attempted to brake, but it proved no use. Adrien had no time to react or move out of the path of the truck and got struck head-on. The vehicle came to a halt briefly but then peeled off in the direction it was originally going. Adrien was sprawled out on the pavement. The drunk man immediately took off running and disappeared into the bushes.

Jenna leapt up. "ADRIEN!" she screamed.

She ran into the street by Adrien's side. He was covered in his own blood with a road rash all down the left side of his body. His clothes on that side of him were melted from the road, but he was still miraculously alive.

"J-...J-" he mumbled in an effort to speak, but he gurgled as fluid filled his lungs.

He coughed, choking up more blood onto his shirt

that was covered in soot and marks from the road. As he unsuccessfully gasped for more air and continued to bleed out, it became clear that he was dying rapidly. Jenna fearfully witnessed his eyes start to glaze over, and she frantically fumbled around to find her phone; she realized she dropped her purse when she was knocked down.

She ran back over to her purse and dumped out all of its contents to find it more quickly. She found it, then hastily dialed 911. She turned back around to the street and dropped her phone in disbelief. Adrien was no longer there. He had vanished, and nothing but the blood-stained road remained.

Chapter 3

"Above all else, guard your heart, for everything you do flows from it."

Proverbs 4:23

A navy blue Toyota pulled up, and a young woman got out of the car and slung a leather messenger bag around one of her shoulders. Dressed in a suit, she carried a badge, her red hair set in a thick French braid off to the side. Michelle was her name, and she was a homicide detective for the Yarmouth Police Department.

She took a few steps out of the car and laid her eyes on the array of red and white flowers that were scattered across the sidewalk. Some of the petals were mashed and smeared, transferring their pigment to the pavement. The petals temporarily changed color as the lights from the emergency vehicles flashed rhythmically. She found the trail of crushed flowers haunting, the sign of a celebration that took a turn for the worse. Michelle pulled out a smaller leather case from her bag. Unzipping it, there was a wide array of pens and pencils strapped on the inner flap, with an electronic tablet and a legal pad on either side. She utilized the hole in the back of the leather case—purposed for her tablet's camera—to snap a few quick photographs.

She took a deep breath and faced the crime scene tape. She gazed for a long moment, captured by the intense yellow of the tape with bold black lettering that had become far too familiar to her. Michelle loved her profession, but every case involved real people that suffered real loss, and it didn't get any easier for her to see. She sighed and pulled out a pen to use her notepad, jotting down a few notes before one of the officers approached her.

"Good evening, Detective Smith. Sorry to call you away from your family on your vacation time, but I feel you are the best fit for this one," the officer explained.

Michelle's teenage brother was in town visiting after his first year in college, and her dad—who happened to be the chief of police for the Boston Police Department—and mom were all together for the week, staying at Michelle's home in Yarmouth.

"The girl who called this in has been questioned already by yours truly, but if she is willing, you can get in a few questions too. She refuses to go down to the station. She's over there, on the other side of the ambulance. Her name is Jenna." The officer pointed in the direction of the vehicle.

Michelle looked up at him from her notes. "Thank you, Lieutenant."

As Michelle began to walk towards the ambulance, she was approached by another one of the first responding officers to the scene. Her close friend, Anna.

"Hey—uh, before you go over there." Anna motioned to her to come close. Michelle leaned in to listen. "Remember that dream you told me about that you had a few weeks ago? Well, just be prepared. This girl looks exactly like the one you described," she whispered in a tone that suggested that she was a little disturbed.

Michelle's heart fluttered, and a lump grew in her throat as suddenly her nerves had increased. She looked back at Anna and calmly nodded, having tried to conceal her reaction. She tucked away her belongings into her bag and then maneuvered her way around the crime scene investigators and the quarantined area to the girl in question.

Jenna was sitting on the curb, shaking, covered in a gray fleece blanket. She was staring at the ground so intensely that she failed to blink. As Michelle drew closer to her, she broke her stare from the pavement, looking up and making eye contact with Michelle. Michelle briefly stopped in her tracks. She had never seen or met Jenna before in person, but had a dream about her recently. Her appearance was so vivid, that aside from the basics of her hair color, hair length and eyes, she saw accurately down to even her unique facial features and the moles and freckles on her skin. Michelle was careful not to look at Jenna suspiciously, but she now knew that the lieutenant was right. This case was for her.

Michelle reached back inside her bag and pulled out an

unopened water bottle. She cracked open the top and kneeled down to eye level with Jenna, her hand outstretched, offering her the water to drink. Michelle left her hand out for a while and then set the bottle next to Jenna after she didn't receive a response or reaction from her.

"Care to tell me what happened here?" Michelle asked in a soft tone.

Jenna did not respond verbally, but tensed up and retracted further into the blanket that was wrapped around her.

"Before I physically see anything else, I want to hear from *you* what happened. I would like to be able to help you, Jenna," Michelle said as she sat down on the curb next to her.

"You wouldn't believe me..." Jenna said with a touch of melancholy, her voice cracked and dry.

Michelle eyed the water bottle and gestured again for Jenna to drink. She still refused. Michelle felt an inkling and inquired if she should say it aloud.

"You don't want to drink this...because you feel like you don't deserve it. You feel as though whatever happened here is your fault, don't you?" Michelle said gently.

Jenna jerked her head toward Michelle and dropped the blanket from her shoulders as she jumped to her feet. "What makes you say that?!" Jenna yelled, her teeth gritted and face contorted in anger.

"Whoa, whoa, whoa," Michelle said while standing up as well. "Don't get me wrong, hon. I just have a sense for things like this, a discernment if you will. I am in no way suggesting that you are at fault here. Just know that you have no control over the evil decisions that other people choose to make. You understand?" Michelle said assertively.

Jenna shifted her weight awkwardly. She then glanced over to the road where Adrien had laid. Her shoulders rose as she tensed up, then her torso contracted violently when she began to sob uncontrollably. Her sudden cries attracted the eyes of everyone around them. People began to whisper and murmur amongst themselves. Michelle lightly touched her on the shoulder and led her further away from the crime scene, so it was no longer in her line of sight.

"I already told them what happened!" Jenna choked out between sobs as she motioned to the other officers. "I can tell they don't believe me! What's the point in telling *you*?" She wiped her tears with the back of her hand. "It doesn't make sense. He was here, and then he literally vanished from under my nose. He…he was *dying*. I didn't get to say goodbye to him." She bent over with her hands on her knees, tears streaming from her face and onto the pavement below. "I shouldn't have left him!" She sobbed to the point where she began to dry heave.

Michelle sympathetically patted her on the back until her crying slowed.

"I'll tell you what," Michelle said as she quickly took out the small leather case again, flipped it open, scribbled in her notepad and ripped out a page to offer it to Jenna. "Call me tomorrow morning after you have gotten some rest. I would like to sit down with you at the station. Do you need someone to escort you home?"

Jenna took the piece of paper from Michelle then shook her head no. Her shoulders were slumped and her eyes were fixated on the pavement as she turned to leave the crime scene. The investigators had gathered her purse and belongings as evidence so all she had with her was the clothes on her back and the piece of paper Michelle gave her. Some of the people that saw Jenna and Adrien at the restaurant beforehand were now bystanders at the crime scene, curious as to what happened. She walked by the blood-soaked road, trying hard not to look over again. Everyone watched silently as she slowly made her way down the street.

Anna walked over to Michelle with her arms crossed. "I'm assuming, by the brevity of that conversation, you did not get much out of that."

"Right," Michelle sighed and started to walk towards the taped-off area. "Poor girl..."

They both gently lifted the caution tape and entered into the area that was under investigation.

"So, tell me what we are working with here," Michelle queried.

"Well...we have no witnesses other than the young woman who just left. There was clearly a hit and run here. But...what she said doesn't add up." Anna pointed to the pavement. "The victim was bleeding out quickly after he landed here. It was most likely internal bleeding from the initial impact, multiple lacerations from the rest of it. The amount of blood suggests that this man is deceased. However, she said that he disappeared, but there are no traces or any evidence of the body being moved in any direction." Anna threw her hands in the air in frustration.

"Wow," Michelle exhaled sharply. "I have never seen or heard of *anything* like this. The time frame doesn't seem accurate, but it almost has to be as swift as she said if there were no other witnesses. If there was an attempt to somehow move or conceal the body...a substantial amount of time would have to go into making sure that no trail was left behind. Someone else would have certainly witnessed it, in that case." Michelle brought her hand up to her chin in inquisition as she ran over the quick briefing she received over the phone before she arrived. "What about the assailant? Do we know who supposedly pushed the victim?"

"We got a very vague description of the assailant from our sole witness. Caucasian male in his early thirties, dark brown hair. She said she had never seen the man before and couldn't give any more details about him. We have a team of deputies sweeping the area for any possible suspects." Anna flipped quickly through a notepad in her hand for a last analysis before she shut it closed. "Where in the world do we go from here?" Anna asked, completely stumped.

"Collect as much of the biological evidence here as we can. Then we wait for a body to show up," Michelle said while she kneeled down and looked more closely at the pavement.

She not only saw the blood that was shed, but also

clothing fibers and flesh from road rash on the ground as well. Michelle shuddered, imagining the awful suffering the victim must have endured.

***

Jenna traveled a few blocks down the road and rounded the corner, the restaurant was in sight. She saw the limo parked in the parking lot and approached it quickly. When she reached the front of the vehicle, she peeked in and saw that the driver was fast asleep. Banging on the window, she startled the driver awake and beckoned him to let her in. He unlocked the doors for her and lowered the privacy window partition.

"I am so sorry, Miss," the limo driver apologized. "Are you guys ready to—where's the young man?" The driver looked around confused, searching for Adrien. He then looked at Jenna and saw the state of her appearance: disheveled hair, makeup running down her face and red, puffy eyes.

"Unfortunately, he is not coming," she sighed in despair. "Can you please take me back to his house?" her voice quivered.

He rose the partition and drove out of the parking lot. As the limo began its route back to Adrien's home it passed by the street where the road had been closed, flashing lights from the emergency vehicles were ricocheting off the other buildings. Jenna closed her eyes, sick of seeing the colored lights, and laid out along the seat of the limo. Without any effort, she fell asleep on the leather cushion.

***

Having arrived at Adrien's home about an hour later,

Jenna woke to the sound of the limo door being opened for her. She sat up in the seat and rubbed her eyes. She innately looked around for Adrien. Her stomach turned at the smell of his cologne as it lingered where they were sitting together just a few hours prior; her reality was unbearable. The driver cleared his throat as he waited with his hand out to assist her.

Jenna found it hard to focus, but she managed to grab his hand and was assisted out of the limo. The driver nodded, then got back in, pulling out of the driveway. She realized that she left the note the detective gave her in the seat and started to wave the driver down. There was not enough energy left in her, so she lowered her hand slowly in defeat and stood alone in the darkness while the taillights disappeared into the night.

Adrien's house was on six acres of land and was about two miles from any other homes or public roads. The clouds had now covered the moon and stars so the night sky was pitch-black. The crickets were chirping, and the sound of the waves were crashing nearby. Jenna stood still for a moment, her mind and thoughts were clouded from the trauma she experienced.

She then walked to the front door to reach into the hiding spot where she knew Adrien placed his spare keys, and she pulled them out. She unlocked the door and entered into the living room, halfway searching. A part of her was looking around, hoping to see that Adrien somehow made his way home safely. Her memory replayed how he looked before he vanished: no ambulance or emergency room would have been able to save him in the state that he was in, as he was too far gone. She collapsed onto the couch and passed out.

***

A few hours later, Jenna woke from her sleep. She felt pressure—a heaviness that seemed to escalate as she came to. It was not long before she realized what she was feeling: someone was on top of her, holding her down onto the couch.

Heart racing, her eyes jolted open. A hand immediately clamped over her mouth and muffled the scream that instinctively escaped from her. She writhed and exuded all of her strength in efforts to move, her eyes straining while trying to make out the shadowed figure in the darkness.

"I figured I would find you here, *Jenna*," a familiar voice rang in her ears.

She could smell the odor of sweat and alcohol as it was emitted from the shadowy figure. It was too dark to see, but her eyes started to adjust to the darkness. She then saw the drunk dark-brown-haired man who attacked Adrien. Her eyes widened as she fully recognized who he was, tears welled up in her eyes then flowed down the sides of her face while she fought to break free. He stared down at her angrily then gripped her even tighter; this pushed her further down into the cushions on the couch. Jenna screamed again through the man's palm that was still covering her mouth.

"Look what you made me do, Jenna!" he yelled at the top of his lungs, just a few centimeters from her face, as he kept his hand over her mouth.

She flinched and drew her breath in fear, the pressure in her head rising as her face turned red from the tension. He furiously stared her in the eyes for a few moments, and then he roughly released her. She sat up on the couch as far as she could before his body blocked her from moving any further.

"How could you?!" Jenna screamed. "How dare you show your face in his house!" She shoved him away from her, and he stumbled back from the couch. She got up and approached him aggressively. "What did you do to him? Where is he?!" She slapped him across the face with all of her strength, her hand stung as a result.

He retaliated and grabbed her wrists together, so he could restrain her from being able to move again. "For all I know he could still be plastered on the bottom of that truck," he retorted through a clenched jaw.

Jenna gasped and squirmed more within his grasp. "How could you do this?!" Jenna cried out as she tried to break free, his tight hold on her making her wrists bruise.

"He never even knew about me," he said as he pulled her in closer and shook her. "Did he?!"

"I-I..."

"You came home to *me* last night, slept with *me* as if I still mattered to you. Then this morning you tell me that you couldn't be with me anymore, that you were 'in love with him?' I just so happened to drive by and see you with *him* at that restaurant. I watched as he slipped that little ring on your finger, Jenna..." His beady eyes darted to the ring on her finger, and he snatched it off her hand. "What made him better than me, anyway?!"

He chucked the ring across the room, and it ricocheted

off the wall, the delicate metal clanging as it bounced across the tile floor. It was then lost in the darkness. She gasped and tried to run after the ring, but he yanked her closer to him. She flinched away from his face and shut her eyes tightly, then she opened one eye to peek at him from the side.

"I can't believe you killed him!" she choked out through more tears.

"And you told no one that it was me, you didn't want to even admit you knew me, did you?! I know you have no one else and no other place to go! You are NOT leaving me!" His forehead was pressed hard against hers, as he spat and yelled in her face.

Jenna whimpered and tightly closed her eyes again, grimacing as she bit into her lip.

"If you tell anyone about what happened tonight, you might end up just like him. Dead. I'm not playing games anymore," he threatened menacingly.

He tugged her out of the room with him. She continued to fight and squirm, so he picked her up and tossed her over his shoulders. She screamed while banging on his upper back with her fists. He carried her over to his car and threw her in the backseat as she kicked and cried out for help. He tore away at her dress and used the fabric to tie her hands together, then stuffed some in her mouth. He tied the rest around her head to quiet her screaming.

Before she saw it coming, the man wound back and brought the force of his body weight and strength against her. With the back of his hand, he smacked her across the cheek.

Propelled into the backseat, her head collided with the cold, black leather cushion; the blow knocked her unconscious. He slammed the door shut, then he jumped into his car to peel out of the driveway, leaving a cloud of dust in their trail.

Chapter 4

"You are all children of the light and children of the day. We do not belong to the night or to the darkness."

1 Thessalonians 5:5

*A*top a hill, an old multi-story building deep within the secluded forests of Massachusetts was swallowed whole by overgrown vines. The thick stone walls were fortified, and the very small stained glass windows were few and far between. The land was filled with stone statues and tall columns, also covered in vines, mature trees mostly concealed the structures. There were many rooms in the house with antique furniture collecting dust. Within one of those rooms was Adrien, stored away in solitude.

Adrien lay alone and motionless in utter darkness. His blood-soaked clothes began to reek. His heart was still beating sparingly but began to slow even more, almost reaching a complete halt. His eyes opened to the darkness. Straining his eyes, he continued to see nothing, his memory failing him. He did not know where he was. Filled with confusion and fear, he had no choice but to lay in the weight of the silence. At that moment, he was unable to move as he sensed what felt like chains of darkness heavily weighing down on him, dragging him into an abyss.

His fingers twitched as he gained control over the muscles in his hand. Little by little, Adrien's senses were awakened, and he began to feel. Realizing that he was abnormally cold, he started to shiver uncontrollably. As he shook, he realized that he could not move to his left or to the right more than mere inches. Once he found that there were sturdy walls preventing him from moving any further, he began to hyperventilate, feeling trapped.

The next sense that awakened was his sight. He could see the cushioning and the fine lines in the wood grain as it formed around him. He saw at a depth he had never seen before, shocked at the details he could make out in the darkness. Upon his examination, he realized that he was—in fact—laying in a box.

His memory of the crash and the excruciating pain of the impact briefly surged back to him. He gasped even more deeply for air and frantically pushed upwards and out of the box where he lay.

"Jenna!" he called out desperately.

Adrien lifted into the air effortlessly and landed nimbly on the stone floor beneath him. He quickly turned around to look at the box he was just within and fell back to the ground in shock.

"No..." he said breathlessly, staring at a wooden casket

lined in dark red fabric and adorned with iron filigree on the outside.

He looked down at his body reluctantly, in fear of what he would discover. The rush of pain was so fresh, but the tattered clothing that was stained a rusty red suggested that a significant amount of time had passed, time that he had no account of. There was also no sign of Jenna or the drunk man they encountered, either. Anxiety coursed through him as he desperately searched around his body for wounds. He could not find any, but he realized that his skin was extremely pale and ice-cold, like a corpse, seemingly absent of life.

Feeling a torrent of adrenaline, Adrien leapt up and ran for the door; he met it at an abnormal speed and crashed through it. He shattered it into pieces and tumbled to the ground, landing face-down in the rubble he had just created. He exhaled sharply, causing a cloud of fine dust to kick up into the air. He looked behind him to the doorway, wondering how it was possible that he destroyed a stone door so easily.

Adrien began to panic as he looked all around him, filled with confusion. "Where...where am I?!"

The anxiety continued to skyrocket inside of him as the darkness rested over him like a thick cloud. His first instinct was to flip the light switches on, but there were none around. The walls were lined with lamps that lit by flame, but they had all been extinguished, however, he could still clearly see his surroundings in detail. There was a corridor before him with a few doors that were still closed. Adrien slowly rose to his feet and cautiously walked down the hallway, opening the doors and peeking inside of them. The walls were covered in old, worn-down wallpaper that was starting to peel away, and paintings in intricate iron frames populated the walls. Bookshelves towered the length of some of the walls, and the shelves were all packed with books. Some of the books were laid open on end tables; it was evident that someone still lived there.

He passed by an iron staircase that led down to a lower level, then he spotted a very large door to his right. He walked toward the door and paused as he grabbed the door handle, intently focused on what he could hear on the other side of it. He heard crickets chirping outside and even cars driving nearby. He swung open the door and walked out onto a balcony. More darkness followed. Looking around, he saw trees for miles. He could have sworn he heard a road nearby. He leaned over the balcony and looked down, seeing that he was on the second story of a mysterious building. Still hearing cars, he now realized that what he was hearing was not near, but very far away. As he pondered the impossibility of this all, his immersion in the dark setting sent chills down his spine.

He then heard a slight rustle of fabric from behind him. His adrenaline spiked again, but his heart did not race. He quickly turned around to see a pair of gleaming red eyes staring back. Adrien practically jumped out of his skin in terror, immediately recognizing who was peering at him.

"YOU!" he cried out in terror.

Adrien's hand shot up to his mouth as he felt discomfort

after speaking, something was pressed up against the inside of his upper lip on both sides. He was too distracted to focus on the discomfort for long. He tried to back up but was already as close to the edge of the balcony as he could be. Removing his hand from his mouth, he used both hands to steady himself as he pressed against the railing, being careful not to divert his eyes from what he figured must have been an illusion.

The red reptilian eyes. The white hair. The black scarf. The object of Adrien's nightmares stood clearly in front of him, less than ten feet away. The white-haired man stood so still that he seemed to be like that of a scarecrow. His black, woolen scarf was covering his face so that only his eyes and the bridge of his nose were visible.

Adrien shook his head in an attempt to wake himself up; it did not work. A lump grew in his throat as he tried to formulate more words to speak. He never imagined that this situation would arise; he was convinced that this man was truly out there, but a part of him hoped he was only a figment of his imagination. This man was the epitome of what he feared and loathed the most: the darkness itself.

The man started to walk towards Adrien; he walked so elegantly that he seemed to glide above the ground. Adrien tensed up in response, and he wanted to look away but was unable to.

"I...I've had n-nightmares about you!" Adrien stuttered anxiously, he was close to falling over the balcony as he attempted to move even further away.

The man stopped, with about three feet left between

them. His eyes narrowed. "I presume you were right to have nightmares," the man responded in a calm voice that was as smooth as honey.

The man lowered the scarf from his face and was revealed to be relatively young. He looked in his mid-twenties, only a few years older than Adrien himself. He had a chiseled masculine jawline, hollowed cheeks and strong cheekbones. As Adrien stared, the man's eyes morphed into another color: though the green proved less threatening, the eerie vertical slit of his pupil still remained.

Adrien jumped back, then scrutinized him fearfully with curiosity. He also noticed the macabre physical state of this man. He then looked back down to himself to realize that his own physical appearance, specifically his skin, was very similar to the man's outward show. His stomach turned—not fully understanding—but knowing something undeniably disastrous had happened to him. He knew that he must leave this place, immediately.

Adrien made a break for it. He pushed past the man and ran back into the house, going straight for the stairs. He kept reaching places sooner than he thought possible, as he was moving quicker than he ever had before. He made it downstairs but was unsure which way was out. He continued to run around, slamming into walls and clipping corners with his shoulder. He failed to understand how to recalculate his movements.

Suddenly, something moved in front of Adrien so quickly that he did not see it, and he crashed into what felt like a wall that had no give. Stumbling back, it took a few moments for him to regain his focus to what was in front of him. There was a black-haired man of slim build standing there, smirking. Simultaneously, yet another man appeared next to him; he was very muscular, had blonde hair and was covered in tattoos, including one large tattoo that was on one side of his face, encompassing his right eye. The blonde man didn't hesitate in grabbing Adrien by what was left of his shirt and lifted him off the ground.

"Let me go!" Adrien yelled, his eyes widening in fear.

The blonde man curled his upper lip in disgust and raised his chin. "Hmph. Figured Latimer would need us," the blonde man snidely remarked. "I knew he wouldn't choose to control his *neophyte*." He looked Adrien up and down with disdain.

"Why hello, Adrien," said the man with the black hair, his tone was a drastic change: borderline friendly.

"H-How do you know my name?" Adrien asked, his mind spiraling in confusion.

He did not know what to make of all of this and still expected to wake up from this nightmare. Those two men also had the same intense reptilian irises as the white-haired man. The black-haired man had brown eyes, while the blonde had blue. The white-haired man, Latimer, then appeared again in the midst of them all.

"Set him down, Coran," Latimer demanded.

Coran reluctantly set him down and shoved him. Adrien grunted, having hit one of the bookshelves. Books came tumbling down from the shelves onto the floor, some hitting him on the way down. He covered his head as the books fell, but they seemed like they were made out of styrofoam; he barely felt them.

"Adrien wants our help, he just...doesn't know it yet," the black-haired man said.

"Yes, Cade...perhaps we should throw him into a crowd of people, huh? See how he manages," Coran chuckled sadistically.

While the two men talked amongst themselves, Adrien noticed that not only did they both have the same ailing appearance that Latimer did; there was also something else that was odd about them.

"Come on, Coran," Cade replied. "You know that's not even how *we* catch our prey."

Adrien then spotted it. Both of the men had long, pointy canines. Fangs. He quickly put his hand up to his open mouth, then feeling the two elongated sharp teeth on either side that caused him his discomfort as he spoke. He felt like his heart should have been racing in panic, but again—it was not.

"What's going on? What did you do to me?!" Adrien interjected in angst, his eyes set on Latimer.

"If it weren't for me, you would be dead," Latimer quickly responded.

Having previously been distracted, he could now see that Latimer had fangs as well. Whatever these men were, he was also. Adrien looked down at his trembling hands. He both looked and felt like what he would have described as death, so how could he not have been dead? He looked back up at them all, speechless.

The blonde man, Coran, turned towards Latimer. As he did, Adrien was drawn to the large tattoo that was on his back. The tattoo was very vibrant with a mixture of orange, red and black ink. Time seemed to slow further as Adrien stared in a trance. The design was a koi fish that filled almost the entirety of Coran's back, along with other intricate designs around it. He was immediately brought back to his conversation with Jenna at the restaurant about the koi in the channel.

Adrien broke out of his stare at the alluring tattoo design, remembering Jenna again. He feared that she was in danger; that man not only attacked him but came for her first. Adrien started to scan the room, searching for an exit.

"Latimer, you have more to lose than we do if he proves to be too much of a trouble for you. This city means more to you than it does to the rest of us," Coran said.

"Look," Adrien said, beginning to grow annoyed and impatient aside from just frightened. He then spotted what looked like an exit door. "As much as I'd *love* to stand here and listen to you guys talk about me," he grumbled sarcastically. "I'll be on my way now."

"You cannot go out there by yourself. You are far too perilous," Latimer explained calmly.

"What are you talking about?!" Adrien's anger raged like a stoked flame. "Let me leave!" He forced his way past all of them and made a break for the door.

"Cade, Coran," Latimer mandated.

Cade and Coran both swiftly appeared before Adrien and blocked his way out yet again. Adrien's frustration and anger exploded, and he instinctively hissed at them, exposing his fangs.

"Calm down," Cade said while gesturing with his hand. "Please. We are just trying to help."

Coran, however, was not as level-headed. A deep growl brewed from inside of him and he hissed back at Adrien. Adrien watched as his eyes turned red, he seemed to be able to control their color on a whim. Leaping at Adrien, Coran delivered a few quick, but powerful blows, knocking him to the ground. His head cracked against the stone as he made contact with the floor. His vision slowly went in and out. Latimer walked up and knelt down by him just as his vision went black.

***

Adrien slowly woke up. He was still laying on the floor in the same place. The house was eerily silent, and no one seemed to be lurking nearby. Without any more hesitation, he decided to take advantage of the moment. He rushed towards the door he was trying to reach before and burst through it. It was then daytime, as many hours had passed when he was unconscious. Something didn't feel right to Adrien; in fact, something felt very, *very* wrong.

Adrien shrieked in agony while the heat beamed down on him, as it felt like he had stepped directly onto the sun. Boils started to appear all over his skin and his face started to burn up. He turned around swiftly and leapt towards the house. He sailed in the air and through the entrance. He crashed to the ground, sliding across the floor and back into the safety of the shadows.

He flipped over and crawled quickly backward, further and further away from the sunlight that was slightly spilling in through the open door.

"What the…" Adrien groaned in agony. "No way! Oh my God!" He kept crawling backward in a frenzy until he ran into something behind him.

"You are finally awake, Adrien."

Adrien turned his head abruptly and saw that it was Latimer. He leapt to his feet.

"The sun! It…it burns!" he wailed in perplexion, holding onto his face and the other areas of his body where the sun started to melt away his flesh.

"Of course it does," Latimer said unfazed as he walked over to the door.

He was careful to avoid the light spilling in and shut the door promptly. As Latimer did this, the wounds on Adrien's body and face healed quickly, and his skin looked completely untouched.

"W-What am I?" Adrien poked and prodded himself, no longer feeling any pain from the burns that had just vanished.

Adrien recollected all of the changes that had occurred to his body: a corpse-like appearance, intense speed, night vision, accelerated healing, the fangs and most convincingly his aversion to sunlight. Daytime. The light. How could he suddenly not enjoy what he had always found so much comfort in?

Latimer stared at him with his arms across his chest. "I suppose you have already perceived what you are." His eyes examined Adrien from head to toe. "And right now you must be very weak. You are famished; you have yet to feed." Latimer sounded slightly concerned.

"Feed?" he repeated in disgust. "Are you implying *that's* what you turned me into? A vampire?!" Adrien responded angrily.

Latimer was staring at him silently, not replying with a yes or a no to confirm the answer. He looked slightly ashamed and regretful.

"So you're telling me that I cannot go home, that I cannot see my fiancé, that I cannot marry her, that I *cannot* have a family... like I've always wanted. Is *that* what you're telling me?" Adrien probed bitterly as he stepped closer to him. "I would rather be dead!" Adrien screamed, pointing his finger in Latimer's face.

Latimer remained calm and breathed in slowly before sighing. "Adrien, you ultimately have a choice. What do you choose?"

"What do you mean by that?!"

"You can leave tonight, but I warn you—you will undoubtedly kill the one who matters most to you. Or you can stay here with me. Abide by my rules."

"Doesn't seem like much of a choice to me." Adrien exhaled sharply and grabbed onto his head in frustration. "Why am I here? Was this something you planned?! What do you really want from me?! Who...are you...really?"

"In due time..." Latimer said calmly. He started walking towards the back of the house and up the stairs.

Adrien reluctantly followed him, not knowing what else he could do. He cautiously walked up the stairs as they creaked under both of their feet. After they reached the top of the stairs, they made their way down the quiet hallway and entered the room where Adrien first awoke. The door that Adrien destroyed had already been replaced, and there was no longer any trace of the rubble he had made. Adrien noticed, after seeing more of the house, that the room was immaculate and without a trace of dust—like it had been carefully and meticulously prepared, for a guest.

"For now, please get some more rest. I am going into town tonight. I will bring to you what you require," Latimer stated.

Latimer then backed out of the room. The closing door echoed as the stone was shut behind him. Adrien flinched at the sound; it continued to ring in his ears while he stood apprehensively in the darkness.

Chapter 5

"The path of the righteous is like the morning sun, shining ever brighter till the full light of day. But the way of the wicked is like deep darkness; they do not know what makes them stumble."

Proverbs 4:18-19

July 25th: a quarter until two in the afternoon

Michelle sat in silence, staring at the telephone in her office. She was partially slumped down in her chair, as she had been in the same place for quite some time. Anna briskly walked by and saw Michelle through the glass window. Anna stopped and walked back to the door to lean in.

"I think you should get some rest. You have been up since last night, and isn't your family still in town, too?"

Michelle looked up at her, slightly startled. "Oh. No, actually they left this morning. Perfect timing, I guess."

"So, you're just going to continue to sit there and wait?"

"I want to make sure I don't miss this call," Michelle said as she quickly turned back towards the phone and sighed, rubbing her forehead impatiently.

Anna walked into the office and sat down on the other side of Michelle's desk. "It's almost two. If she hasn't already called you...I don't think you will be getting a call at all."

"Yeah, I kind of gathered that, too." Michelle leaned over to her printer and grabbed a piece of paper from the tray. "I already pulled her address from her driver's license, but wanted to give her a little more time before I searched for her."

"You aren't able to call her yourself first?"

"I found out where she works. She didn't show up to her shift this morning, so her manager gave me a number they have in their system for her. The number isn't actually in her name. It's under the name Adrien Reed. That's the name of the victim from last night. He has two lines but lives on his own. Looks like he's been paying for her phone. I called, but no answer."

"Do you think she did this herself? The victim was very wealthy. Perhaps she believed she could get something out of his death," Anna hypothesized.

"No, I don't believe so, but even so, the fact that he has disappeared leaves things open-ended. I honestly have a feeling that she is in danger. You already know about the dream I had about her; something very significant is going to come from this."

"Yeah?" Anna sat up straighter, even more interested in what she had to say.

"I just saw her so...*vividly*. Then there was something about a fire. That's it. I just have to keep pushing and trusting in what I was shown and I will be led to the truth eventually."

Anna was confused for a second, then laid her eyes on the cross pendant that was around her neck. "Oh. I see. You sure have a lot of faith in that stuff," she said awkwardly. "Good luck with that. I'm going to head home for the day...don't push yourself too hard." She got up from the chair and headed towards the door.

Michelle sighed while grabbing her necklace and watched her walk out of the room. The name Adrien seemed so familiar to her, but she couldn't seem to figure out why. Frustrated, she began to reflect on her dream that she had experienced a few weeks prior instead. Not much happened that could be formulated into something that made sense. She saw Jenna clearly. She was dressed in a fancy dress and in the foyer of a very nice home. She seemed to be nervous about something while frantically reading a piece of paper. Suddenly, there were flames; however, Jenna was no longer in sight. There wasn't any screaming or noises other than the sound of a raging fire consuming the house and burning it to the ground.

"What does this mean?" she whispered aloud to herself.

She rocked in her chair, her necklace now in her mouth as she sat and concentrated. After taking a few personal moments alone in the silence, she picked up the paper she printed and scanned the page of information she pulled on Jenna. She recognized the city in her address: Chelsea, Massachusetts. It was around an hour and a half away and northeast of Boston. She quickly gathered up all of her stuff and left.

***

Michelle spent an hour and a half on the road replaying her dream again and again in her head. The drive seemed to go by quickly, and she reached Chelsea in no time. Michelle turned onto the street and parked in front of a building. Leaning up against her steering wheel, she strained to look up at the tall building through her windshield and was confused by what she saw. Her eyes jumped from the number on the building and back to the GPS on her phone. She confirmed the correct location. She got out of the car and walked up close to it.

The apartment building had been condemned. It was quite evident that no one lived there. It was riddled with broken windows, one of which had curtains from the interior of a room waving in the wind against the red brick exterior. Some of the windows were boarded up while others were covered in foil. There were overgrown bushes and broken glass all over the ground near the building, as the area had been unkempt.

A few women walked behind Michelle on the street and she turned around to ask them, "Hey, excuse me? Are you from around this area?"

They stopped and nodded, looking her up and down suspiciously. Michelle looked down at herself and saw her badge clipped onto the waistband of her pants, then she hurriedly tucked her badge out of sight.

"Can you tell me how long this place has been like this?" She pointed up to the condemned building, and their eyes followed the direction of her finger.

"Oh...It's been about a year, ma'am. A lot of people went homeless after they had to shut it down. The place was a dump, though," one of the women chimed in.

"I'm sorry to hear that. Did any of you happen to know a woman named Jenna McBrayer who may have lived here?"

"We don't know anyone with that name." All of them shook their heads.

"Okay, thank you, ladies." She nodded at them.

They all continued briskly on their way down the sidewalk. Michelle started to walk around a few blocks in search for at least someone who knew Jenna or had seen her. She spent about two hours investigating and interviewing anyone she passed. She then returned to her car with no new information and plopped down into the driver seat.

"Great," she sighed and looked up, "now what?"

She pulled out her notebook, flipping to a page that was titled with Jenna's name. She jotted down a few notes then shut her notepad. All she could do was wait and hope to hear from Jenna herself. She let out a large drawn-out yawn, then fastened her seatbelt to begin her hour and a half drive back to Yarmouth.

***

In Bourne, Massachusetts, there was a large, elaborate, modern mansion sitting on a plot of land at the edge of a cliff. Parked outside was a brand-new silver and black Audi R8, the same car that had left Adrien's estate in a hurry just the prior night. Jenna sat in the kitchen of a home that felt foreign to her. Though she had spent nearly a year there, she now felt completely out of place. It had been a long day for her. Her cheek was still flushed red and inflamed from where the man had hit her. She fought so much that night after returning to consciousness, that she passed out again and spent most of the day sleeping. Her eyes ached in pain, having stared endlessly without blinking, replaying in her mind the tragic events that happened.

She stared down at her fiddling hands just beneath the table and then switched her attention to the man on the other side of the room. Hot grease splashed all over the kitchen as he clumsily tried to tend to the food cooking on the stove. An awful smell enveloped the room as the food was scorched to the pan. Some of the grease popped and splattered on his suit. He cursed and shot a sharp glare in her direction. She quickly looked away from him and out the window. The sun was almost completely gone as the day began to turn over to night.

Yesterday morning, Jenna was sitting in the same seat when she told this man that she was leaving him. Yet, she found herself back in the same spot, but now suffering a heartache that she could not fully put into words. She believed it all to be her fault, that she sort of deserved every bit of this punishment.

The man before her was named Brock, he was one of the wealthiest bachelors in Massachusetts. He owned multiple businesses: pharmaceutical and real estate—the real estate company was given to him by his father not long out of high school. Jenna had met him about a year ago, then she moved in with him a few months later because she needed a place to stay.

Brock knew a secret about her family that she couldn't bring herself to reveal to Adrien. Brock had always known about Adrien; he found it thrilling to compete for her, but couldn't accept when she chose Adrien over him. Jenna had never come clean to Adrien about Brock.

Brock turned around from the counter, carrying two plates of food that were obviously burnt to a crisp. Jenna watched the steam lift from the plates and had the sudden urge to puke. Adrien had wanted to marry her on that day, and now the hope of that would never be fulfilled. She started to tap her hand on the glass table uncontrollably, as the tension within her mind approached its brim. He set down both of the plates and took a seat on the other side of the glass table.

"You should be the one slaving over that hot stove...not me," he said as he quickly slid one of the plates in her direction.

She held her hand up to the table's edge and let the plate hit her palm, preventing the dish from sliding off the table. She scoffed at the plate of charred meat in front of her.

"You can't just act like nothing happened! Do you expect me to just forget what you did?!" Jenna crossed her arms over her chest.

He stared emotionless at her for what seemed like an eternity, then his face started to turn red. He jumped up from the table and kicked his chair into the wall behind him. Jenna flinched as the chair slammed so hard into the wall that it chipped off the wall paint and a chunk of sheetrock beneath it. Brock's hand darted across the table and grabbed her chin. The force almost made her bite her own tongue, adrenaline pumping through her veins as fear filled her.

He forced her to look around the room. "Take a look around, Jenna!" he said furiously. "What have I done?! I'll tell you what I have done! I opened my home to you and practically gave you the world! But, what did you do? You tried to leave me." He huffed and paused for a moment, his dark eyes searched her up and down. "You know I *always* get what I want." He released her chin and sat back down in the chair, brushing off his suit and preparing to eat.

She trembled in fear, not understanding how she could have ever seen an ounce of good in this man. How could she have allowed him to fool her enough to trust him? She stared back at him, teary-eyed, and shook her head in disbelief. Her face heated up; she refused to cry in front of Brock again.

"Adrien didn't deserve this!" she yelled.

"Oh, please." He took a large bite of food, pointed his fork at her and continued to talk with his mouth full, "I helped you finally stick with a decision. That's all."

"You are so sick! I *made* a decision!" she responded angrily.

"Well, it was the wrong one." He spat the food back out onto the plate. "Argh! This is terrible!" He took his napkin and rubbed the food from his tongue and crumbled it up. He looked back up at her. "You know what? Now that I think about it, what I did was quite merciful. Now he never has to know. You will never have to crush his little heart. You're welcome."

He slammed both of his hands down on the glass as he got up from the table. Jenna jumped, startled by his volatile nature. He started to walk out of the room, but on his way out he tossed the crumpled napkin onto the tile floor just a few feet from the trash can.

"Clean this up." He gestured to everything in the kitchen as he had his back turned to her. "Then get dressed. We're leaving."

He continued out of the kitchen and went to the living room, then he sat down on the couch and propped his feet up on the coffee table. He turned on the television and switched to the news. Jenna closed her eyes for a few moments to calm her nerves, then she took a deep breath before she got up to start cleaning.

Chapter 6

"Like a city whose walls are broken through is a person who lacks self-control."

Proverbs 25:28

It had been an hour after the sun had set, and the old stone home in the middle of the forest was enshrouded in darkness. A fire was burning, and soft light was coming from the crackling embers within the fireplace. Adrien slowly opened his eyes; he hoped that he was waking up from this nightmare in the comfort of his own home. That, unfortunately, was not the case. He sat upright in his coffin, which was elevated on a stone slab that had four steps down to the floor. Earlier, he had tried to rest on the floor or on the couch that was also in the room, but he couldn't find any comfort until he finally gave in and got inside of the coffin. He left the lid open, for he did not have the courage to close himself within it.

Though he was able to lay still, he was awake almost the

entire time, replaying the last few normal days of his life that he could remember. He reflected on his home, his "lighthouse" that he held so dear, his morning swims and the warmth of the sun as he would frequently lay on the beach. He could not help but cringe at those thoughts, now knowing how his body reacts to the sun. He reminisced about his recent times with Jenna, up to the moment that he slid the engagement ring on her finger. His heart ached but physically felt completely absent within him.

He swiftly lifted his hand to his neck and felt around desperately for his pulse. Minutes went by...nothing. The darkness surrounding him seemed to pull him further into the realization, as it was surreal. Just as he was about to remove his hand, there was one strong beat. His heart seemed to beat powerfully, but just once every few minutes. This gave him just a sliver of hope.

All of a sudden, he was startled by a sensation of liquid running down his cheeks from his eyes. He quickly wiped his cheeks off with his hands and looked down at his fingers to see that they were smeared with red liquid. It was his blood—no, it was his *tears*. Tears of blood. He exhaled sharply in disbelief as he continued to discover the changes that occurred inside of him, dreading what his near future would further reveal.

Wiping his hands and face off on his already bloody clothes, he sat still while he stared at the wall in front of him. His silhouette was projected against the surface from the light of the fireplace; his gigantic, exaggerated shadow looked menacing, like it belonged to a monster. He wondered how this was now his reality. How could it be true?

Doors opened, and then the sound of multiple pairs of boots heavily thumping on the floor followed. Shortly after, voices traveled from downstairs. Finally breaking his gaze from the wall, Adrien looked to his right and saw fresh clothes folded for him on the table next to an armoire. Without hesitation, he jumped out of his coffin. He ripped off his bloody clothes and threw them into the fireplace to change into the clean ones. He paused to gaze at the intensified crackling of the fire, his eyes widening as his old clothes were consumed by flames.

Out of nowhere, an uncomfortable rumbling overcame his body and sharp pangs traveled through his muscles. It felt as though the pain was within every single cell of his body. The discomfort quickly escalated into an excruciating pain that took his breath away. It was a while before he recognized that it was hunger; it was not just refined to his stomach as he was accustomed to. Terrified, he staggered around in the room and caught himself on the arm of the couch. The pain then faded away just enough so he could stand up straight. He then rushed out of the room as if running from what he just experienced. Not knowing where to go, he gravitated towards the voices downstairs.

Latimer stood at the head of a long, ornate dining room table where Cade and Coran were sitting.

"His first experience must be within confinement in this house," Latimer asserted. "Or he will be dangerously unpredictable."

"Not to mention, we know you won't take full advantage

of your control over him," Coran concluded, clearly bothered.

"We will break his Hunter nature soon enough. I found someone for him like you asked, Latimer," Cade reported, then looked at his watch. "He frequents Nye Park near the shelter and meets our requirements. His observed habit suggests we have ten minutes until he is in the area, we sh—"

Cade stopped talking, and they all looked over to the entrance of the room. Adrien was trembling as he stood silently in the large stone archway, his eyebrows furrowed in confusion and fear.

"So..." Coran got up and walked towards him. "My dear little Adrien," he said mockingly. "I heard about your little run-in with the sun today! How splendid!"

Adrien's fear vanished as anger overcame him, and he lifted his upper lip and growled. Coran's hand shot toward him and clutched his shoulder with a death grip. He viciously growled back, making sure he showed more teeth.

"Stop, Coran. You seem to be of no help other than provoking him," Cade said, perturbed, while getting up as well.

"I'm just waiting for this punk here to hiss at me again!" Coran snarled as his grip continued to tighten on Adrien's shoulder.

Adrien yanked his shoulder from Coran's grasp and walked around him to address Latimer, "So, your little *vampire* friends come here to taunt me because they've got nothing better to do?" he protested bitterly.

"They are here to help you," Latimer calmly explained.

Adrien felt the grumbling again, but it had intensified significantly since the last time. He bent over and groaned in agony. "W-what is this?!" Adrien continued to moan in pain.

Cade, Coran and Latimer all looked at each other and then back to Adrien.

"I will go on my own," Latimer declared while glancing at both Coran and Cade as he turned to leave.

"Both of you go. I will stay here with him," Coran offered.

"Trusting you to be alone with him would be quite careless," Cade scorned.

"You know, I just like to show a little tough love," Coran chuckled. "I'm not going to hurt him. Go on."

Latimer eyed Coran sternly over his shoulder then looked over to Adrien, his eyes remaining stern. "Very well then. Cade and I will be back shortly," Latimer affirmed as he left.

Cade rolled his eyes and followed suit. Coran approached the door as they exited.

"Ohhh no, come on! Don't leave me here with this guy!" Adrien pleaded after them through weighty breaths.

Coran closed the door behind them and turned around to face Adrien with his arms crossed. "I don't know what it is about you. Latimer has not told us why you are here...why he decided to turn you. You hold some sort of importance and...I am unsure *why*." Coran lifted his own hand and rubbed the scruff on his chin. He then walked up closer to Adrien with narrow eyes and surveyed him. "The truth is…you are a liability. A risk that I am not fond of."

"So what are you going to do about that?" Adrien questioned coldly.

"Just don't push it. I don't want to have to kill you."

"I…am not convinced that's something you *don't* want to do," Adrien said as he instinctively backed away from him.

Coran scoffed. "Latimer has helped my family and me a great deal the past few decades. I will repay him in any way I can."

"Your *family?*" Adrien whispered back to him in disbelief.

"I have a wife. A kid. If you screw this up, royally enough that is, we will have to leave. All of us will."

Adrien was taken aback by this information. His eyes lit up as some more hope was quickly restored to him. Coran noticed the change in his expression.

"Hey—don't get any ideas. My wife and kid are…like *us*… It is not at all what I had hoped it would be either."

"What you hoped? You made them what they are?" Adrien guessed, without thinking.

Coran pursed his lips and sighed. "My wife, yes. My daughter…well, I had to enlist help to turn her."

"Why?"

"A rule of our nature. If we try to turn someone we share a bloodline with, we will end up killing them instead. One hundred percent of the time. This life is terrible, even when you have the ones you love with you. A little bit of Hell on earth, if you ask me. I wouldn't wish this on anyone, not even my worst enemies. So... it's unfortunate that you are here. Not only for me, but mainly for you," Coran revealed chillingly.

Adrien scoffed, remembering the koi fish tattoo on Coran's back. It was odd how fitting it seemed now.

"What is the best way out of this, then? There *must* be a way out. If not, what's the point? Why choose to still live like this?" Adrien questioned him.

Coran eyed him up and down and tried to figure him out. He had a tribal tattoo that looked like an animal claw had slashed around his left eye in black ink. He was also dressed in all black with a leather vest. His muscular arms were pumped with testosterone, riddled with elevated veins and an innumerable amount of tattooed arts. Though he had a tough appearance, Adrien could see the pain and confusion in his eyes from the question.

Adrien didn't want to have anything to do with it. "Just let me leave," he pleaded.

"That's not going to happen."

"Come on." Adrien started to pace. "Look, there is this woman...her name is Jenna. She means the world to me. I asked her to marry me—just last night. I need to see her. You *must* understand," the tone in Adrien's voice saddened as he spoke.

Coran toughened his stance, suggesting that he was not budging on the subject. "You don't know what you need," Coran said sternly.

"And *you* do?" Adrien snapped back.

Coran's eyes narrowed as he stood in silence.

It was not long before Adrien grew frustrated and very impatient. He then noticed that he was no longer in any more pain, as it seemed to come in waves. He pondered, trying to think of a way to get out of that place with Coran watching him like a hawk.

He sighed heavily. "So, uh..." Adrien looked around, attempting to change the subject. "I take it that Latimer lives here on his own."

Coran nodded, looking around as well.

"Why the big home if it's just him?"

"Latimer is actually an architect. It's what he was as a human, also. He built this place on his own, from scratch...if you think this is too much, wait until you see the home he built for me and my family."

"He *built* you a home? How come you don't know more about me if you are as close to him as it seems? Why the secret?"

Coran silently walked to the other side of the room and then leaned up against the table, keeping his eyes on Adrien.

"Do you know Latimer's been following me almost my entire life?" Adrien continued to prod. "I first saw him when I was three. I thought it was all just my imagination but...here we are."

Adrien could tell by the look in Coran's eyes that he truly didn't know the answers to those questions. Either that, or Coran had mastered his poker face. That wouldn't be too far-fetched, after all, he must have been much older than what his appearance suggested, just like Latimer. Coran was still leaning up against the table, his head cocked to the side and his eyes squinted even more at Adrien.

Adrien then pondered about the youthful appearances of Latimer, Cade and Coran. "Is it truly like the myths? Are you...am I...*immortal*?" Adrien continued in his questioning.

Coran rolled his eyes, letting out a long, drawn-out sigh while he dropped his head back to look up at the ceiling. "You sure ask a lot of questions," Coran grumbled.

"Well, wouldn't you if you were me?" Adrien retorted, eager for him to respond with useful information.

Coran, who was across the room, was then unexpectedly in Adrien's face, his eyes filled with fire. Adrien's hair blew slightly from the breeze of Coran's quick movements; he stumbled backward, startled.

"Be careful. Keep asking and you might get an answer you *really* don't want to hear," Coran advised chillingly.

They stood in silence again, staring at one another. Adrien found it hard to continue to look Coran in the eyes. The red of his irises were just as intense as Latimer's, and though Adrien had not fully seen himself, he knew that his eyes must have looked close to the same. He then remembered seeing all of the vampires with variances of eye colors when he first came in contact with them.

"Why do your eyes keep shifting color? Sometimes they are blue...but now they are red," Adrien asked.

Coran rolled his eyes. "Camouflage. It proves useful at times...we stand out less," he said nonchalantly.

"How can you control that?" Adrien prodded some more.

Coran narrowed his eyes in annoyance, then folded his arms over his chest.

Adrien sighed, then began to walk out of the room.

"Where do you think you're headed off to?" Coran called out after him.

"If you refuse to answer any more of my questions, I'd rather not just stand here and stare at you all night. That a problem?" he remarked sarcastically over his shoulder as he continued towards the staircase.

Coran chuckled and followed him. He stopped at the bottom of the stairs and watched Adrien as he walked up to the second floor. Adrien then stumbled as a weakness suddenly traveled through his entire body. The pain of hunger returned to him with a vengeance and his knees buckled, causing him to collapse forward just a couple steps shy from the top of the staircase. Adrien grunted as he grasped at the iron steps to prevent himself from sliding down them. Coran snickered. Adrien turned his head and glared in his direction. Coran then shook his head as he walked back into the other room.

Adrien looked forward again. The span of the last two steps seem to expand in his sight, and his arms began to tremble. With all of his strength, he pulled himself up the remaining steps and propped himself against the post on the very top of the stairs. His efforts were so extreme that he began to feel himself perspire. With his past experience, he was reluctant to wipe his sweat away.

His hand shook as he lifted it to his forehead. He gently wiped his skin and nervously looked at his hand. It was just as he fearfully anticipated, his sweat—just like his tears—was made of blood. His stomach dropped, and he looked away from his hand as the pain continued to pulse throughout his body. He wanted to be rid of the agony, but he was dreading what needed to be done in order for that to happen.

A few minutes passed while Adrien dealt with the agony. He exhaled sharply, then he breathed in deeply as the pain lifted, the wave passing. He looked to his right and saw the door that led to the balcony. Getting up quickly but quietly, he then leaned up against the door and listened for the same noises from the previous night; he could still hear the cars from the city. His hand hovered over the handle and he gently cracked open the door.

At that same moment, a phone rang downstairs. Adrien side-eyed the staircase in his peripheral while he continued to slowly open the door; he heard Coran answer his cell phone. Coran began to laugh in conversation with whoever was on the other end. Adrien then heard him walking and his footsteps moving further away, seemingly down another flight of stairs. He was speaking of a room in the basement being prepared. The others were about to return. It was now, or never.

When the door opened just enough for him to barely fit through, Adrien ran out to the edge of the balcony. He grasped the railing and hung over the edge, calculating how far the drop was. Taking note of all of the vines along the exterior wall, he realized they were fit to climb and grabbed onto them. He quickly moved down the vines, making as little noise as possible until his feet touched the ground. He was free.

Adrien rushed into the forest and followed the sound of the cars in the distance. He ran as quickly as he could, barely weaving between the tree trunks and branches. He seemed to have become more accustomed to his enhanced speed, but he was unable to gauge how far he was actually running.

The smell of salt was overwhelming as it filled the air, and he could sense that he was close to water. He saw that the trees were thinning out and picked up his pace until he made it out of the forest. Adrien gasped and put on the brakes as hard as he could. He fell and slid along the ground, barely stopping as the tree line ended right at the edge of a cliff. His legs dangled over the ledge as the rocks near him plunged into the waters below. He was on one of the islands just offshore of the mainland. The city was not far off; about one mile of water was now between him and the mainland.

"Well, well, well. Look what we have here," Coran said over Adrien's shoulder.

Adrien leapt to his feet and jerked around, previously unaware of Coran's presence. He backed up as far as he could to the edge of the cliff and teetered as his heels had crossed the precipice. There was about a twenty-foot drop into the choppy waters below.

Coran sighed. "You just don't get it." He paced back and

forth, then he stopped. "You will have to learn for yourself out there. Go on." He gestured toward the city. "Go ahead."

Adrien looked at Coran suspiciously and then back to the choppy waters below. Adrien was not afraid of the water—he had spent almost every day in it, whether it was his pool or the ocean behind his home. Looking back to Coran one last time, he leapt backward off the cliff. Adrien kept his eyes on Coran as he descended; he saw Coran lift a phone to his ear just before the rocky wall of the cliff obstructed his view.

The fall was seemingly short as Adrien plunged into the dark waters quickly. Due to Adrien's new body temperature, what would normally be freezing cold waters felt abnormally warm. The feel of the water on his skin was something he never felt before—he could feel every bubble, every molecule on his body as the current flowed. Adrien began to swing his arms over his head in a freestyle swim; his arms cut into the waves as they propelled him towards the shore of the city on the other side. His new speed not only applied to him on land but also in the water as he reached the other side in record time.

Adrien emerged from the water and sloshed up on the shore. Dripping wet, he turned around to look back at the cliff for Coran. He was no longer there. Adrien's eyes searched the waters to see if he had followed, but there was no trace of him. As he turned around to continue his journey, he was startled by Coran. Coran was standing in front of Adrien, completely dry, with a cocky grin plastered across his face.

***

After Jenna cleaned the mess that Brock made, they got in the car and drove a few miles away from the house to the city. Brock had taken her to a quiet French café.

"Why are we here?" Jenna said as she looked around in discomfort.

He had chosen this location because it was normally very slow, especially this night of the week. They were the only ones that were sitting in the restaurant, and he had the waiter take them to one of the tables near the back.

"You know...you and I used to have a pretty good time. I would take you out, you would look good on my arm, I'd buy you things...you never complained. Things will return to normal soon," he said confidently while he was eyeing the menu.

The waitress came back up to the table and Brock ordered them food. They sat in silence until their food arrived. He paid the check in advance and started to eat. Jenna didn't touch her food, staring blankly at the wall behind him.

Someone else came into the cafe and sat a few tables over from them, ordering a black coffee. Brock looked over, uncomfortable with her proximity to their table, then he begrudgingly continued to eat his food. Jenna grimaced as she watched Brock chow down on his meal. Feeling tense, she could sense that someone must be watching her. She looked over to her left and a few tables over, her eyes jumped as she recognized the woman.

Michelle was staring at Jenna in confusion, and then her eyes flickered over to Brock, narrowing even further. She started to get up from her seat but Jenna quickly signaled to her to stop with a subtle jerk of her head. Michelle got the hint immediately; the situation was precarious. Michelle's eyes bore into the two of them as she grabbed a piece of paper from her bag to scribble on. Once she finished writing, she impatiently bounced her knee under the table until her coffee arrived.

Brock finished his food, and then he looked over to Jenna's untouched plate. He shrugged, grabbing her plate of food and consuming it quickly for himself. Jenna's heart pounded in her chest as she was short of breath from the tension—so thick that it was hard for her to breathe. She glanced back over to Michelle who was inconspicuously sipping her coffee and writing in her notepad. The first piece of paper she was writing on was folded neatly and sat next to her hand. She clicked her pen, then she slightly tilted the notepad just enough so Jenna could read the message that was on the paper.

"Hey!" Brock blurted out as he pushed his chair back, creating a loud and obnoxious grind between the metal and the tile floor. "Time to get out of here."

Jenna inadvertently gasped and her heart pounded even faster. Brock noted the direction she was looking and he glowered at Michelle suspiciously. Michelle had already flipped her notepad closed and was looking off in the opposite direction. The waitress then came with Michelle's check and blocked Brock's view of her.

No longer paying attention to Michelle, Brock motioned to Jenna for them to leave. As they left, Jenna dropped her purse on the floor. Michelle watched them leave in her peripheral, waiting a few moments before getting up to grab Jenna's purse. She slipped the folded note into the bag and followed them.

**

Adrien stared at Coran, confused as to how he was able to get over there so quickly without taking a plunge in the waters as he had.

Adrien began to speak, "How did you—"

The wind picked up and a sudden gust carried a strange scent just under Adrien's nose. His mind went instantly blank; he could no longer think, as his blood seemed to boil within his veins. His throat constricted and the veins in his neck started to protrude. Without forethought, Adrien bolted off towards the city. There was still a short area of woods between the shore and the city streets, but with his speed, he closed the gap quickly while leaping over tree stumps and dodging branches. An innate nature took over him as he no longer had control over his actions. Just as Adrien broke through the brush and to the road, he was quickly pulled back into the bushes. A car sped by, the person driving it blared their horn as they believed they were about to run over a man.

Cade had just shown up and had Adrien in his grasp. He had him from behind in a chokehold, with his hand clamped over Adrien's mouth. Adrien hissed and growled, his eyes intensified as he attempted to see what smelled so enticing on the other side of the street. It was a busy road, but there was no one walking the street other than the two—no, three people not far off. He couldn't see them clearly as the shrubbery still blocked his view. Their scent wafted in the air around him, driving him completely mad. His vision was crimson and all he could think about was devouring them.

Never had he experienced such a volatile reaction, especially from hunger. His muscles twitched and contorted. It felt as if he was being torn apart from the inside as every cell within him demanded to continue across the road. Latimer walked into Adrien's view and gestured for him to be silent; Adrien stopped hissing for a moment. Cade removed his hand from Adrien's mouth.

"For the love of God, let me go!" Adrien shouted and started to snarl again, catching stronger whiffs of the humans' scent. Cade clamped his hand back over Adrien's mouth and wrestled him still as he squirmed to break free. Adrien was still very strong though his body was weak.

"I will not allow it," Latimer mandated. "Besides, you do not want to kill the female," he assured Adrien.

Adrien was confused. He squirmed just enough to manage to peek through the bushes and make out the faces of the people walking along the other side of the road. He recognized them. Adrien felt like a bowling ball dropped in his gut.

It was Jenna, and she was walking with the very man from the night before. His *murderer*. The taillights flashed on a silver and black Audi R8 a few feet in front of them as the couple approached the car. Adrien, filled with rage, exuded all of his strength to break free; it took both Cade and now Coran to restrain him.

Before Adrien knew what had happened, he felt extreme pressure as they lifted off into the air. The wind blew violently through his hair as he looked down, seeing the city grow smaller the further they climbed in altitude. The alluring scent quickly faded as he was enveloped by moisture from the clouds, the city completely vanishing from his sight.

Chapter 7

"Dear friends, I urge you, as foreigners and exiles, to abstain from sinful desires, which wage war against your soul."

1 Peter 2:11

Jenna and Brock continued to travel down the sidewalk. A third set of footsteps quickly approached them just as they reached the car. Brock turned around defensively, and Jenna slowed down while peeking over her shoulder.

"Excuse me, ma'am!" Michelle shouted, catching up to them.

Jenna turned to fully face her. She was nervous, not certain of what Michelle planned to say to them. Michelle walked with confidence, her badge still tucked away and out of sight. She approached Jenna with her hand outstretched and holding the purse that she left behind.

"Hello. I'm sorry. I noticed that you left your purse in the café…I took it upon myself to bring it to you." Michelle's gaze did not break from Jenna's eyes and she could clearly see the fear within them.

Jenna started to speak, "Oh…w-well, thank—"

"Take your purse and let's *go*, Jenna," Brock barked out impatiently and then sat in the car, starting it up and revving the engine.

Jenna went to grab the purse from Michelle, but Michelle did not let go of it until Jenna looked up and held eye contact with her. Michelle raised her eyebrows and glanced down at the bag in both their hands before looking back up to Jenna. Jenna folded her lips and breathed in deeply. Exhaling slowly, she lightly nodded her head. Michelle loosened her grasp on the purse and Jenna quickly turned to get into the car.

Brock sped off just as Jenna closed the door. She took a deep breath and held tightly onto her purse, wondering what the folded note that Michelle had placed within it could possibly say. She carefully looked at Brock from the corner of her eye; he was angrily holding the steering wheel while glaring at the road. She looked back down to her purse and felt a slight glimmer of hope; she planned to share the entire truth with the police this time. She only just needed an opportunity to do so. Hopefully, whatever was in this purse would be the opportunity she desperately needed.

Michelle watched as the car drove off. She prayed intently that what she gave would suffice for Jenna, then she quickly took out her notepad to jot down information. Content with her efforts, Michelle then sensed something. Looking to her left and across the street through the passing cars, she fixated on the woods lining the other side of the road. Not knowing why, she felt an overwhelming sense of danger.

***

Dazed by the struggle and the flight, Adrien was dragged by his arms back into the old stone home. Though he was nowhere near their scent anymore, the aroma of Jenna and Brock's blood was still burned within his senses. Adrien screamed in agony as he was overcome with pain from the hunger, but now it was worse than ever before and was not letting up. They laid him down on the floor in the foyer.

"I am grateful for your assistance tonight. I understand you have other matters to attend to," Latimer expressed to Cade and Coran.

Coran nodded, catching one last glimpse of Adrien before he left out the door. He shook his head and smirked as he exited.

Cade lingered a bit longer. "You think he let him go on purpose?" Cade asked, slightly gesturing his head in the direction Coran went.

"I am certain he did," Latimer replied.

"Huh. At least we got to him just in time." Cade then leaned over and whispered to Latimer, "There is something... *abnormal* about Adrien. Aside from the fact that I have far more years than he, for as weak as he is, he should not have almost escaped my grasp. I had a hard time restraining him even before he recognized those people." He then backed up a few steps and spoke at his normal volume, "I'll leave you to tend to him. I shall return whenever you need, Latimer." Cade walked out, closing the door behind him.

Latimer watched Cade leave and pondered about what he said. He then thought back to the morning when Adrien was exposed to the sun, his skin healed in a rate that he had never seen before...a rate of healing abnormal for even a vampire.

Adrien belted out another shriek of pain, breaking Latimer from his thoughts. He approached Adrien. Bending down to grab onto his arms, he hurriedly slung them over his shoulder and lifted him up to his feet. Supporting most of Adrien's weight as he led him out of the room, Latimer took him underground to the basement.

There was a small room at the end of a very long hallway; a dark nook that was barred up like a jail cell. Cade and Latimer had already returned home just as they received the call from Coran that Adrien was loose and heading toward the city. They dropped off their bounty before leaving again. The aroma Adrien sensed before flooded back as Latimer led him closer to this room. Adrien's vision went crimson again, his throat tightened in response to it.

"I must explain something to you, Adrien," Latimer began to disclose. "There are two kinds of vampires. We are called Harvesters. We like to reside in one place. In order for that, we have to sustain control. We kill much less than those we call Hunters...it makes us less...savage," Latimer explained as he dragged Adrien along. "We live our lives strategically to avoid suspicion. This is the way it will be for you; eventually, you will build a resistance and will not have to feed as often as your body beckons you to now."

Adrien barely listened, carnally focused on the smell of blood that drew ever nearer. He began to feel and hear the warm pulse emanating from the person locked away within the cell. Adrien's conscience finally grasped what was about to happen.

"No! NO!" He attempted to stop, fighting back against Latimer, but now he was too weak. "There must…there must be another way! Please!"

They reached the cell doors. Latimer opened the cell and pushed him in, closing the door behind him. Adrien turned around and pressed himself up against bars, grasping onto them while he continued to plead. He looked at Latimer desperately, his face pressed between the iron.

"Please don't let me do this!" Adrien begged.

"This is…unavoidable," Latimer said as he clenched his jaw. His concerned, regretful eyes tried to avoid contact with Adrien for long. He turned his back to him and sighed. "It will be over quickly," Latimer blurted out as he walked away. He hastily reached the end of the hallway and traveled up the stairs without as much of a glance back towards Adrien.

Adrien shut his eyes tightly and attempted to hold his breath, but the scent still seeped through, permeating the surface of his skin. He heard the very light whimper of a man who was terrified in the corner. Adrien slowly turned around and looked at the man cowering in the dark.

Choosing to breathe freely again, Adrien fully took in his scent. The man huddled even further into the wall as Adrien took a few steps towards him. Adrien's hands and legs trembled, and his mind battled with what his new nature was inducing him to do. He then inhaled deeply and exhaled with a drawn-out sigh.

"Do you have any idea how *amazing* you smell?" Adrien said, leaning in closer to the man. He was face-to-face with him, his mouth watering profusely.

"Uh-Um! T-Thank you?!" the man shrieked in confusion.

By the man's appearance and state of his clothes, he was quite obviously homeless. Adrien suddenly recognized the man that was cowering before him. When Adrien was eight years old, he had just moved to a new group home. He was immediately teased from being the youngest, for his physical appearance and for his odd behavior from his sleepless nights. Another boy named Chris, who was close to aging out of the foster care system, was the only one who showed him any kindness. Chris was significantly older than Adrien and it was only six months before he turned eighteen and was released into the world.

After Adrien aged out himself, he had seen Chris multiple times in the years he spent volunteering at the homeless shelter not too far from there. This was Chris...in the flesh. Adrien felt a rush of guilt and concern for him; he wanted to help him, to save him from this. However, what was now within Adrien—this darkness—had a hold on him. The desire to see this man delivered to safety vanished as quickly as it came.

"That wasn't a compliment...for *your* sake," Adrien said sinisterly.

Adrien felt as if he was no longer within his own body. His conscience sat aside, helpless in horror, as his flesh took over.

"A-Adrien? Is...is that you?" Chris asked, suddenly recognizing Adrien, despite his drastic change in appearance.

Adrien heard Chris's heartbeat begin to race faster and the blood rush quicker through his veins. It was no longer bearable... Adrien could no longer fight it. Chris saw the darkness in Adrien's eyes and believed that who he thought he just recognized must have been a mistake. This could never be the Adrien he knew. Adrien snarled, lifting his upper lip to flash his fangs.

Chris cried and pleaded, "Please! Please don't kill m—"

Adrien lunged and grabbed him by the neck to yank him closer, his teeth plunged deep into Chris's flesh. A grueling sensation took Adrien aback. He tried to stop but was unable to; he was filled with almost equal amounts of pain and gratification. Chris attempted to push him off, but Adrien's strength was paramount to his. Chris fought, squirmed and gurgled as the life was sucked out of him. As Adrien continued, the blood felt like acid coating his esophagus, and the pain was agonizing. He also felt the warmth from it spreading through his own body. He tried to stop again, but he couldn't. It was not very long before Chris stopped moving completely, and his pulse became absent. He was dead.

Adrien was finally able to pull away from him; he ran to

the other side of the cell and fell down. He shook in the corner with his hands over his head. His throat still burned, but he felt his body strengthening.

"W-what have I done?" he whispered while looking at the dirty ground beneath him.

He had blood on his forehead and all over his mouth and chin. Adrien sat in the corner, staring at the deceased man now laid out across the floor. That man: a man who had been orphaned...just as he, a man that was broken...just as he, dead... just as he might as well have been. Adrien's mind spiraled as he sat in the cold, dark cell. Never in his life would he have thought he would be responsible for the death of another person, and yet there he was...responsible in the most gruesome way he could think of.

Adrien then remembered catching the very last of the vampire's discussion as he came from upstairs earlier in the night. They spoke of this man near the shelter and had planned to take him. Adrien then thought about all of the people that used to frequent the shelter and how many would seem to drop off the face of the planet, never showing up again. He rejoiced at the time, believing that those people were getting off the streets. He looked around the dark and dreary room, wondering if many of them actually ended up in that very cell...with the same fate as Chris.

Adrien grew nauseous but lacked the ability to throw up. The pit of emptiness in his soul grew. He wondered how in the world Jenna could have ever loved a man who could turn into someone capable of doing something like this.

"Jenna..." Adrien's mind flipped focus instantly. "Jenna! What was she doing with that guy?!" he spoke aloud to himself.

His emotions were heightened and he did not know how to control them. He was just remorseful beyond repair but now he was filled up with an envious rage. Now that he had his full strength, he burst out of the cell, ran up the stairs, back out of the house and through the forest. He did not see Latimer when he came up out of the basement, but he was not going to wait around for him to attempt to stop him.

Adrien was now much quicker after feeding. He glanced over his shoulder expecting to see Latimer coming after him, but there was still no sign of him. In the back of his mind, he was shocked by how quickly he got over killing Chris. He started to realize just how much had changed; besides the physical aspect of him, something was altered in him psychologically, and it was not good. In light of what just happened, he knew deep down that he should stay away from Jenna. However, the blood gave him a high that also clouded his judgment.

Adrien made it all the way to the cliff that overlooked the bay and faced the mainland. He tried to focus, wondering how the others were able to fly. Gravity still governed him as he winded up and leapt as high in the air as possible just to come straight back down. After a few more attempts, he decided that he didn't have time to try to figure it out. He turned to look behind him again, paranoid that he was being followed. Still no sign of Latimer.

Standing on the edge of the cliff, he looked along the

shore on the other side of the body of water before him. He tried to make out what he could see from where he was standing first, scouring the area. Something caught his eye far northwest of him. He saw a modern home that was situated on a cliff with a very nice sports car parked in the driveway. A black and silver Audi R8 was lit up by the moonlight, the same car he witnessed Jenna and that man walking towards earlier in the night.

Without anymore hesitation, Adrien dropped down into the water and swam diagonally in the direction of the mansion. As he reached the other side, he emerged from the water, the current pushing him up against the steep wall of rock. He grabbed ahold of the wet rocks and quickly climbed them. The climb was so effortless that Adrien felt like he could have held onto each rock with just the tips of his fingers and still have more than enough strength to ascend. He reached the top and flung himself over the ledge, landing into the soft, plush grass of the well-manicured lawn. Rain clouds started to roll over and it began to lightly drizzle.

There were many large windows on this house, and it seemed like all of the lights were turned off. Adrien circled around the home and then spotted a window on the side where warm light was spilling out onto the small patio just outside of it. Adrien slowly snuck up to this window and grew anxious as he drew closer.

SNAP!

Adrien froze in his tracks, not taking his eyes away from the window before him. After a few moments, there seemed to be no movement from that window in response to the noise he made, so he broke his forward gaze to look down. He had stepped on some twigs lying on the lawn. He walked around them and was careful to avoid any more of them as he continued to approach the home.

He reached the patio and saw the window from the side, unable to look into the room right away. Climbing over the railing, he pressed his back along the edge of the wall of the house. He slowly slid closer to the window, then leaned over to peek through.

His heart fluttered. He recognized Jenna; she was laying on a bed, her back to the window with disheveled hair and her body partially clothed. She was slightly shaking. As Adrien watched silently, he realized that she was crying while she was balled up in the fetal position on the mattress.

"What did he do to you?" Adrien muttered angrily under his breath.

Adrien's heart ached as he listened to her sobs. Stepping out from behind the wall and squaring his shoulders to the window completely, he reached forward and placed his hand flatly on the thick glass.

"What I wouldn't give to be able to touch you right now," Adrien whispered, his grief-stricken voice quivered. "To be close to you...once again."

Looking down, he eyed the handle of the door next to the window, desiring more than anything to open the door and sweep her up into his arms. He was then reminded of the danger that he posed to her as the scent of her blood began to seep through the walls and the glass window. His vision turned crimson, yet again, and his mouth began to water. It was nowhere near as intense as it was before when he was starved and weak, but Adrien felt the beginnings of his loss of control. His new nature wanted to take over, to break through the glass and tear into her throat, rather than wiping away her tears.

Adrien quickly turned and leapt off the patio, sprinting back towards the cliff. Not only was his vision crimson again, but his throat had also begun to tighten and he felt the veins protruding from his neck; the signs he had quickly learned to mean danger. He reached the edge of the lawn and glanced back to the house just before he dove off the cliff and back into the water. Once he plunged into the bay, he kept swimming, desperate to get as far away from her as possible.

Anguish weighed down his arms as he slowed to a halt about halfway back to the shore. He could not help but replay the image in his mind of Jenna sobbing, making it harder for him to go on. The sound of her weeping still rang in his ears as the rain had started to come down even harder in a torrential downpour. Adrien rolled over in the water and began floating on his back in a near comatose state.

He stared off blankly into the storm clouds. Thick rain droplets hit his face, neck and all that was exposed above the surface of the water. The more time that passed, the more he finally came to grips with this: this was no dream, there was no waking up from this. This was his life now—there was no way out.

Chapter 8

"They are wild waves of the sea, foaming up their shame; wandering stars, for
whom blackest darkness has been reserved forever."

Jude 1:13

*L*atimer was hidden within a secret chamber of the house that only he was aware existed. He frequented this room, going there in his time of mourning. Having fallen to his knees, he was ensnared by what was displayed on the wall before him, staring as time continued to slip away. He was aware that Adrien had taken up and left the house, however, he could not have pulled himself away from this; filled with a crippling guilt that multiple centuries have failed to fade by any degree. Latimer eventually closed his eyes, finally able to break his gaze from the contents of the wall. Sighing heavily, he got up and exited the room to go to the ground floor. He sensed that Adrien was on his way back.

The darkness of the night and the storm clouds loomed above Adrien as it was still pouring rain. He walked up while fully taking in the exterior of the home for the first time. The stone house towered above him as he looked at the faded columns and statues. The vines that blanketed the walls looked constricting, suffocating. He wanted to go back to his own home, but he thought of what his trip there would be like: how many people he would come across, what he would do to those people, the danger he now posed to them. His old home was also filled with walls of windows. It was unsafe for him during the day. Latimer was right: he could stay or go; leaving would render himself worse off. As much as Adrien despised it, this was now his home.

Adrien dripped water across the floor as he entered the house. He stopped and turned his attention to his right. Latimer stood silently in one of the doorways. Adrien looked at Latimer blankly, then he turned to walk away to his coffin room upstairs.

"Adrien…" Latimer called after him apprehensively.

Adrien stopped and sighed impatiently before he looked over his shoulder at Latimer. "*What?*" he responded dryly.

Latimer's brows tilted in concern as he noted that Adrien was soaking wet, his wet hair in clumps and his shoulders slumped in depression. Latimer opened his mouth to speak, but no words came out. He closed it, unsure of what he should say.

"What is it with you?" Adrien asked, turning around to face him completely now. "You look at me that way…like you feel sorry for me." Adrien was bitter as he briskly walked up to him. "*You* did this to me. Why?"

"One day I'll be sure to explain. However, as I stated before...it is not the time," Latimer solemnly responded.

Adrien threw his hands up in the air. "I just want answers! I believe I am owed as much!"

"I understand," Latimer assured, now with one of his arms across his body supporting the other arm and part of his face behind a balled fist. Latimer wanted to tell the truth, but could not convince himself to speak it.

"You do, huh?" Adrien scoffed. "I don't think you do." He glared at Latimer, then started to leave the room.

"Wait..." Latimer called after him again. "You are very troubled at the moment, this I know. After you change into dry clothes, I have something to show you. I believe it would please you."

Latimer turned around to walk into the room belonging to the doorway he was standing in. Adrien tilted his head and narrowed his eyes at Latimer as he walked further into the room and out of his sight. Adrien was not certain what could possibly please him in there. His hands tightened into fists as he made his way upstairs to change. There was a strange connection that Adrien had with Latimer due to him being his creator; in this particular moment he had an ingrained desire to be compliant with him. Once Adrien had changed into dry clothes, he reluctantly went back to the room that Latimer entered.

The room had a few couches and chairs arranged in a semicircle. There was also what seemed like piles of junk covered by sheets in the corner. Above the sheeted objects was a chandelier that was slightly recessed into the ceiling, and the light gave off a delicate sparkle.

Latimer had been waiting for him to return. He walked over to the pile of sheets and pulled them off one by one and clouds of dust swirled into the air. A grand piano, a viola and a cello were hidden beneath the sheets; they were antiques that had been kept in pristine condition.

The polished walnut wood of the cello glistened under the light. Adrien immediately gravitated towards it, running his fingers along the length of the cello in the air just above it, his eyes glowing in admiration. This cello, aside from its pristine condition, was eerily similar to the one that he learned on in his childhood. Adrien looked over to Latimer, his brows furrowed and lips pursed in confusion.

"It belongs to you now." Latimer gestured to the cello as a ghost of a smile briefly crossed his lips.

Adrien's eyebrows relaxed and he let out a half chuckle while he sat down on the chair behind the cello. The bow was standing upright in a stand off to the side of the instrument. He gently picked it up. Adrien sighed out of relief, this feeling—of the many he had felt the past forty-eight hours—was the only one similar to what was normal for him.

He moved the bow back and forth along the stiff strings, beginning to play one of his favorite pieces. Latimer, with a slight grin, took a seat on one of the couches to watch him play. The weighty, powerful notes danced from the cello, escaping the room and echoing throughout the walls of the entire house.

In those moments, Adrien found himself forgetting his present state and losing himself in the music. It was not long before he began to picture his last memory of Gabriel again. This time, instead of the memory feeling distant and in the past, he felt as if he was living within his memory at that very moment. He could feel the warmth in the house, he could smell his father's cologne as his back was turned to him and he grasped the handle of the front door to leave. It ended there, but it also repeated. Adrien was astounded, as he hadn't remembered those details before.

Hours passed until the night turned to day. Adrien had not stopped playing, though the daytime made him feel slightly lethargic; he was safe within the confines of the thick stone walls. He had never been able to play so long so tirelessly before, and—unlike what he believed was possible anymore—he was thoroughly enjoying himself. He did not feel the need to stop and had no plans of doing so.

***

July 28th: one o'clock in the afternoon

Jenna sat on her bed while anxiously twiddling her fingers, reflecting on when she and Brock had gone to the café a few nights ago. When they returned to the house, Brock forced himself on her and she was not able to fight him off. After he left the room, she curled up and cried until morning. She shuddered as she thought of all the things she had to endure from him: the forced kisses, the yelling, the threats. A tear ran down her cheek, feeling a slight relief from it being over—for now. That day, he had finally left her alone so that he could tend to business matters.

She looked atop the dresser to her purse, unmoved since it had been placed there. Her cheeks burned and her eyes dried from staring so intently at the black leather bag. Her courage grew, so she hurriedly got up to yank the purse off the dresser. She found the folded note from Michelle and quickly unfolded the paper. Michelle's cell number, work number, email, work address and home address were on the sheet of paper, along with a couple of sentences: *Contact me as soon as you can. All my doors are open.*

Jenna's hands trembled as she lowered the paper. She got up and walked to the phone that was on a table within her room. This was the first time she had the opportunity to try and make a call. Her palms were sweaty as one hand hovered over the handset, the sound of Brock's threats ringing in her ears. She gulped as she lifted the handset and began to dial the numbers.

A terrible sound traveled through her ear as she held the receiver up to her head. The monotonous dial tone was evidence of a phone that had been disconnected. Jenna slammed the phone back down and peeked under the end table; the cord was still plugged in the wall correctly so that was not the problem. She went into the hallway, looking for another phone and found the nearest one. Also disconnected.

Now in a state of panic, Jenna ran across the house and to the garage. Brock had a collection of luxury cars that she could use for her escape. She rummaged through the drawers in the toolboxes and then all the drawers in the kitchen once she could not find any car keys. They were missing, as they had been strategically hidden or taken. She slammed the drawers closed.

Filled with grief, she leaned against the cabinet and slid down until she sat on the floor. Her head was in her hands, grasping onto the roots of her hair by the fistful.

Suddenly, Jenna heard the doorbell ring. She jumped to her feet, startled. The entire property, aside from where the house faced the cliff, was confined by a tall, vine-covered, concrete wall. Cautiously, she walked towards the front entrance and peeked out of the glass. No one was directly at the door, but someone was at the end of Brock's long driveway; they were looking through the gate. Jenna squinted to see who was ringing at the gate and she saw red hair glistening in the sunlight. It was Michelle. The other night when Michelle had watched them drive off, she recorded Brock's license plate number in her notes. When she hadn't heard from Jenna yet again for a few days, she decided to pay a visit to Brock's home.

Michelle was about fifty yards away, she had her hands shielding her eyes as she peered through the bars of the front gate towards the house. Jenna's heart fluttered as she quickly opened the front door and jogged down the steps. Michelle's posture straightened up as she saw Jenna coming to her rapidly.

"Hey! Are you alright?!" Michelle yelled to her.

Jenna picked up her pace and eventually reached the barricade. "Thank God you're here! Have you found Adrien?" Jenna hurriedly blurted out.

"We have not, but we are still searching," she disclosed sadly. She then tilted her head while looking around at Brock's pricey estate. "Jenna...you have to understand that this does not look well. Can you explain to me what's going on before I continue to make more assumptions?"

"Assumptions?" Jenna wondered aloud.

"Well, I have a feeling that you are not at fault, but with my profession, I cannot run on feelings alone. I'm sure you can imagine how this could be seen to an outsider. Jenna, I have a lot of questions and I need you to answer them truthfully."

"Yes, ma'am. Absolutely," Jenna responded eagerly.

Michelle began her questioning, "The man I saw you with the other night...who is he to you?"

"He is the one who killed Adrien...he abducted me from Adrien's house not long after you released me from the scene of the accident and he brought me back here. Since then he has not let me go and has threatened me if I tried to leave him," she claimed urgently.

"You see," Michelle sighed. "I did some more digging before I came here. I found out that you actually have been living here, with him, instead of what is displayed on your license. Is this true?" she asked.

Jenna's eyes flickered but she retained eye contact with Michelle. "Yes..." she said apprehensively.

"So, he abducted you to take you back to where you've been living?" Michelle questioned further.

Jenna gulped, her eyes widened, seeing then exactly what Michelle meant by it not looking good.

"Were you seeing both of these men?" Michelle prodded.

Jenna dropped her head in shame. "There are many decisions I have made that I wish I could change. I got myself into this situation, unfortunately, Adrien has suffered the most from it."

"Well, now we at least have a viable motive," Michelle concluded.

Jenna stared at her for a few moments. "Will you arrest him?" she asked nervously.

"Do you have any bruises? Any proof of him keeping you hostage or abusing you?" Michelle asked.

"No..."

"Voicemails, witnesses that can testify to this, physical evidence of anything?"

"No..."

Michelle sighed. "We will take him in for questioning but, unfortunately, we will not be able to keep him detained without any evidence. As much as I hate to say it, the same applies to Adrien's case."

"I..." Jenna looked down to her feet. "I appreciate your honesty..."

Michelle noticed that Jenna backed up a few steps from the gate. "Jenna, I *really* believe you should come with me. Though we are limited with what we can do right now, if what you say is true, then you are in grave danger. We need to get you out of there."

"I will have no place to go," Jenna said hopelessly, "If you can't keep him locked up then it will be even worse for me. Please do not question him if nothing permanent can be done yet."

"There is a women's center that deals with situations like this. They provide housing, resources…please let me escort you there," Michelle urged.

Jenna stayed silent and continued to back up a few more steps. Michelle knew that Jenna was not going to come with her, and also felt a sudden nudge—an unmistakable urgency to leave.

Michelle fidgeted around with her cellphone then shoved her hand through the bars of the gate. "This is unconventional, but take this," she offered. "I assume, in your situation, it is hard for you to contact me. Now you have a way."

Jenna reluctantly stepped forward and grabbed the phone from her, slipping it into her pocket.

"Ahhh, hold on!" Michelle turned and rushed to her car to dig through her console. She came back with a silver charging brick and cord in her hands. "Take this, too. Call my office whenever you need me…or you can shoot me an email. I am *not* giving up on you, Jenna."

Michelle turned around and rushed to get back into her car. She leaned out of her window as she began to drive away, staring Jenna deep in the eyes. "Please. Be careful," Michelle advised before she drove off quickly and turned the corner at the end of the road.

Just as her car was out of sight, the big, black metal bars of the gate abruptly jerked and began to move. Jenna jumped back as the gate doors creaked open. She hadn't even heard a vehicle approaching. Her muscles burned as her body filled with adrenaline. Her mind screamed for her to run into the house but she couldn't move. She managed to stuff the charging brick into her pocket though. The sleek, luxury car pulled up next to her and the tinted black window lowered, revealing Brock's dark, angry eyes.

"What the hell are you doing out here?" he said, his eyes darting around her suspiciously.

"I-I..." Jenna stuttered, her heartbeat pulsing rapidly in her throat. "I really just needed to get out of the house for a bit... get some fresh air."

"So, you stand at the gate?" he questioned her skeptically. His eyes narrowed. "That's bull. Get in the car."

Jenna lowered her head, then walked around to the passenger side of the car. She glanced at the road behind them that was no longer blocked by the gate doors and thought, for a millisecond, about making a break for it, but the same fear she had minutes before remained. She opened the door and sat in the seat. Brock eyed her as the car idled in the driveway, then he grabbed her face to pull her in for a kiss. The stubble on his chin felt like a hundred little needles stabbing her. She tensed up slightly, but she knew it was better for her not to fight it. He finished kissing her, then pulled away. Her face was still in his hand as he squeezed it just enough to make it painful, her cheeks pushing up under his grip.

"Don't tell me you were planning on leaving me, Jenna?" he asked in a calm voice, with a menacing undertone.

Jenna's eyes scanned his face in fear. She shook her head no with the little movement she could manage to make within his tight grasp.

"Good girl..." he said while letting go of her.

He turned back to the steering wheel and pressed the gas pedal. As they pulled further into the driveway, the reflection of the gate closing was in Jenna's view in the side mirror. Her heart dropped as the gate loudly shut behind them.

***

Adrien had been playing for three nights and three days without any pause. Cade joined them on the third night and stayed for the performance. Adrien had felt pains of hunger here and there, but the distraction of the music and the replaying memory of his father helped him suppress his hunger. Coran brought his family over to the house when the fourth night began, upon receiving word of Adrien's artistry.

Coran's wife, Xylia and daughter, Kiana entered into the music room along with Coran. They moved very gracefully and were both very beautiful. They had long, silver hair and were almost spitting images of one another. Xylia was wearing a long, elaborate dress decorated in copper sequins, and she was adorned with jewels around her neck. Kiana was also wearing an elegant knee-length dress of lace and satin almost the same silver color as her hair. Taking their seats within the room on the couches around Adrien, they reveled at his music.

As Adrien continued to play, he looked at the family and deeply longed for what they had. His gaze landed on Coran's daughter, Kiana, more intently. He saw that she looked merely a teenager. He wondered how many years she actually had on her and was filled with pity, seeing melancholy in her eyes. Xylia, aside from her age, looked no different.

Adrien's eyes then landed on Coran, who had noticed Adrien's once-over of his family. Coran lowered his head to look at Adrien intensely through his brow in an attempt to remind him of their conversation before. It was evident that what Coran had said was true: this life had taken a toll and had weighed down upon them all.

Latimer noticed this entire exchange and the sudden negative shift in Adrien's demeanor. He got up and sat at the piano next to Adrien. Latimer's hands quickly bounced along the keys; he smirked at Adrien just before switching to an upbeat tempo. Adrien, who was at first confused, adjusted to the new tempo with Latimer. This was the first time that Adrien had gotten to play alongside anyone else, and this excited him. Coran and Xylia got up to dance while Cade and Kiana both laughed at their antics, clapping to the beat of the music. For a time the night was filled with joy and laughter as the music and the dancing continued for hours.

After those few hours passed, Adrien was all of a sudden thrust back into his memory, but it was no longer the loop of his father leaving. It was later in that same night before any news of Gabriel's death had reached the babysitter. Adrien was half-asleep in his crib. He felt a presence, but kept his little eyes shut; a hand gently reached into his crib. The hand caressed his forehead, but the touch was jolting, and the skin that met his was ice-cold.

Out of nowhere, the grumbling that Adrien had been able to suppress the past few days returned with a vengeance. He began to squirm in his seat and bore down harder onto the cello bow, the wood fiber splintering under the pressure. The bow snapped in half and the cello dropped to the ground, making a loud resounding crash. Everyone stopped to look at Adrien who was bent over, kneeling on the floor in front of his chair.

With weighted breath, blood—as sweat—beaded on his forehead. It dripped to the floor beneath him. The music had been enough to distract him from this, however, it was no longer helping. The cello that was once in pristine condition was scuffed up and chips of wood were missing from one of the edges. Adrien choked out an aggravated grunt and yelled in anger, drawing back his fist, he then punched straight into the stone floor, barely missing the cello.

Cade jumped to his feet. "When is the last time he fed?"

Latimer stood up from the piano bench. "This is the fourth night."

Cade, Coran, Kiana and Xylia all looked at each other and were obviously impressed. Adrien himself hadn't even realized that many days had passed.

"We may already have us a Harvester just yet," Coran chuckled. He looked at Adrien with a sliver of astonishment.

"Well, obviously it's time for him to feed now. Thankfully," Cade said as he tapped his fingers to his temple, "I came prepared." He rotated, gesturing with his hand out of the room.

Kiana rushed over to Adrien. Kneeling down to his level,

she placed her hand under his chin and gently lifted his face so she could look him in the eyes. Adrien was confused by this interaction, his eyes flickering over to Coran who was standing and watching with his arms crossed, with a look now void of emotion. Adrien then shifted his eyes back to Kiana who was looking at him intensely.

"This gets...a little easier with time. I promise. Soon enough you will be able to go weeks without having to do this," she said to him in a gentle voice.

She pulled out a red silken handkerchief from her clutch and wiped away the blood from his forehead. She then opened up his hand and pushed it into his palm. She closed his fingers around it, giving it to him to keep. Jumping to her feet, she then crossed her arms as she walked out of the room. While passing her father, she shot a sharp glare in his direction. Coran winced, then stormed out of the room behind her.

Xylia walked up and lightly touched Adrien on the shoulder. "It was nice meeting you and having the privilege to hear you play. You are delightful! Until next time, darling." Xylia glided out of the room after Coran and the three of them left the house together.

Adrien removed his other fist from the floor. The hunger pangs caused him to grit his teeth so hard that it felt like they should have shattered into pieces. Latimer avoided making eye contact with Adrien and sat back down on the bench, he swiveled back towards the black and white keys. His hands hovered over them for a moment, then he began to lightly press down on them, quietly playing another song.

Cade lightly motioned with a finger at Adrien to follow him as he walked out of the room. Adrien got up slowly and followed Cade into the foyer as he tucked the handkerchief into his back pocket. Once they were both in the hall, Cade faced him.

"Sooner or later, you are going to have to learn to catch your own prey. Has Latimer spoken to you about this?" Cade stood with his arm across his body and one hand resting on his cheek.

"No. Honestly, we have not spoken much about anything," Adrien responded through his teeth he was still grinding together from the pain.

"That's very odd. Latimer seems to be more jubilant than I have ever seen him before. I figured you two got along very well," Cade's eyes glistened as he said this.

"*That's* happy?" Adrien expressed in disgust.

Cade chuckled. "Anyways, you are clearly famished. You know where to go. For the next one, you will be on your own."

Cade went back into the music room and left Adrien to himself. Adrien looked down the hallway to the door that led to the basement. He did not smell any human blood, but just the thought of knowing what was waiting for him down there threw his body into another upsurge of pain. Within seconds, he found himself down in the basement just outside of the bared room in the cellar.

The darkness took over him and only the monster was

present. This time it was a woman in there for him.

"Please, help me!" the woman cried out.

She could only slightly see Adrien in the darkness but could tell that he was not the one who captured her. Adrien didn't speak, but he opened the cell door for her.

"Thank you, sir!" she responded in gratitude.

She clasped her hands together, giving thanks to Adrien then quickly tried to run past. He caught her by the arm. It took little to no effort for him to keep her from moving further as she struggled to run, she felt like a feather just blowing in the wind in comparison to his strength. The woman reluctantly turned to look at Adrien, now in fear, realizing that he was not a savior there to aid in her escape.

Adrien's eyes flashed red in the darkness and her eyes, in turn, adjusted to see his face fully. She saw the richness of his red irises and the abnormality of his pupils. His mouth was parted, fangs visible. She shrieked in terror just as Adrien bit down into her neck. The surge of warmth and acid overcame him again until she was gone. This time was just as quick and painful as the last.

As soon as she was dead, as soon as he was finished, he was overcome with grief yet again. It rushed back to him like a flood as it was suppressed just moments before. He ran back out of the basement and slammed the door shut behind him after he reached the top of the stairs. He leaned with his back pressed up against the door and his eyes were forced shut in shame. His body began to feel jittery and a whirlwind of emotions rushed to him all at once again.

Adrien took a deep breath, then snuck by the music room to exit the house. As he walked through the door, both Latimer and Cade were standing out front, facing the forest. Adrien tensed up, freezing where he stood. Latimer peeked over his shoulder at Adrien, then continued to look forward.

"You know, Adrien...I am giving you the free will to do as you please," Latimer said to him, knowing where he was planning to go. "But what you are doing is dangerous...I strongly suggest against it."

Cade looked back at Adrien, and for a moment he saw a face that did not seem to fit the amicable vampire. His frigid glare sent chills down Adrien's spine, his face was full of enmity. There was no sign of the friendlier face he associated with Cade from the start. Adrien looked away from Cade hastily, then silently slipped away into the bushes, disregarding Latimer's advice. After Adrien fed, all of his emotions were heightened, and the greatest of those beyond his grief was his affection for Jenna.

"Latimer...shouldn't you forbid this?" Cade asked in frustration.

"I refuse to control him," Latimer sighed.

"I know. But, you do know what we have to do if he reverts to a Hunter, don't you? We have worked relentlessly to establish this as our territory, so it would be our duty to exterminate him."

Latimer sighed, then he stared off into the brush where Adrien disappeared.

***

Adrien's journey was quick this time; he knew exactly

where to go and which room to go to. He staked out a vantage point that gave him enough distance to safely watch Jenna through the window. He did not see Jenna right away, though. There were more lights on in the house this time, and he spotted Brock through a window of one of the other rooms walking around.

Adrien's blood boiled as he saw him. He thought, for a moment, that he would sneak into the house and take him out, but his attention was quickly diverted by movement in Jenna's room. Jenna had just walked into her room and laid out across her bed after she shut the door behind her. After waiting a few moments and glancing back at her door a few times, she reached into her pants pocket and pulled out a silver cellphone. The corners of her mouth slightly rose in a seemingly forced half-smile.

Adrien stared in awe, his heart that barely beats seeming to flutter at the sight of her. Her face did not look the same to him as it did when he was human. She somehow looked even more beautiful to him now than before. He stepped out of the foliage a bit without realizing that he was gravitating closer to the house. Jenna's eyes jumped in Adrien's direction as her head turned to look outside the window. Her eyes lightened up in excitement and confusion. She got up off the bed and rushed to the patio door.

Adrien jumped back into the bushes as he realized that he'd been spotted. Jenna ran out onto the patio and stood on her tiptoes, looking to the top of the hill at the foliage that Adrien was hidden within. He caught a whiff of Jenna's scent and immediately vanished into the night, not giving himself a chance to do the unthinkable.

Jenna heard the bushes rustle and she gasped, climbing over the patio railing before she ran up the hill. She pushed her way through the branches to the other side. Looking around and as far as her eyes could see, there was no trace of Adrien anywhere. "Adrien?" she whispered, her voice shaky.

There was no answer, there was no response. She could only hear the sound of crickets chirping and the waves crashing along the base of the cliff. After a few moments, she went back to her room and shut the door, still staring out into the backyard and at the foliage. Thinking back to all of the times Adrien had sworn about seeing the white-haired man within the darkness, she started to doubt. Jenna was not entirely sure what she saw but started to think that she only saw what she wanted to see, that she was starting to see things just as Adrien once had. She lay back in the bed. As she stared at the blankness of the ceiling, a single tear ran down the side of her cheek, then she closed her eyes to fall asleep.

Chapter 9

"For the revelation awaits an appointed time; it speaks of the end and it will not prove false. Though it linger, wait for it; it will certainly come and will not delay."

Habakkuk 2:3

*J*ust under five months passed quickly after Adrien became a vampire. He was plagued with nightmares again, but his nightmares were different than before: he was haunted by all the people whose lives he had taken. Majority of them continued to be the ones he used to devote his time to helping. Their screams and pleas for mercy still rang in his ears and with each kill, it added on, not one replaced the other. Adrien felt slightly insane while he was human because of his nightmares of Latimer, but those paled in comparison.

He wasn't able to drown out the voices. The only thing that helped, just like what helped with his hunger, was music.

Adrien had begun to write more of his own songs. For a change, he found a purpose in this form of creation, giving relief to all the destruction he caused. Adrien and Latimer developed a habit of playing together most nights. Across many of those nights, Latimer opened up, sharing bits of his past with Adrien.

He originally lived in France as a very successful architect. In the mid 1600s, he traveled to New England, present-day Massachusetts. There, he continued his architectural work as well as immersing himself in the prosperous fur trade at the time. Latimer was responsible for most of the architectural foundation of present-day Massachusetts before he was turned into a vampire. He managed to purchase property on an island just before the unfortunate event that led to his transformation. On this land, he built their current home with his enhanced strength and speed. He was able to complete the building in record time. Latimer had yet to share in more detail what happened to him, his early vampire years, or why he chose to become a Harvester.

He had coached Adrien with the stealthy and strategic lifestyle they had as Harvesters: feeding strictly on humans who were virtually unknown to society, sometimes staging accidents and covering up their tracks to avoid suspicion and exposure— this included killing Hunter vampires. When the Harvesters took someone for themselves, they called it reaping. Adrien learned to control his blood-lust more and was able to go a few weeks without reaping, but when that one night did come, it was complete, and utter hell.

In the process of Adrien's learning, he mastered the gift of camouflaging his eyes. Harvesters were able to temporarily shift their eyes back to the color they were when they were human, a mechanism that required a lot of focus and proved useful when walking amongst humans in public. It was something he was only able to do once he became a Harvester, as Hunters do not have the ability to do so.

Latimer, on multiple occasions, had spoken about the Hunters and why they posed a threat to their way of life. If any Hunter stepped into their territory, it was their due diligence to take them out as quickly as possible. Hunters are far more feral and messier when they feed, not as concerned about covertness and have a stronger bloodlust. They do not cover their tracks meticulously because they are nomads and are constantly on the move. This makes it very hard for Harvesters to be able to reside in their cities at ease, so it is imperative to make sure their territory stayed void of roaming Hunters.

Latimer met Coran's family quite recently, in 1959. He gave them a twenty-acre plot of land and built them a two-story home situated around a large courtyard in the middle. Coran's house was strategically placed near the northern border of Massachusetts, over one hundred miles north from Latimer's. Coran and his family would regularly split up and sweep the borders of Massachusetts for security measures against the Hunters. They had a ten thousand square foot black brick house filled with: black marble floors and red accents on the inside, from the columns, to the carpet, to the paint. Their main living room was extravagant, it had vaulted ceilings and waterfalls that lined the walls.

Coran and his family had been put in charge of relations

with Harvesters in their neighboring states as well. Every few years they hosted an elaborate gala to discuss their reaping and security strategies with their allies. Their nearest alliance was with a faction further north, under the leadership of a vampire named Lazaro. Lazaro had arrived about a century after Latimer established himself. It was typical that one would alert the other as soon as Hunter activity was discovered so that they could coordinate a plan of execution.

Cade lived quite differently than the others. He was a meticulous planner and strategist living on his own within the city in a small apartment. Cade spent a lot of his time alone, observing and documenting. Being that he was in close quarters with humans, he was the most acquainted with them and had the best knowledge on who they could pick off inconspicuously. They came to him to discover the best time and place to securely reap their harvest.

Adrien still hadn't mastered his ability to fly like the others. Something was inhibiting him from being able to do it no matter how many times he tried. This bothered him, as Adrien desired to bring a drawing pad along with him on his trips to see Jenna, but his dips into the sea to venture over there made it impossible without soaking the pages. One night, Adrien posted up in his usual spot and found his drawing pad sitting there for him already. One of the others, mostly likely Latimer, had placed it there for him. For months, Adrien would sit and draw Jenna as he would watch over her, leaving the drawing pad hidden in one of the trees there so that it would always be available for him.

He found a vantage point much further away to be certain

that she would not catch a glimpse of him again; he relied on his enhanced vision to watch after her. Some nights he would see her staring out of the window for hours, searching the darkness. The more time that passed, her eyes grew more and more devoid of emotion. She wasn't happy, a captive within those walls. Adrien understood, as he felt like a prisoner himself.

***

December 24th, seven-thirty in the evening

Adrien was within the music room playing his cello, perfecting a new song he started to piece together the previous night after he reaped. As he played this song, he closed his eyes for the memory of his father. It was the same sole memory he always had of him. It usually started with him watching his father as he reached for the doorknob and turned it to leave, however, tonight it started earlier than he had remembered before. He could feel that his father just gave him a hug and kiss goodbye and he had just swiveled around. This time Adrien caught a glimpse of his father's face, but it was blurred and unclear. His father *still* remained faceless. Adrien strained while trying to focus on the blur, attempting to replay it in his head for clarity, but the memory instead jumped again to Adrien within his crib later in that same night. He lay there, warm until the cold touch of a hand caressed his forehead.

Adrien was unable to keep playing, as it seemed like the weight of a building was placed on his chest. He felt angry at himself for not remembering, angry that no matter what he remembered, his father's face—something so simple—was still missing from the puzzle. He took a few deep breaths before sighing and opening his eyes again.

There was movement just outside of the door. Latimer was walking back and forth in the foyer with his hand up to his mouth. Adrien got up and walked over, leaning up against the doorframe while still holding onto his bow. His eyes followed Latimer as he continued to pace.

"So," Adrien sighed. "Who came here earlier?"

He glanced over at Adrien as he continued to pace, Latimer's eyes briefly growing wide.

"Oh, um...don't worry. I didn't eavesdrop," Adrien ensured him.

Not long before, while Adrien was still laying within his coffin shortly after night fell, he heard footsteps and voices coming from above him, but not directly atop him. Adrien found it odd, not knowing exactly what was up another level as the main staircase did not go up to another floor. Nor was there another staircase elsewhere in the home that he had seen. Latimer was speaking with someone whose voice Adrien did not recognize, but he chose to come down to the music room and tune them out to respect their privacy.

Latimer stopped in front of Adrien. "It was no one of importance," Latimer asserted sternly.

Adrien furrowed his brow, wondering why Latimer felt the need to lie to him. "No one of importance, huh?" he straightened up and fully stepped out of the doorway and into the foyer. "Whatever they said clearly bothered you." He could tell Latimer was worried, and in turn, it caused him to become worried as well. "Latimer...what's going on?" he pried.

"Can you stay here?" Latimer asked, dodging the question.

Adrien silently searched Latimer's face. Though Latimer expressed fear and concern before, now his expression was stone cold.

"Yeah, I'll stay h—"

Before Adrien could finish his statement, Latimer had gone out the door. There was something wrong with him. Latimer was not only concerned, but he was also spooked. What could possibly incite this sort of reaction? Adrien rolled his eyes in annoyance, sick of Latimer's secrecy.

He set his bow back down by his cello and then walked to another room. Just the month prior, he managed to convince Latimer to get them a television. Latimer originally looked at Adrien as if he had three eyes, but eventually he caved in to the idea. Adrien plopped down onto the couch and flipped through the channels. He was fascinated by the visuals and the shots shown of the daytime. This was his only way to catch a glimpse of what he missed so much. The bright, warm sunlight that used to darken his once tan skin, being able to see people without having the desire to kill them; it was something he took for granted before.

He tapped on the control until something caught his attention. He stopped on the news channel where they were showing captivating shots of the snow softly falling around the buildings that were covered in colorful Christmas decor. In the background, the newscaster was speaking of more snow in the forecast.

Adrien quickly drowned out the voice of the newscaster, as he started to daydream about this same time a year ago. He took Jenna to a cabin in the mountains near Clarksburg, Massachusetts. They spent their nights in front of the fireplace sipping hot chocolate and dreaming about their future together while watching the snowfall through the windows.

Christmas Day, in particular, was Adrien's favorite. They had nothing planned and just stayed at the cabin the entire day. After opening their gifts to one another, they strolled outside. They were building a snowman together when Jenna suddenly challenged Adrien to a snowball fight by throwing the first projectile. They chased each other around the yard, hurling whatever they could quickly pack into their hands at each other.

Adrien accidentally pelted Jenna so hard with a snowball that she toppled over to the ground. When he went to check on her, she had the largest snowball he had ever seen hidden underneath her. She hit him with it straight in the face. They laughed until their stomachs hurt, and as she giggled, the pink in her cheeks and the snowflakes decorating her blond, wavy hair enraptured him. She looked so beautiful, so full of joy. At that moment, he knew for sure that he was going to marry her.

After his trip to the past in his mind, Adrien got up from the couch and made a conscious decision to disobey Latimer's wishes again. Besides playing music, going to see her was the only other thing that grounded him, connecting him to his old life. Adrien ventured out of the home to go frequent his favorite spot of bliss on the hill across the water.

The television was left on and the sound of it still resonated in the empty house. The newscaster had switched story coverage to slightly less local news of a sudden string of murders on the rise. People had gone missing and were turning up dead at alarming rates from the same cause of death. The killings migrated from Maine, then to New Hampshire, then to Vermont; they remained a mystery to authorities.

It was lightly snowing as Adrien left the house; he quickly made it over to his frequented spot with his vantage point of Jenna's room. Searching for her, he saw no sign of her. She was not within her room; the lights were off, but they were on in the foyer.

Adrien walked around the perimeter while remaining concealed in the bushes. There was a steep hill that he climbed up and was able to look downwards into the foyer of the house. The windows filled up the entire wall that spanned at least twenty feet tall. Jenna was seated on a bench, bent over and strapping her shoes. She was wearing a beautiful sparkling gown; her hair was in an updo and her makeup was done. It looked like she was preparing to leave for a party.

"You get more beautiful each day I see you," he whispered.

There had been countless times that Adrien thought of showing himself to Jenna. Since he had grown in his control around humans, he was tempted to reach out to her and at least let her know that he was alive. However, he had withheld from his desire every time. Despite having grown closer to Latimer and the others, he knew that at their core there was an evil, a darkness that he refused to expose to Jenna.

Adrien's eyes glowed in admiration as she strapped her shoes on. She finished adjusting them, then looked around. She seemed jittery and extremely nervous. Peeking into her purse, she pulled out a piece of paper. Her lips moved quickly as she seemed to read through it. Suddenly, she jumped up, quickly stuffing the paper into the bust of her dress. Brock, dressed in a very nice tuxedo, walked up to Jenna.

Adrien adjusted his hearing so that he could listen through the window. The snowfall started to rapidly pick up.

"It's time to go," Brock said.

Jenna nodded, then started to walk towards the front door. The piece of paper she just stuffed into her dress fell out onto the ground while she continued to walk, but she did not notice. Brock saw the piece of paper and paused, bending down to pick it up. He unfolded the paper and began to read it.

***

There was an overwhelming scent of burning wood, metal and plastic. The heat was unbearable. Shards of glass and ash fell down from the sky like sleet. What was once white paint bubbled up and charred to black just before the wall was fully engulfed in flames, consumed by the heat. Pillars of fire towered above as a house burned and collapsed completely to the ground.

"Michelle! Wake up!" Anna roughly shook Michelle, who was passed out at her desk in her office.

Michelle woke up quickly, startled and breathless, gasping for air.

"Michelle! Chief has been calling you!" Anna exclaimed.

Michelle grabbed onto her head, struggling to grasp reality momentarily. The phone in her office was ringing off the hook. Overworked, she was in such a deep sleep that the sound was not enough to wake her. She grabbed the phone and pulled it up to her ear. The voice on the other side began speaking immediately.

"Y-Yes, sir. Oh, an hour? Sir, I don't thi—" The phone clicked and she slowly set the receiver back down.

"What's that about?" Anna asked.

"He, uh—he wants me to take a trip up to Vermont. They need as much help as they can get, their homicide rate has skyrocketed the past few days alone. He told me to be at the airport within the hour to catch the nearest flight," Michelle said, frustrated.

"Come on, I'll take you…grab your stuff."

"Uhh, about that. I really need to be somewhere else tonight," Michelle explained while scooping up her coat and other belongings.

"What do you mean? If the Chief is telling you to be in Vermont, that's where you ought to be," Anna lectured her.

Michelle sighed. "I-I know…I just can't do that right now. I will have to take the next flight tomorrow. He will have to understand later." Michelle rushed out of the door and exited the building.

Anna chased after her. "Michelle, where are you going?!"

The snow was coming down thick.

"No plane is leaving out in this, anyway!" Michelle yelled back to her as she continued to her car.

Michelle got into her car, equipped with snow tires, and pulled out of the parking lot. The roads were filled with cars backed up at the traffic lights. Michelle blared her horn, desperate to keep moving. The nightmare that Michelle just had was all too familiar. It had been many months since she had this one, but this time it seemed more real than before. The details in her dream were the same as before, but she only then recognized them and this absolutely terrified her. She finally knew where the fire would be.

***

Within a dark alleyway, the sound of deep bass thumps traveled through the walls. Latimer walked through this alleyway to a tin door in the back. Entering into the building, he shook the snow off his coat. This was Voyage, a nightclub in the heart of the city. The dance floor was crowded, filled with people who were mostly intoxicated.

At the center of the room was a stage where the DJ was elevated on a platform playing electronic music, the moving lights of many colors were strobing and swirling around the room. The sidewall of the club had an oversized aquarium tank where they had all sorts of exotic fish and sharks swimming around within it. Above the tank was a bar with a glass-bottomed floor. Latimer made his way towards the back of the club and climbed up a spiral staircase to the top floor, where a set of couches adjacent to the bar overlooked the entire room from a balcony.

Cade and Coran were sitting on the couches. Coran had a smirk on his face as he observed the people below. Cade did a double take when he saw Latimer and immediately jumped to his feet, confused as to why Latimer would be there.

"Latimer! What's going on?" Cade asked, concerned.

Coran then saw Latimer and got up quickly as well.

"I have reason to believe there has been a spike in Hunter activity in our neighboring states. They may be heading our way," Latimer explained.

"A spike?" Coran asked, he grabbed his phone out of his pocket and went through it.

"When was the last time you had contact with the New Hampshire and Vermont Harvesters?" Latimer asked Coran.

"I heard from Lazaro just a few days ago, but he spoke of nothing peculiar," said Coran. Coran put the phone up to his head while it rang on the other end. Moments passed and it went to voicemail. He then scrolled through his phone again and continued to call around, no one he called answered. "This...is not good," he said as his free hand dropped and balled into a fist.

"This could be disastrous. What do you suggest we do?" Cade inquired irritably.

***

Jenna, who was still walking toward the front door, now

sensed that Brock was no longer walking toward the door with her. She turned around, her eyes horrified as she saw him reading the piece of paper that should have been in her possession. She felt around for the paper in her dress and confirmed that it was no longer there, and she gulped in anticipation.

Brock's hands trembled as he finished reading what was on the paper. His dark eyes slowly looked up to her and he ripped the paper into shreds. He stomped towards her in heavy, thunderous steps.

Adrien hurriedly moved closer to the window. "What the hell is going on in there?!" he stressed aloud to himself.

Whatever was on that piece of paper was not intended for Brock's eyes to see.

"I thought I was *very* clear about what would happen if you tried to pull something like this," Brock said calmly to her.

Jenna backed up a few steps and lifted her hands. "I…I…"

He lunged for her and ripped her clutch from her. Opening it, he dumped its contents out onto the floor. Out fell a little silver cellphone. "How did you get this?!" he yelled, picking it up off the floor and waving it in her face.

He turned on the phone and looked through it. Going through the gallery, he saw videos that had been secretly recorded of him. Incriminating videos, one of which Jenna had gotten him to confess to everything that he had done and had verbally threatened her. It was hard evidence that she planned to use against him.

Brock slammed the phone down to the ground then stomped on it with the heel of his dress shoe, completely destroying it. He grabbed Jenna by the hair and yanked her closer towards him. Though his eyes were full of fiery rage, they were also filled with tears. Jenna grabbed onto his hand, screaming as she tried to pry his fingers open.

Suddenly, she heard a loud sound like thunder while simultaneously losing all sense of her balance, her ears rang, and jaw throbbed as she drew closer to the tile floor. She crashed to the floor as warm liquid filled her mouth, and it tasted like she swallowed a stack of pennies. Brock hit her directly in the face with a closed fist.

A loud crash came from behind Brock and the foyer filled with cold, crisp air as snow found its way into the house. Brock swung around, seeing a figure that had landed on his floor and standing at the end of the hall atop the pile of glass. Shards of glass continued to shatter as they hit the floor, the large window falling victim to gravity from the gaping hole in the center of it.

"Step away from her! NOW!" Adrien shouted in fury.

"What the—get the hell out of my house!" Brock yelled, not even recognizing who was standing before him.

Jenna, who was still on the ground, groaned while the room spun around her. She propped herself up on her elbow, trying her best to focus. She rubbed her eyes roughly, seeing the red hair that belonged to her beloved Adrien. This couldn't be. She had long accepted the fact that Adrien was dead and that she would never find out what happened to his body. Holding onto her head, she slowly stood back up.

"A-Adrien?" she faltered in almost a whisper. "Is that you?"

Adrien's eyes grew in size; he looked down to his feet in shame. "Jenna..." he whispered back.

"What happened to you?!" Jenna's vision had fully regained focus and she saw Adrien in his full state: his pale skin, red eyes and overall ghastly appearance.

"Get out of my house!" Brock demanded again.

Adrien's throat started to tighten and his mouth began to water. His vision shifted to crimson, and he was thrown into a panic. Jenna was bleeding from her face and mouth, and her blood started to drip onto the tile underneath her. Adrien gasped, then grasped onto his throat, choking himself in a futile attempt to stop this reaction. Jenna took a few steps closer.

"Jenna! Jenna, stop!" Adrien shouted desperately between chokes, having fallen to his knees. He was fighting with every ounce of his conscious to leave, but his body wouldn't allow it. "Jenna, don't come any closer! Go! RUN!" he shouted.

"It really is you!" she exclaimed. She started to run towards Adrien instead.

A vicious snarl ripped through the foyer. Time seemed to slow as Adrien leapt up in a full stride. With tunnel vision, he passed by Brock. Every ounce of him burned as he knew what was about to happen, but he could not stop. The hunger within him was too strong.

He embraced Jenna as he reached her, his fangs sinking

into her neck. His arms and hands tensed as he clawed at her dress, the threads snapped under his fingernails and sequins rained to the ground. Tears escaped from Jenna's eyes as she attempted to speak. The warm and acidic sensation coated his throat and he sobbed as he fed, unable to stop, unable to protect her from Brock...unable to protect her from himself. Adrien was only able to stop when there was no longer anything to fight for. He yanked his fangs out of her flesh and held her body upright as she slumped over in his arms and fell into his chest.

Brock was still facing the wrong direction; Adrien's movements were too quick to follow. He turned around to see Adrien holding Jenna, his lips covered in blood. Yelling in terror, he frantically started to run. Brock fell, slipping on the shards of glass. Hurriedly getting up, he continued to look back in terror as he tried to escape.

Adrien was blocking the main exit to the house, so Brock ran through the kitchen. If he went out the other end of the kitchen it would meet back up in the foyer where Adrien was standing, there was nowhere for him to go. He looked around desperately and saw the door that led down to his basement.

Adrien gently laid Jenna down to chase after him. Just before Brock opened the door, they burst through the wood as Adrien tackled him through it. On the other side was a long flight of stairs. They tumbled down the dark staircase, Brock's bones breaking as he slammed against the metal stairs repeatedly until they hit the bottom. Brock gargled as a fractured rib punctured one of his lungs.

Adrien then jumped on top of Brock. He palmed Brock's face with his left hand and then ravenously tore into his throat. Adrien, so full of wrath, ended up breaking Brock's neck before he could kill him by draining his blood. As soon as Brock was dead, Adrien left the basement and rushed back up to Jenna, who was still lying where he left her.

For just a moment her cheeks looked rosy, and some of the snow from outside had drifted into the foyer and landed on her hair. She looked like she did Christmas Day a year prior, that moment they had on the mountain. Now, her expression was lifeless. There was no laughter and no joy. The rosiness in her cheeks began to fade as her lips turned white and skin quickly began to pale.

"No...no, no, no...JENNA!" Adrien cried out as he joined her on the floor.

The snowstorm started to slow until it was calm, flurries no longer gusted into the home. It was now silent, aside from Adrien's pleas. He pulled her into his lap. Rocking back and forth, he held her close to him, her head pressed firmly in his chest.

"Jenna, please..." he sobbed between every word as he endearingly ran his hand through her hair, "Jenna...w-wake up... wake up!"

There was no warmth left in her, her body felt like his now. Like death. He rested his chin on the top of her head and looked up to the ceiling, he wailed as he held onto her tightly, not wanting to let go of her, not wanting to accept what he had just done.

"No...I...I'm so sorry. I'm so sorry, Jenna," he whimpered in despair.

He held onto her tightly, but gently. Adrien reached into his pocket with one of his hands for the handkerchief that Kiana had given him. He used it to wipe away Jenna's tears and the blood on her mouth and neck, then he lightly kissed her on the forehead.

***

Michelle was speeding through the snow-covered roads since she finally was able to get out of the traffic jam. As she got closer to Brock's house, the terrible feeling in her gut intensified. Her dream earlier in the night revealed details to her she had before but did not recognize in the beginning. Details that made her realize the burning house she kept seeing in her dreams of Jenna was Brock's mansion. It had been months since she had the dream and the first few times she did, it was well before she visited the house.

Michelle's car skidded up to the front of the property. She opened the door to her car and ran up to ring the bell at the gate while shouting and banging on the bars. She strained to see up the driveway and into the foyer. She spotted movement around the house in a quick blur and could see through the front door into the foyer where a slight tint of red was reflecting off the floor and onto the white walls. Her heart dropped. She stopped ringing the bell and grabbed her pistol from her car before jumping onto the gate and starting the climb. She scaled the metal bars quickly and flung herself over, jumping to the ground. She sprinted as fast as she could towards the house.

As she drew closer, she could smell a slight hint of gas. She had placed one foot onto the first step of the front porch when a sudden burst of hot air lifted her off her feet and hurled her backward. A fireball erupted from the house as it exploded, bursting into flames.

Michelle was thrown five yards, landing on her back in the snow. Glass, metal and ash fell from the sky like sleet from the explosion. Some of the scalding hot pieces of metal hit Michelle on the way down and she screamed in agony, having also suffered burns from the initial explosion. The terrible smell from her dream she had less than an hour prior filled the air.

Adrien, on the opposite side of the house, emerged from the basement, engulfed in flames. Though the flames burned through his clothing, his skin healed so rapidly that the flames hardly affected him. Climbing over the heaps of metal and concrete, he made his way to the far edge of the back yard. He limped to the edge of the cliff and dropped to his knees, sobbing with his face in his hands as the house collapsed behind him.

He would never get to see Jenna again, her life cut too short at the hands of the one who was supposed to love her. Did he truly love her? His mind raced as he tried to grasp the gravity of what he had just done to her. The tree that he hid his drawing pad in was right next to him. Adrien stood up and grabbed onto the tree, yanking it out of the ground. Adrien yelled, tossing the tree over the cliff and into the choppy ocean waters below. All the drawings of Jenna sunk into the dark waters along with it. Anger, coupled with despair, raged within him. For the first time, he lifted into the air, defying the rules of gravity that had previously proved to govern him.

Michelle, who was still laying on the ground with some rubble that had fallen on top of her, saw the movement above her. She rotated her head upwards and briefly saw a human figure flying through the sky just before her vision faded and she passed out in the rubble.

Chapter 10

*"For sighing has become my daily food; my groans pour out like water. What I
feared has come upon me; what I dreaded has happened to me. I have no peace,
no quietness; I have no rest, but only turmoil."*

Job 3:24-26

December 24th: nine in the evening

There was a home within the suburbs dimly lit by an array
of Christmas lights decorating the rooms. The smell of
pine within the family room was delightful. The faint
hum of Christmas music played from the multicolor lights
wrapped around the tree adorned with metallic ornaments and
tinsel. The lights were on a timer, and they danced around to the
beat of the soft music, bouncing off all the shiny, wrapped gifts.
The house was empty. The family who lived there was out visiting
relatives on the other side of town until the next morning.

The doorknob to the kitchen jerked and jiggled as the lock
was picked. Four teenagers crept in: three boys and one girl. On
the way to this house, they had heard a very loud noise nearby.

At first scared, they nonetheless continued with their plan. The first boy to step within the house had his hand on the girl's arm, tugging her along with him. They all moved directly towards the family room. As they reached the room, they split up and began to stuff as much as they could into their jackets.

"Man, these people are loaded! Nice choice, Matt," one of the boys whispered to their leader.

"Yeah, grab as much as you can guys," Matt whispered back, shooting a glare in the direction of his girlfriend who he pulled through the door with him. Her name was Valerie.

"I can't believe you dragged me along with you guys! You lied to me!" Valerie piped up, not in much of a hushed whisper as the others.

"Valerie, shut up! Their neighbors might still hear us over here!" Matt leaned down and grabbed another small present as he peeked out one of the side windows of the house. "Seems like no one else even heard that explosion earlier. Weird," he said as he snuck it into his pocket.

"Sounded like a car crash to me. A big one. Good for us, though—it means the cops will be busy somewhere else," one of his friends said.

"You know what?" Valerie interrupted their discussion. "I'm sick of allowing you to drag me into stuff like this. Forget you guys! I'm leaving!" She stormed out of the family room.

"Your stupid little girlfriend Matt...I told you not to bring her," one of the boys angrily whispered behind her back.

She exited the kitchen and walked back outside in the snow. Valerie came from a very poor family and she didn't have the appropriate attire for the winter. She grasped tightly onto her arms and shivered as the cold air engulfed her.

She went around the side of the house and out to the street. For a moment she was captured by the beauty of the house that was elaborately covered in Christmas decorations. She walked forward as she continued to look behind her. She pondered how it would be to experience such privilege, to be as fortunate as the family that was able to live there.

Valerie crashed into something in front of her that she was careless to miss, and an alarm blared. Her heart skipped a beat as she jolted to see where the sudden noise came from. It was a brand-new BMW with a large red bow on top. The alarm echoed through the streets.

The porch light flipped on next door, then shortly after, the same happened to the other houses in the neighborhood. Valerie gasped as she saw the lights. She stepped towards the house, thinking of running to warn her friends. In a split-second decision, she instead ran away as fast as she could.

Valerie continued to run though she was now more than half a mile away from the neighborhood. She saw a secluded park where all of the lights were off and ran through the gate, planning to hide in there. She felt an awful presence and attempted to stop, her feet slipping along the ground before she came to a complete halt. Looking around, Valerie saw a man sitting alone in the dark on one of the park benches. He was slumped over and breathing very heavily. His clothes were torn to shreds, and they looked like they had been scorched, as if he had just come out of a fire. That didn't seem very possible to Valerie, as the condition of his clothes suggested he was engulfed in flames. The sight sent a chill down her spine.

Gulping, she formulated words to speak, "E-excuse me, sir...you must be freezing! Are you okay?" she asked, trembling as she struggled to keep warm herself.

Her question was followed by a resounding silence. The alarm from the car down the road could no longer be heard and the streets were silent again with the slight ambiance of snowfall. The man still sat with his head tilted downwards, not showing any evidence that he heard her or was aware of her presence. She started to wonder if the man was deaf. She was not only scared but very intrigued by this silent man.

The sound of people quickly approaching caused Valerie to turn and see her friends running towards her in a panic. All of the boys had stolen goods hanging out of their coats. They caught up to Valerie and were grumbling and cursing about their close call.

"Valerie, what did you do?!" Matt yelled angrily.

"SHH!! You guys..." She glared at them and then nudged her head in the direction of the man sitting on the bench.

The teenage boys looked over in confusion. They each noticed the same thing Valerie did about his odd clothes. Though he seemed troubled, as misfits, they could have cared less to be concerned for him.

"Less than one minute away from me and you find some freak to hit on?" Matt chuckled and elbowed his friend next to him.

They all snickered and threw out a few curse words while calling Valerie derogatory names.

She scoffed in disbelief. "Look at him! He obviously needs help!" She turned back towards the man and leaned forward, wary to actually take any steps towards him. "Sir, is there any way we can help you?"

"Really, Val? You want us to *help* him?" Matt aggressively stepped towards the bench intending to grab the man to start a fight. "Oh, I'll help him, all right!"

"Get out of here! Or we'll make you!" one of the other boys threatened.

The man hadn't moved, still showing no signs that he was aware of their presence.

The third boy also stepped closer to speak up, "He ain't movin'. What do you say we teach him a lesson?"

The sound of sirens filled the air. All of the boys swiveled around and ducked behind the bushes. They peeked through the branches towards the street. They expected to see cop cars racing towards the house they came from, but that was not the case. The cops were racing in the opposite direction. Adjusting their focus, the boys looked down the road and saw pillars of smoke rising above the treetops from a house that was a few miles away. Cop cars, ambulances and fire trucks steadily passed, continuing towards the smoke.

Valerie didn't turn her focus away from the man as the others did. She watched his shoulders steadily rise and fall as his heavy breathing continued. Something caught her eye, a glimpse of red slowly dripping. As she focused on it, she realized that it was blood that was dripping from his face and onto his legs. Valerie assumed he must not only be freezing but also badly hurt.

She took a few steps towards him. "S-sir?" she stuttered.

The man's head began to move as it tilted upwards. She stopped and gulped as he finally showed any signs of awareness, but her heart dropped and body filled with adrenaline as his face was unveiled from the shadows of his hair.

Adrien lifted his head enough to lock eyes with Valerie. She gasped and stumbled back a few steps in the snow, but she was unable to move any further. Her mind raced—questioning her sanity—wondering if she was face-to-face with a ghost. He glowered at her with his red serpent-like eyes, blood running from them and down his cheeks.

Adrien slowly stood up from the bench. Valerie's feet felt laden with cement as her fear had rendered her motionless. He blinked rapidly at Valerie, unsure of what he was truly seeing. Valerie looked to be about thirteen years old, but to his amazement, she was a spitting image of Jenna. He was still about three yards away from her, but he took a step towards her. His head was cocked to the side as he stared at her face. Valerie backed up slowly, her knees knocking in fear. She continued to back up until she was adjacent to Matt. He was still hiding behind the brush, looking in the opposite direction.

Matt looked over at Valerie as she stepped into his peripheral vision. "Val," he jumped up from behind the foliage. "What are you doing?" He continued to stare her down, but she didn't even glance towards him. "Valerie!" Matt yelled and grabbed her shoulders, shaking her roughly to get her to snap out of it.

The other boys then noticed what was going on and they jumped up from the bushes as well. They turned their attention to Adrien while Matt continued to shake Valerie.

"Yo-uh...Matt!" one of the boys yelled over to him.

"What?!" Matt pushed Valerie as he turned to look at his friend.

Adrien growled viciously as she fell into the snow. Matt turned to look at him. Adrien looked like a ghost riddled in blood; his teeth were exposed, looking like the epitome of evil. They all—except for Valerie—made a break for it. However, none of them even made it to the gate before Adrien reached them. He appeared before them, blocking the exit to the park. The boys slipped on the icy ground.

"No! W-what are you?!"

"What the hell, man!"

"Please...just let us go! We're sorry, man!"

Adrien attacked all three boys so quickly that they never even had a real chance to escape. He fed on all of them as they screamed for help. Their screams were fleeting as it was over very quickly.

Valerie was still laying in the snow, shaking and shivering. She lay still, in hopes that he would leave and forget that she was there. After the screams of her friends no longer echoed through the park, it grew eerily silent. She cried softly, whimpering as she attempted to keep quiet. She heard his footsteps approaching her. Her heart raced; he had not forgotten about her, after all. He was on his way to her, and all she could do was run.

She quickly got up and ran through the park, pumping her arms and legs as fast as she could move them. She did not look behind her, in fear of what she would see. Valerie heard a whirring of wind behind her and then above her. She looked up just in time to see that Adrien, who had jumped into the air, was about to land in the path she was heading. She stopped and turned back around to run in the opposite direction. She pumped her arms and legs even faster, and the frigid air began to constrict her throat as she inhaled more, using all of the strength she could muster.

Valerie screamed as she approached the gate, passing her friends on the way. They were all sprawled out in the snow, red speckles spattered into the whiteness around them. Their horror-stricken faces were frozen at their moment of death. She almost made it to the other side of the chain-link fence, but Adrien grabbed her from behind. Her legs lifted in the air. She kicked, screaming for help and squirming in attempts to break free. To her surprise, he turned her around and embraced her.

"Jenna!" he cried out as he held onto her firmly.

He held onto her so tightly that she could hardly breathe;

he was slowly crushing her. Adrien's cries started to mix with hisses as he was close to her neck, her blood drawing him. A lump had formed in her throat as she desperately wanted to cry out more but was overcome by her fear. His grip grew even tighter, like a boa constricting its prey.

"I-I'm not Jenna!" she wailed, finally finding the strength to speak.

Adrien loosened his embrace and then grabbed her small neck, his hand almost wrapping completely around it. He leaned back to look her in the eyes. She had tears streaming down her face, knowing that she was about to die just like her friends. He continued to growl and hiss, the hisses growing in intensity.

For a moment, Adrien saw past the crimson blinders over his eyes and noticed the fear in Valerie's face. This face that looked so much like the woman that he loved. His sanity had been at a break, but at this moment he realized what he was doing. His brows that were heavily furrowed in anger suddenly lifted and his expression shifted to fear.

Valerie shut her eyes, bracing for what was next. She stumbled backward as the grip around her neck was loosened. The hissing and growling stopped abruptly as the wind around her whirred. When she opened her eyes, she saw that she was now by herself—Adrien was nowhere in sight.

Valerie dropped to her knees in the snow, her entire body burned from the adrenaline coursing through her veins. Looking to her left, she spotted her friends again, sprawled out in the blood-stained snow. Her legs were too wobbly to stand up, so she shuffled over to them on all fours.

"Please, please, please..." she pleaded desperately under her breath.

She reached her boyfriend Matt and tugged on the collar of his coat. He did not move. She began to yank him in efforts to wake him up.

"Come on! Matt!" She ripped open his coat and leaned her head down on his chest, but there was no heartbeat. "Matt?" Valerie's lips and voice quivered.

Quickly shuffling over to her other friends, she did the same thing. They were all dead. Valerie sat back in the snow, the pain from the loss of her friends distracting her from the freezing temperature. Her mind raced, unsure of what to do next. The smoke still billowing into the sky caught the corner of her eye and she remembered that emergency vehicles had headed in that direction earlier. Her legs still wobbled as she stood to her feet, but her strength returned to them after a few moments. She sprinted towards the smoke.

***

There was a muffled sound, but the noise started to grow louder and louder. Slowly, Michelle woke up. Soon enough, she recognized the sound: people yelling. Her mind raced in confusion for a moment, forgetting where she was. She opened her eyes, her ears ringing and her body stinging, grim reminders for her. Her vision was blurred. Blinking, she hurriedly attempted to see more clearly as there was a frenzied movement of colors and shapes swarming around her. It was still dark, just an hour after the initial explosion happened. There was a crowd of people rushing around her. An EMT knelt next to her with various instruments, checking her vital signs. Now that Michelle was fully aware but unable to move, the EMT glanced over and noticed Michelle with her eyes open and blinking frantically.

"Ma'am, can you hear me now?" he asked.

The EMT made eye contact with Michelle, and her brows furrowed in response to him.

"Mm," Michelle managed to grunt out.

He twisted around to look at the people already rushing over with a stretcher and gestured for them to hurry before he turned back to Michelle. Michelle, through a lot of pain, started to squirm and twist her body as she attempted to sit up. The EMT lightly placed his hand over her right shoulder.

"Please, take it easy," he requested.

The stretcher arrived and a team of people gently lifted her onto it. As they lifted the stretcher and rotated her, she could see the aftermath of the explosion, her eyes filled with tears as she saw the rubble strewn across the ground and ash falling from the sky.

Smoke still billowed from the wreckage that was once a beautiful mansion. She was rushed over to the ambulance parked in the driveway of the Reynolds estate. They slid her into the back of the ambulance. With her heart racing, she stared at the piles of rubble, smoke and ash as long as she could before the double doors shut her in. An IV was inserted into her forearm and she slipped out of consciousness.

***

Adrien ran. He ran as far as he could go before the grief caught up to him once again. He was currently in the forests of Clarksburg, near the cabin on the mountain that he stayed in with Jenna the year before. He could no longer move, paralyzed by the guilt that flooded him like a torrential storm. He had left carnage in his wake, the three teenage boys not being the last people that he killed; he continued murdering more innocents after them—anyone who happened to cross his path. Valerie and Michelle, so far, are the only ones that had survived him being in their presence that night. The total number of his victims for the night he was now unsure of; he had lost count. Adrien fell on his face in the snow, the voices and screams of his victims were ringing in his ears. Grabbing onto his head, he hollered, not knowing how he could bear the torment any longer.

Suddenly, Adrien heard movement from around him. Jumping up to his feet, he turned around, searching for who was nearby. There was no sign that there were humans close, as he did not pick up their scent. The wind whirred again and the sound of branches cracking echoed through the forest. He looked up, as it sounded like something was within the trees. He started to suspect that it was Latimer or one of the others since they must have been aware of the turn of events by now. No matter how near or far, Latimer could feel Adrien's emotions and knew what had happened to him. Latimer must have known where he was.

"Who's there?" Adrien called out in apprehension.

The snow crunched directly behind him. He could then smell human blood but it was oddly faint. He listened intently and heard the sound of someone breathing. Adrien's eyes shifted and his neck stiffened. He jerked around to face who was behind him.

"GRAH!" Adrien belted out as a branch, sharpened at the tip, pierced his abdomen.

Adrien grunted as his attacker continued to force the branch further through his body. They were so close to him that he could not see them clearly. Their forehead was pressed up against his as they growled deeply in his face. They then lifted their leg to kick him in the stomach with great force off the sharp branch and backward into a tree trunk. The tree rumbled and more branches snapped from the tree, collapsing to the ground around him.

Standing in front of Adrien was a man. His legs were set wide apart and his shoulders broad. He held loosely onto the sharpened branch that was now dripping with Adrien's blood. He was wearing an iron mask that covered his nose all the way down to his chin. His white tank top was stained with the bloody handprints of a multitude, giving evidence of the struggles of his victims. Atop his head was an eccentric hairstyle: a mohawk with low-cut designs on the side and his black hair faintly dyed green on the tips. He glared so viciously that his eyes were mere slits.

Adrien winced as his wounds healed, then he lifted his eyebrows in realization. He came across something he had never seen before: a Hunter vampire. Adrien's eyes jumped around frantically, seeing that the male was not alone.

About five yards behind the male stood a female Hunter.

The woman was in all red, her stance very feral as she was positioned to quickly attack if need be. Her neck was wrapped in a multilayered leather choker with a red jewel dangling on the end of it. She also had the same iron mask fitted on her face. The male went by the name of Kyle and the female's name was Gina.

Kyle twirled the branch in his hands as he approached Adrien. He quickly knelt down and shoved the branch lengthwise against Adrien's neck, forcing his head back into the tree trunk.

"W-who are you?" Adrien mumbled as the branch put an uncomfortable pressure on his Adam's apple.

Kyle's eyes moved up and down as he examined him, his eyes steady on Adrien's. His gaze was intense and his eyes were red like the other vampires, but his irises were outlined in a deeper red—nearly black. Human blood dripped from underneath Kyle's mask and down his neck; he must have fed recently.

Adrien gulped. "W-what do you—"

"How ya reckon ya got grounds ta keep speakin'?" Kyle's iron mask moved as he talked. His voice was deep, gravelly and heavy with a Southern accent. He put more pressure on Adrien's throat, crushing his windpipe. Adrien gasped for air. "Her an' I?" he nudged his head back in the direction of Gina that started walking their way. "We was sent here. Our leader has quite an eye on this here state. When we all come back, we gon' kill any Harvester that choose ta get in our way. Ya understan'?"

Gina leaned over Kyle's shoulder and stared at Adrien intently. "Lucky for you, that's something you're not. Care to join us?" Her voice was deep but very smooth and feminine. The tone in her voice made it seem more like a demand and less of a choice.

Kyle looked over to Gina, annoyed. "Let me handle this here, sweetheart," he said condescendingly.

Adrien coughed violently from the continued pressure on his throat, he shook his head side to side quickly in rejection to her offer.

"Ya gon' join us or ya gon' get what's comin' ta ya." Kyle's eyes darkened and his head lowered. "And it ain't gon' be purty." Kyle finally lifted the stick off Adrien's throat.

Adrien coughed and cleared his throat as he healed. "Please...kill me," he breathed heavily and continued to cough, rolling the back of his head against the tree trunk as he gazed off in the distance.

Gina didn't break her stare at Adrien, but Kyle turned around to see where his attention was going.

"What in the world ya lookin' at, boy?"

"Please..." Adrien said more desperately, "please...kill me..."

Kyle leaned back. "This one here dun lost his mind," he chuckled while standing up.

Gina sighed and turned to walk the other direction.

"We sure as well don't take no orders from ya," Kyle turned around, but then eyed Adrien from over his shoulder. "Stick roun' here, an' ya best believe we'll be seein' ya again. Imma kill ya then—on my own terms."

They both vanished instantly, leaving Adrien alone once again. He groaned in grief, then shortly afterward felt himself becoming lethargic. This meant daytime was quickly approaching. Turning his head, he breathed in deeply, then sighed as he watched the horizon in the east, waiting patiently for the sun to rise.

Chapter 11

*"Light is sweet, and it pleases the eyes to see the sun. However many years
anyone may live, let them enjoy them all. But let them remember the days of
darkness, for there will be many. Everything to come is meaningless."*

Ecclesiastes 11:7-8

A drien stared at the horizon, comatose, his
breathing growing heavier as the darkness in the
sky began to lighten. As he gazed into the distance,
his eyes spotted something familiar. He saw the cabin that he
had rented close by. A passion within him burned as he saw it,
desiring to be within it, to immerse himself in his memories.

He slowly stood to his feet and trekked to the top of the
hill to the cabin. The front door was locked, so he broke through
it. In what was usually a hotspot for families who wanted to
spend Christmas in a home away from home, the cabin was
completely vacant. He then remembered something of his that
he could take, and it was in the underground wine cellar.

The boards of the cabin floor creaked under his feet as he jogged his memory of the cabin's layout. He found the door leading to the stairway below, just outside of the kitchen. Adrien looked to his left and saw the morning sunlight beginning to spill in through the kitchen window. He distinctly remembered the gentle warmth on his skin from the sun through that same window while he was human. He and Jenna danced to Christmas music and laughed as they attempted, and failed miserably, to make blueberry pancakes in that kitchen. This was the first time since he was burned that he had seen sunlight like this, outside of the safety of the stone home. He stood staring in a trance as the sunlight crept closer towards him, inch by inch.

He pondered: what if he didn't get into the cellar? Maybe, through death, he would get to see Jenna again? The light crawled inches from the tips of his toes, the mere proximity of the UV rays heating up his entire body, causing steam to rise from him. He suddenly realized that he didn't truly know what would happen to him if he died: if there was an afterlife, if he would feel peace, nothing, or possibly *more* anguish. This sudden thought of the unknown started to terrify him.

He instinctively bolted through the door. He breathed heavily within the safety of the dark, not only fearing the unknown, but thinking of the time he stepped out into daylight as a new, naive, vampire. He remembered the excruciating pain of his skin bubbling—melting off his face. If there was ever a way to go, he knew that's not what he'd choose. His shoulders were elevated as he leaned tensely against the cellar door, looking down the long flight of stairs. He straightened up, then walked down into the cellar.

He immediately began to reflect, thinking about Jenna again. Memories he had of her were baked into this cabin. He walked over to the other side of the room and searched along the wall of alphabetically organized bottles. Finding his place, he pulled out a bottle of wine.

The cabin had a tradition where they would press a special wine and label it with the guests of the people who had stayed there. They gave one bottle to the guests as they checked in and then stored another complimentary bottle in the cellar for when they came back for another stay. Adrien, in advance, had them adjust Jenna's last name for their future complimentary bottle. He planned to take her there again after they got married.

The wine bottle he held in his hand glistened with a gold embossment of their names: Mr. & Mrs. Adrien and Jenna Reed. The pit in his stomach grew. He set it on the floor next to him and then sat down by it. Crossing his legs Indian-style and pressing his back to the wall, he leaned his head back, then closed his eyes to rest.

***

CRASH!

Adrien jolted awake. He immediately sensed that night had now fallen, he had slept through the day. Jumping to his feet, he looked upwards, the sound of boots along the floorboards were echoing above him. The sound quickly approached. The door to the wine cellar flung open, flying off its hinges and crashing to the floor in front of Adrien. Cade leapt down the flight of stairs to the bottom of the cellar and landed in a hostile crouching position, hissing, ready to attack. Shortly afterward, Latimer entered the room and traveled down the stairs as well.

Adrien wasn't fazed by Cade's hostility, but he glanced at Latimer and was surprised that he did not seem angry. Instead, he looked worried and simultaneously empathetic.

"Cade...let him speak," Latimer requested.

Cade sighed and then stood up, crossing his arms over his chest. "Fine," he said venomously. "You may speak."

Adrien said nothing as his eyes moved between the two of them. They were dim: what little life was left in them was no longer there. Both Cade and Latimer noted this.

Cade grew impatient. His anger brewed ever more with Adrien's silence. Cade lunged towards Adrien and slashed at his torso, tearing away a chunk of his flesh. Adrien screamed in agony and then instinctively leapt out of his way as Cade tried to go for another blow. He grabbed Cade in a headlock. Adrien was stronger than he; however, Cade was more of a skilled fighter. Cade maneuvered out of the headlock and dropped down to sweep kick Adrien's feet from under him. He landed roughly on his back onto the wooden floor.

Latimer stood out of the way, observing at the base of the staircase, knowing that Cade would not kill Adrien without a direct order from him. Cade had Adrien pinned to the ground. He retracted his arm to slash down at Adrien again, but Adrien used his legs to push Cade off with a mighty force that sent him flying through the cellar ceiling. Cade crashed into the kitchen, bursting a waterline in the process. Water spurted and gushed into the room, quickly flooding the floors.

Water poured down like a cascade into the cellar from the hole in the ceiling. Adrien stood to his feet slowly as the water saturated him from head to toe. He looked at Latimer blankly.

"Adrien, speak to me. Please," Latimer appealed to him.

Adrien closed his eyes briefly, then bent down to grab the wine bottle still sitting near the wall. He then started to quickly walk towards the staircase, pushing past Latimer and sprinting to the top.

Cade charged Adrien from the kitchen, tackling him as soon as he exited the cellar door. Adrien used his strength to prevent from falling, but they continued to tussle through the foyer until they broke out of the cabin through the front window. Glass rained down with them. When they hit the ground, they separated. Cade rolled and then flipped himself to his feet while Adrien lay dazed on his back. He groaned, then sat up. Latimer emerged from the cabin as well, his eyes filled with worry.

"You have nothing to say?!" Cade fumed as he stepped forward. "You have jeopardized *all* of us!"

In between Cade and Adrien laid the wine bottle, slightly sticking out of the snow. Adrien rushed over—trying to grab it—but Cade saw what he was reaching for and beat him to it. Cade yanked it out of the ground and analyzed it.

His eyes narrowed to slits as he read the text. "All of this... for some cheating *tramp*?" Cade asked acidly.

He gripped tighter onto the bottle, then swung it into a tree trunk, causing the bottle to shatter into thousands of pieces. Adrien watched the shards spread all over the snow and the burgundy liquid splatter from the bottle. The label with the gold embossment of their names fell to the ground along with a heap of glass. Adrien growled as he ferociously looked at Cade.

Cade chuckled, planning to provoke him even more. "Well—on second thought—you did well by killing *her*, at least. After all...she did deserve to die."

Cade's words echoed through the forest. Adrien's blood boiled in anger. He yelled, charging for Cade. Cade grinned as he braced for Adrien, and when Adrien reached him, he lunged forward and grabbed onto his neck as he simultaneously pivoted and tossed Adrien behind him.

Adrien was flung more than two stories into the air, dead branches bending and snapping against his body as he soared through the treetops. He slammed into a tree trunk, then plummeted to the ground, breaking through more branches on the way down. What sounded like thunder resounded from the impact of his fall. Cade quickly closed the gap between them and picked him up from the ground. Cade then shoved Adrien into the tree trunk.

"How *many* did you kill?!" Cade's eyes were filled with fury; it looked like he planned to finish the job, whether or not he was given an order.

"Drop him! NOW!" Latimer demanded, his voice boomed with authority.

Cade immediately dropped him and huffed, diverting his attention to Latimer. "You knew as soon as this happened— you tried to keep it from the rest of us! But why? You have the power of *complete* control over him, Latimer! All of this could have been avoided! What a mess we have to clean up now!"

Adrien looked up at Latimer. "Control?" He stood up, staggering towards him. "You can control me?"

Latimer stared at him stoically.

"Why didn't you stop me? HUH?! You could have stopped me from killing her!" Adrien exhaled sharply, feeling betrayed.

"I do not believe in hindering your free will to such an extent, no matter the reason," Latimer justified firmly.

Adrien scoffed, shaking his head in disdain from his answer.

The trees rustled as Coran suddenly appeared with Xylia and Kiana. He ran up to Latimer.

"Hunters!" Coran exclaimed. "We just missed them. Just a little over a mile from here."

Xylia stepped forward. "We split up after we caught their scent. Kiana and I went just a little further north and discovered humans working a crime scene. There was a massacre last night."

Kiana piped up, "Twenty-five humans, just one location. Seems like the work of the Hunters who may have passed through here."

Cade grabbed onto the remnants of Adrien's shirt and yanked him towards himself. "Or was it you?! You are no longer better than them, after all!"

"Cade," Latimer reprimanded him.

Cade let go of him. "Latimer...*you*, more than any of us, have worked for centuries protecting this place from Hunters—establishing a home here. What is so special about Adrien that causes you to forget what has been, and will always be, our duty?!"

Adrien cleared his throat loudly, and they all turned to him to listen to what he had to say.

"I-uh..." Adrien paused, then he continued to speak, "I ran into two Hunters—last night..." he trailed off. "*Twenty-five* people?" he asked in disbelief.

"Hunters have a blood thirst sizable in comparison to ours," Coran explained.

"I...I don't want to become like that. I can't..." Adrien said as he realized the path he had taken.

"How many...*did* you kill?" Cade asked again.

"That no longer matters," Latimer interjected. "You came in contact with them, who were they?"

"It was a male and a female. They wore iron masks," Adrien said.

"Iron masks?" Xylia asked. "That makes no sense. That would lower their sense of smell for human blood."

"Perhaps it is intentional, to keep them focused on a task," Latimer theorized. "What else can you tell us?"

Adrien scratched his head, racking through the

conversation in his mind. "They spoke of having a leader—and there are more of them. He said they are all going to come back, they will kill us all when they do."

Cade's eyes shot daggers in Adrien's direction. "What the redhead just spewed out *can't* be true. Hunters don't gather, they don't coordinate with one another and they certainly would not align under a leader."

"If the leader created them all...it *would* be plausible," Kiana said, matter-of-factly.

"Believe what you want. I am telling the truth," Adrien hissed back at Cade.

"We tried to contact Lazaro from Vermont once more, but we have still not heard from him," Xylia said.

"I was able to contact another Harvester named Ransom. He is from further west, but he is very close to Lazaro. He has also not heard a word from him. Ransom should be here within the next few nights," Kiana stated.

"Good. Thank you, Kiana," Latimer said. "Cade and I will plan a trip further north. We will check on them in person. Everyone else stays here in case of an unexpected infiltration," he ordered.

"How many do you think there are?" Coran asked with uncertainty.

Latimer stiffened in his stance. In his mind, he went back to the previous night when he set out to tell the others of the possibility of Hunters coming their way. An unexpected visitor had come to the house just before then. This visitor was one Latimer hadn't seen for nearly two decades, someone that not a single one of the Harvesters—or Adrien—knew about. This someone was not a friend.

Latimer made eye contact with them all as he showed no signs of fear. "I believe they will come in numbers *far* greater than ours."

Chapter 12

"For there is a proper time and procedure for every matter, though a person may be weighed down by misery."

Ecclesiastes 8:6

December 26th: ten in the morning

*M*ichelle woke up in the hospital. Sunlight was spilling into the room and a tray of food was sitting next to her on a table. Bruised and sore, she slowly sat up in bed, just as Anna walked in.

"Michelle!" Anna dropped her bag on the floor and ran to her side. "Thank God! How do you feel?"

Michelle's throat felt like sandpaper, and her body was exceptionally weak. "I'm fine...Jenna, is she—"

Anna placed her hand on Michelle's arm. The look on Anna's face spoke just as loud as any of her words would have. Realizing the answer to the question, Michelle lowered her head and inhaled deeply, her breath shaky. She sighed and tightly closed her eyes as hot tears escaped from them and streamed down the sides of her cheeks. She felt like she was supposed to save the girl, and she failed. She thought: maybe she didn't try hard enough—maybe she should have been more aggressive with her approach.

"I'm sorry..." Anna whispered sympathetically.

The room was silent for a few minutes as they both stared grimly in opposite directions. Michelle looked back over to Anna; Michelle had yet to speak to anyone about what she had witnessed.

"I..." Michelle began to speak, but then she stopped, unsure of how to explain to Anna what she had seen; the man in the sky. Was she merely hallucinating? "Last night, I—"

"Michelle. It's the 26th," Anna interjected.

"Is it? I've been out for that long?" She said, concerned, she sat up even straighter. "What have I missed?"

Anna stared at her with eyes wide and mouth agape, then she cleared her throat. "A lot happened on Christmas Eve. Many more are...dead."

Michelle gulped. "*Many* more? W-what do you mean?"

"Well...first it was the incident at the Reynold's estate with the explosion. Then there was a girl who came to the scene of the explosion that night. She had run for miles, her face was as white as a ghost, terrified of what she had witnessed. We went to where she directed us. Three teenage boys, murdered in cold blood just three miles away. She is here at this very hospital being treated for hypothermia. You and her are very lucky. We received a total of six emergency calls just in that one night all within hours of each other. Eight people found dead around the city, attacked in alleyways or on the main roads...you two are the only ones who survived."

Michelle ripped the hospital blanket from her legs. "I have to go!" She started to yank the tubes out of her hand and remove the tape from her arms.

Anna stepped back from the bed, knowing she would not be able to convince Michelle to stay and continue to recover. Michelle hopped out of her bed and saw the plastic bag with her clothes laying on the table. She rushed over to it and yanked the privacy curtain around her before she began to change.

"That's not all..." Anna said while walking towards the curtain.

Michelle stopped, becoming woozy from her sudden burst of energy. She hunched over, leaning her weight on the chair in front of her. Turning her head slightly, she eyed the curtain from the side in reluctance, wincing as she waited for Anna to continue.

"Christmas morning, we received another call. Further north, in Clarksburg, a house was discovered with more victims. The people were murdered in the same way we found the others. All of the doors were locked from the inside, though. We found a broken window and two pairs of bloody footprints that left the scene of the crime, but the tracks suddenly disappeared," Anna explained. "That makes it thirty-three deaths...all in *one* night," she murmured.

Michelle shook her head in disbelief and rested her face in her hands. "What's happening?" she asked in fear.

"Listen to this: the first string of murders followed a trail up to Clarksburg; we were originally thinking the same person was responsible for all thirty-three homicides, but that is impossible," Anna added on.

Michelle pulled back the curtain and approached Anna quickly. "Why?"

"Based on the times of death, the massacre happened when the other string of murders were still in motion. Many must have been involved in this mass murder," Anna concluded.

Michelle stood silently for a few moments as she pondered. "I need you to take me to that girl," Michelle said as she leaned over and grabbed one of the muffins off the plate of snacks by her bed. "The one you mentioned earlier."

"O-okay. Follow me, she's just down the hall." Anna began to lead the way.

It took only a few minutes for them to make it to the room where the teenage girl, Valerie, was staying. Michelle hurriedly stuffed the blueberry muffin into her mouth as they approached the room. The room was dark; the lights had been turned off and the curtains were shut. They slowly peeked around the corner and saw the girl casually flipping through channels.

Michelle noticed that her face looked eerily familiar. Her eyes were spacey as she was not fully paying attention to what she was looking at. Her stare at the TV on the wall broke as she saw Michelle approaching her in her peripheral vision. She looked at Michelle head-on; her eyes were puffy, red and swollen from crying. Michelle gasped under her breath, noting her striking resemblance to Jenna McBrayer. Michelle suddenly had déjà vu, this was similar to the night she first approached Jenna when she was on the street curb many months ago.

Valerie sat the control down in her lap and pulled her knees up to her chest. Her legs were still covered by the hospital blanket. Crossing her arms over her knees and biting her lip, she looked at the two women shyly. Anna stayed within the doorway of the room and did not enter any further.

"Miss?" Michelle asked tentatively as she approached.

Valerie raised her eyebrows at Michelle in response. She noticed that Michelle looked pretty beat up herself. She had bandages on her face and was walking with a slight limp when she came in.

"Hi...my name is Michelle."

"Valerie," she responded dryly.

"Nice to meet you, Valerie. I came to see you because I heard from my colleague over there that you experienced something quite frightful two nights ago." Michelle leaned against the foot of the hospital bed. "I saw some...unusual things that night as well. Do you mind telling me what you saw?"

Valerie pursed her lips and pulled her legs into her chest even tighter. She sighed and her eyes jumped around frantically, her expression transforming into extreme anguish. "My friends are dead," she said quietly.

"How did they die?" Michelle responded gently.

Valerie whimpered, and her eyes began to water. "It looked like a man. He was very pale, he had dark red hair and eyes…his clothes were torn or burned off his back or…something. He…*killed* them."

"Burned?" Michelle pondered, knowing that this was only a few miles from the explosion. "Did this man say anything to you?"

Valerie breathed in deeply, her eyes squinting. "Yes. He called me…some name. I don't remember, but…he looked at me like he knew who I was."

"Have you seen him before?" Michelle prodded curiously.

"Never…" Valerie sighed.

"Hmm… is there anything else you remember?"

"Um, he seemed to be crying before I came up to him. But…there weren't any tears it was…" Valerie trailed off. She looked at Michelle wearily as she shifted uncomfortably in the bed.

"What was it?" Michelle prodded.

"It was *blood*," she said as she shivered.

Michelle gulped, not sure how to respond to that. Her mind wandered, running over a list of possible diseases that might cause someone to cry tears of blood.

"Hmph. That's very odd," Michelle said. "How did you—"

"Oh!" Valerie exclaimed. "Now I remember! I remember who he called me." Valerie lifted one of her hands and scratched her head. "He...he called me Jenna."

Anna looked at Michelle from the corner of her eye as she heard this. Michelle's eyes widened before she glanced at Anna, then she looked back at Valerie.

"J-Jenna?" she asked in disbelief. "Does this name mean anything to you?"

Valerie sighed. "Yeah, well...my sister's name is Jenna."

Anna's head swiveled towards Michelle, her mouth was hanging agape.

"As in...Jenna McBrayer?" Michelle tried to clarify.

"Yes ma'am," Valerie confirmed.

Anna entered the room and stood at the foot of the bed with Michelle, eager to listen more closely. Valerie had no clue that her sister was now deceased.

"My family and I haven't had contact with her in years." Valerie continued, "She disowned us, sort of. My family was—and still is—very poor; we barely had enough money to put food on the table. So, she left us and started dating this rich guy named, um..."

"*Adrien,*" Michelle whispered in epiphany.

***

December 27th

Adrien stood alone on a hill, the dead branches of an oak tree looming above him while snowflakes delicately fell to the cold ground beneath him. He wore a black, short-sleeved V-neck with tattered jeans that were torn short near his ankles. His bare feet dug into the snow. He found himself there, watching two overnight employees that were wrapped in winter coats work their shift. The stone that marked the land had etchings carefully carved out of the rock:

"Jenna Marie McBrayer
March 15ᵗʰ 1998-December 24ᵗʰ 2018"

That stone sown in the cemetery soil solidified it. Though her death was certain, it was only then that the horrid truth had settled in his mind for good. It at first seemed surreal, just like every moment since he became a vampire. He observed with a heavy heart as the men piled shovels full of dirt and snow atop her coffin. Her *coffin.*

Each release from the shovel was followed by the chilling sound of the earthy slush echoing off the metal frame. Soon, the sound became unbearable to him. The workers finished filling the hole and they patted the freshly laid ground with the back of their shovels.

The grave workers were then startled with a deafening noise of splintering wood that echoed across the entire graveyard. They turned around and saw a very large oak tree topple over. It crashed into the ground, shaking the soil beneath their feet. Adrien was no longer near, having uprooted the tree in anger before he ran away.

Adrien traveled to a place he hadn't seen in over five months. His home when he was human. Before that night, he had avoided coming back to his house. Now knowing that he would never see Jenna again—that the wine bottle along with all of the drawings he made of her were destroyed—he was desperately in search for all the places he had memories with her. He feared he would forget her face just as he had forgotten his father's.

When he reached the home, he was greeted by something; an unexpected feeling. When he would daydream about his old home while lying in his coffin, he remembered it as a place full of light and life. But now there was the same glooming semblance of the darkness he had become all too familiar with; he couldn't seem to get away from it. This darkness followed him no matter where he went.

He stood just on the other side of the front door with his hands across his body, holding onto himself as he felt he was falling apart, piece by piece. The overgrown grass and shrubbery that had begun to envelop the front of the house was a testament to the time that had passed. If only he knew. If only he knew what lay ahead of them both when they got into that limo many months ago. If only he knew, they would have stayed. Maybe they both would be there...flourishing in wedded bliss, living their life the way they dreamt it would be.

Adrien drew even closer to the door. Pressing his forehead against it, he looked down. His hand hovered over the knob as he took a few deep breaths, and then he slowly turned the smooth brass to enter.

He walked in through the foyer of the room he had formerly called his lighthouse. The cello and other instruments had begun to collect a thick layer of dust. As he walked around, his heart seemed to flutter at the memories that flooded back to him: days playing his cello for Jenna as she lay on the chairs off the balcony or on the white sofa in the center of the room, the warm, sparkly lights would illuminate the room through the countless deep conversations that they had.

Out of habit, he sat behind his cello and strummed on the strings quietly with his fingertips while looking around. He remembered the first time he played for her, the way that her beautiful eyes glistened proudly. That same night they decided that they would no longer just be friends, that their feelings for one another were deeper than a simple platonic relationship.

While he sifted through memories, something gleamed in the darkness and caught his eye. His stomach dropped. The engagement ring that he had given to Jenna was laying on the tile floor under one of the end tables. The seat creaked as he leapt to his feet and went to pick it up. Examining it, he blew the dirt and dust from the band.

He turned his head and saw the couch directly to his right. It was disheveled, evidence of an altercation that happened while he was not around.

"She must have come back here," Adrien whispered to himself.

Dropping to his knees by the couch, he buried his head into the side of it. Bloody tears streaked down the side of the once flawlessly white cushion. After a few minutes, he stood up. He stuffed the ring into his pocket before leaving the room. He had suddenly remembered something that he held as a treasure on the tableside of his bed and he was intent on getting it from his bedroom.

Adrien passed by the pool, the waterfall and the gazebo as he traveled down the hill towards the rooms of his house lining the beach. The waterfall no longer worked since it had frozen over. The pool had a thin layer of ice and piles of leaves covering the surface of it as well, nothing like how he had last seen it.

He approached his bedroom. Once he entered, he went directly to his nightstand. Atop the table were nicely framed photographs of him and Jenna. Adrien hated to take photos, but eventually, Jenna convinced him to take some with her and get them developed. These were the only two physical photos of them that he possessed. He lightly touched the glass on the frame above her face, accidentally smudging blood over the smooth surface. A few more tears escaped from him as he viewed them, but this time he smiled. Now he at least had something to cherish.

The moment was cut short as Adrien heard footsteps approaching. He hid quickly, locking himself within the bathroom in the bedroom. Completely baffled by the possibility of someone on the premises, he wondered who in the world could possibly be there. Why would they be there? He was so distracted that he did not sense them coming ahead of time.

The door to his room opened and closed. Listening carefully, he heard that the footsteps on the carpet were delicate and more than likely belonged to a female. Soon after, their aroma seeped through the doors and the walls; it was a human, no doubt. Growing even more curious, Adrien carefully moved closer to the door and knelt down. The old style to the door handle allowed him to peer through the keyhole. His face lightly touched the smooth metal, and his eyes jumped in confusion. That hair, that face...this woman looked so familiar, but from where?

Michelle dropped her purse down on the table at the entrance of the room and let out a big sigh. She had her hands in white latex gloves and held firmly onto her small brown leather case. She looked around the room intently and flipped the leather open, pulling out a pen. She took notes on what she observed.

Michelle had been very busy the past two days with the aftermath of the explosion and the mysterious deaths around the city. Adrien was now the main suspect. She had searched for clues with no further leads on his location. Michelle researched more on Adrien, finding out more detail on his past and the places he had grown up. She visited the shelter he used to volunteer at, but no one had seen him around.

Her suspicions arose even further once an anonymous donation was made to pay for Jenna's funeral. Going there earlier in the day, she had her eyes peeled, expecting to see Adrien there. She did not see him of course, as she was the only one present at the ceremony. Michelle's next resort was to visit his home again. Though his home was already searched months prior, she decided to venture there again that night, in case anything was missed the first time around.

"Rich, huh?" she said aloud to herself and scoffed. She continued in a sarcastic tone, "That's an understatement."

Adrien was fascinated by the detail in old ornate furniture, so his house was full of it. The mirrors, the chairs, the door handles and frames were all intricately carved out, some lined in silver or other precious metals and rare materials. There was also a slight Moroccan influence in the tiling in certain areas in the home, especially in the bathroom that Adrien was currently hidden within.

Michelle made her way around the room cautiously. She saw a piece of clothing that was on the floor, kneeling down she then lifted it eye level with the tip of her pin. There were a few hair strands stuck to the shirt. After briefly examining it, she set it back down. Eyeing her purse from over her shoulder, she straightened back up with the intent to go grab a plastic evidence bag for collection. However, something caught her eye in her peripheral. She saw the black table by the bed with fancy crystal frames that were displaying professional photographs.

She walked up to the nightstand and mulled over them, setting her stuff down beside them. Instantly, she recognized Adrien. Michelle saw pictures of him before, but for some reason, she never connected the dots until then. Many months ago, she met him at the park after accidentally hitting him with a soccer ball. She also remembered that it was the same day that Jenna claimed the incidence of his disappearance. He seemed like a nice guy, her heart sank at the thought. Paying mind to his features, they seemed to match the description that Valerie had given of the man who attacked her and her friends.

She shifted her attention to the next photo and breathed in sharply. There was a fresh bloody fingerprint on the glass just above Jenna's face. Without moving an inch, her eyes shifted to the surrounding area, raking the surface of the rest of the table. There were more small splatters of blood pooled on the surface in front of the picture. The sound of Valerie's voice resonated in her mind: *He seemed to be crying before I came up to him. But...there weren't any tears it was...blood.*

Michelle's heart began to race as she realized that Adrien must have been there just moments before her. Without moving her head, she looked down at her feet, being careful not to move too suddenly. She spotted a trail on the ground and partially followed it with her eyes; she looked to the side and could see from the corner of her eye that the trail led to the door directly behind her. Michelle had studied the floor plans of the house before she visited...she knew that the door did not lead to an exit. She knew that he must have still been there.

Michelle looked forward and stayed calm...she closed her eyes, attempting to quickly formulate a plan in her mind. She didn't know the potential danger she was dealing with, but her firearm was left in her purse and she could not approach him without it. She opened her eyes, knowing that it was now or never.

Michelle turned her back to the nightstand and walked over to the entrance where she sat her purse down. Opening the purse, she pulled out two plastic evidence bags and set them on the table. She then reached back in and felt for her pistol, quietly disengaging the safety once she took hold of it. The door to the bathroom creaked. Michelle swiveled around wielded her pistol in the direction of the bathroom.

"FREEZE!" she yelled.

She expected to see a man standing before her, but all she saw was a blurred movement so quick that the bay window seemed to swing open on its own. It opened with such force that it flew off the hinges and the glass shattered on the ground outside where it landed.

Michelle sprinted to the window, leaping over a coffee table that was in her path then climbed over the threshold and out to the other side onto the beach. Her boots crunched in all of the broken glass scattered around her. The sound of the loud waves crashing to shore made it hard to hear anything else as she focused on her surroundings. She carefully aligned the barrel of her gun to her line of sight and, with labored breath, she searched in all directions, the adrenaline rush so intense that her blood felt like electricity coursing through her veins.

There were three fresh footprints in the thin layer of snow covering the sand and then the trail abruptly ended. She looked up into the sky and saw only clouds and a few falling snowflakes.

"What *are* you?" Michelle asked, perplexed as she stared into the sky, allowing the flakes to softly land on her face.

Michelle thought back to the night of the double homicide that took the lives of Jenna and Brock. She remembered what she saw within the house moments before the explosion, that same blurred movement. She remembered what she saw in the sky after the explosion, too. There was no doubt in her mind now that it was Adrien, and that she was just now only a few feet away from him.

She walked the perimeter of the building cautiously, still leading with her pistol until she reached the door to the bedroom on the other side and re-entered. Gathering all of her stuff quickly, she noticed something. The nightstand. It was completely wiped clean, and the frames had been taken. Rushing over while fumbling with the contents of her purse, she took out a cotton swab to retrieve a sample of the blood left on the nightstand.

"Shoot!" she shouted, noticing that not only were the frames taken from the table, but her small leather case and all that was in it: her case notes, her tablet, were swiped along with them.

Michelle packed away the cotton swab with the blood sample and grinned, suddenly realizing that her possessions being swiped would work incredibly in her favor. Zipping up her purse, she left the room, closer to the truth more than ever.

***

Cade and Latimer just returned from a trip up north scoping out their allied territory to find out why none of their Harvester acquaintances were responsive. They had come back with a grueling discovery and had just gotten off the phone with Coran and the others as they shared what they found.

Adrien stormed through the front door to the stone house with the picture frames and leather case belonging to Michelle in his hand. He was flustered and concerned, wishing that he had killed the woman that was in his old house. He paced back in forth in frustration, not entirely sure all of what she had seen.

Latimer walked into the room with Cade, mid-discussion, "What we discovered will not lie ahead for us; we already know of the threat, at least. The others up north must have been caught off guard," Latimer mourned.

"But why would the Hunters have retreated? And where did they go?" Cade inquired.

Latimer then looked over to Adrien, his eyes following down the length of his arm, and seeing the frames and case firmly grasped in Adrien's hands. Adrien stopped pacing and looked down at the frames in his hand as well after seeing that Latimer noticed them. Adrien then noticed what he had also grabbed accidentally: Michelle's stuff. He quickly brushed it off, dropping it to the floor as he continued to hold onto the frames. Latimer watched it land, then looked back up to Adrien.

Cade looked at the frames and saw the picture of Jenna. He scoffed. "I am overdue for my reaping. I will see myself out," Cade said. He elbowed passed Adrien on his way out of the front door.

Adrien glared at Cade as he left, then turned back around to Latimer.

"Adrien, are you alright?" Latimer asked, concerned.

Latimer and Adrien had spoken but a few words to one another since the night they confronted him in the cabin. Adrien found it hard to get over the fact that Latimer knew what he was about to do the fatal night of Jenna's murder and did nothing to stop him when he had the power to do so.

Coran had further explained more of their vampire biology. He explained that each creator could control the actions of the ones they transform into vampires—like a puppet. They could take away their free will on command. Their venom used in the transformation could be likened to a parasite in the brain. This parasitic venom is what gave creators the ability to have all power over those they produced. Adrien pondered this all and his anger built again. He walked up to Latimer, getting close in his face.

"Tell me something," he said, very agitated. "Why didn't you just let me die that night?" Adrien's eyes darted around Latimer's face, seeing that Latimer's mouth slightly twitched at the question he continued to bring up time and time again. "I didn't want this. You have no idea....you have NO IDEA!" Adrien screamed so loudly that it felt like his mouth would come unhinged.

Adrien staggered backward from Latimer a few steps, his face morphing from fury to anguish. He grit his teeth and looked down at the photographs in his hand. A tear of blood escaped from one eye then the other shortly after. Though Adrien had cried a few times since he had turned, this was the first time that he had done so in front of Latimer. Latimer's eyes that were already dim, withered further at the sight of this; though already pale, he somehow lost even more color from his complexion.

"This pain...I...*can't* stand it anymore," Adrien lamented, his voice so broken that it was hardly audible.

Latimer did not know what to say, but his mind raced,

knowing exactly what he should have shared with him. He lowered his head in remorse and sighed deeply, still not uttering a single word. Latimer's silence angered Adrien even more.

"Nothing to say, huh? You were probably all pathetic and lonely in this place by yourself. So, you decided to screw up my life for your own sake." He spat on the floor just next to Latimer's shoe. "You are nothing but a selfish creep!" Adrien stared Latimer indignantly in the face, expecting him to show some sort of emotion or response beyond his usual stoic reply.

Latimer squinted his eyes at Adrien. He then broke eye contact and placed his hands in his pants pockets, shaking his head in shame. "You are right…I am…very selfish," he responded quietly, then he promptly walked off in the other direction.

Adrien's heart softened as Latimer walked away; he immediately felt terrible for disrespecting him. He followed behind Latimer who had already disappeared to the second story of the house.

"Latimer…" Adrien called after him in an apologetic tone.

Adrien reached the top of the staircase and neither saw nor heard Latimer. He slowly walked down the corridor, listening intently for him and where he could have gone. As Adrien passed by one of the bookcases, he felt an abnormal draft. Turning to investigate, he saw the bookshelf was out of place; it was slightly shifted to the side so an aperture in the wall was now exposed.

"What in the world?" he said to himself, curiously feeling around the edge of the bookcase.

Adrien grabbed onto it and pushed it to the side just

enough so that he could squeeze behind it. Surprisingly, there was a hidden hallway; a metal door that was rusted and worn down was at the end of it.

"Latimer?" Adrien called out.

There was no response, only silence. Adrien slowly walked toward the door in front of him. He cautiously opened it and peeked around to see an elaborate staircase that spiraled up to another story, a story that he was unaware of. With his head still peeking through the door, he looked up towards the top of the flight of stairs at a glow of bright light coming from above. The staircase looked to be made of a material that he had yet to see around the stone house. It was made out of an off-white high-end marble and it had golden rails. He opened the metal door fully and began to walk up the stairs.

As Adrien ascended, the light brightened even more. As he emerged at the top of the stairs, the sight took his breath away. The walls were white and columned, and there were some walls with decorative panels of detail and colorful paintings reminiscent of the French Renaissance. There was soft white drapery around fancy furniture that glistened to perfection. Yet, there was still another door on the other side of the room. Why wouldn't Latimer tell him about this room? Adrien was enamored by it all as he gravitated to the next door in front of him. He paused in front of this door, feeling a pit in his stomach. Anxious, he proceeded and opened this one as well.

This room was just as beautiful as the last, if not more. There were mosaic tiles all along the floor and the ceiling; the ceiling was lined with white lights. There was a decorative fountain with trickling water and white sheer drapery all around. The wall was lined with what looked like hand-painted portraits.

Adrien followed the line of portraits down the wall, observing them curiously. All of the portraits were of young adult men and women individually displayed. The first set of portraits looked like they were dressed in garb from hundreds of years ago; as he moved along the line, their attire grew more and more modern.

Adrien got to the last portrait in line and he could not seem to take his eyes off it. The man in the portrait in front of him looked so enticing, so familiar...he reached forward and touched the painting, running his fingers along the elevated ridges of the paint. He was completely enraptured by it. Wait a minute. This man...he may have known who this was. But...no, it couldn't be.

From the corner of his eye, Adrien saw that there was actually one more portrait, but it was on the wall adjacent to the others. He looked fully to his right and saw none other than... *himself*. There was a detailed portrait of himself isolated on its own from when he was human, painted of him from a few years ago. A lump in his throat grew so big that it felt like he had swallowed a tennis ball.

Suddenly, he heard movement behind him. He looked over his shoulder and saw Latimer emerge from the side and stand in the middle of the doorframe. The look on Latimer's face was filled with apprehension.

"Latimer..." Adrien managed to say as he turned to face

him boldly. "What is this?"

Chapter 13

"Answer me when I call to you, my righteous God. Give me relief from my distress; have mercy on me and hear my prayer."

Psalm 4:1

West Africa: September 1678

It was midday, and the sun was beaming while the wind blew through the rich, green foliage. The sound of a hefty waterfall roared into a plunge pool below it. In this shallow pool, water lilies abounded and frogs hopped around on the pads.

A twenty-three-year-old Latimer, whose skin was tanned and freckled by the sun, ran through the tall grass in a clearing while laughing playfully. He stopped to catch his breath briefly. An older man that he favored pushed aside the branches of the trees to enter into the clearing; he came from a small journey to this specific spot.

"At last! Latimer, my son…I have searched tirelessly for you. May I ask why you withdrew here? " he asked, looking around at the scenery.

Latimer turned around, startled, and looked at his father. Latimer's eyes were agleam, full of joy.

"Well, I…" Latimer glanced back over his shoulder to the direction he was facing as if he was looking for someone, or something, as he tried to catch his breath. "Nothing, Father. Is there something you wish from me?"

Latimer's father, Monsieur Remy Alderic Belmont, started to walk back through the trees to the path he followed there. Latimer began to follow him but took one last glance over his shoulder, flashing a bright smile towards one of the trees. A beautiful woman was peeking from around one of the tree trunks and smiling back at him. Latimer winked at her, then hurriedly vanished into the trees to catch up to his father who continued down the path.

"I come bearing great news. You are to return home, your journey begins tomorrow," Remy said to Latimer, his hands clasped together and resting behind his back.

Latimer gulped, flustered by this news. "Tomorrow? Return to France?"

Remy stopped walking. "My son, you sound troubled by this news. My anticipation was your delight. You are not pleased to learn of this?"

"Much is still here for me, I cannot simply leave," Latimer said quickly, his face beginning to pale.

Remy's eyebrows raised.

"I—uh…my duties here cannot be complete, not yet. There is undoubtedly much left for me to do," Latimer elaborated.

"Son, architectural work has now slowed. The hands we have now outweigh the tasks remaining. Returning home is an order. For over twenty months, your service has been exceptional, now it is time for you to rest from all your toil."

Latimer stared back at his father, uncertain what to say, but he was torn by this information.

"Well, son, come on—follow me. Their king has planned to present you a gift."

"Yes, sir. You continue on. I will follow after you shortly," Latimer assured him nervously.

His father raised his eyebrows at him once again in suspicion. His eyes flickered at him and the trees surrounding them. Sighing, he nodded before he turned his back to walk away. Latimer waited until his father was out of sight before he turned around and rushed back through the trees and into the clearing. He ran up to the tree where the woman was hiding, but she was no longer there.

"Adaeze?" he called out, spinning around in all directions to find her, to no avail.

Sprinting up to the waterfall, he slightly stepped into the pool, wondering if she hid in the small cave behind the curtain of water, or behind one of the large boulders surrounding the area.

"Adaeze?!" he called out even louder. "Where are you?!"

Adaeze came from around one of the boulders with both of her arms across her body, the thumb of her right hand nervously strumming at the array of beads and rings decorating her neck. Her skin was smooth and browned to a rich bronze. Her face was decorated modestly with paint, a soft rouge design on both cheeks accenting her almond brown eyes. The design on the left side of her face continued from her cheek to her eyelids and flowed just above her eyebrow.

"Latimer..." she said in a soft, heartbroken tone.

"Did you hear my father's words?" Latimer asked, walking closer to her.

She closed her eyes and drew in a long sigh before she opened her eyes again to look at him. "This day I have dreaded... Latimer, will I ever see you again?" Her eyes glistened as they began to fill with tears.

"Never will I return," Latimer stated with a heavy heart.

Adaeze lowered her head to stare at the ground. A tear fell from her face and into the dirt near her feet strapped in golden sandals. Latimer grabbed her, placing a hand on each of her shoulders. She looked back up to him, sniffling in attempt to stop the tears from flowing.

"But, my darling—day unto day, there I will be." He grinned largely, filled with joy.

"How is that so?" she said, confused by his joy and optimism.

Latimer squared his shoulders and straightened his

posture. "Apart from you, I am nothing. I cannot go if you are not by my side, my beautiful bride." He reached forward and caressed her cheek.

She leaned into his hand endearingly and held it as it warmed her face. "I long to leave with you," she said, her eyes growing large in the excitement of that possibility. "However, my father will not allow this, and neither will yours. Our time is now brief. To convince them to allow us to be as we are...in this I have no confidence."

Latimer and Adaeze met a little over half a year after he came to West Africa. They were both immediately fixated, falling quickly for one another. For the past twelve months, they had snuck off together, keeping their relationship mostly hidden. Just last night they decided to recruit a trusted friend of theirs to marry them in secret. This day marked their second day as husband and wife. They decided on everything so suddenly, but didn't think through the possibility of Latimer being sent back home so soon.

"To that, I pay no mind!" he said, now grabbing onto her hand and pulling it up to his lips. "Never have I had the blessing to feel this way for any woman. I cannot bear to be separated from you now. My wife, my beloved. I love you more than mere words can express, Adaeze," he whispered, his lips lightly brushed against her knuckles.

Adaeze pressed up as close to him as she could and they embraced warmly. "I love you too, Latimer. Oh, how I long to truly be with you, forever..."

They kissed each other tenderly with the sound of the waterfall beside them. Soon thereafter, night fell. They found a soft spot in the grass and gazed at the stars until they fell asleep in each other's arms.

***

Latimer woke to the sound of birds chirping the next morning. He rolled over to see that he was by himself. Getting up quickly, he looked around for Adaeze who had left him in the clearing on his own. Remy walked into the clearing, seeing that Latimer was dirty from lying on the ground and still wearing the same clothes from the day before. He pursed his lips in disapproval as he approached him.

"My son, you never returned. I informed you of your impending gift from the king, did I not?" he said in a firm voice that was evidently disappointed.

Latimer cleared his throat and then opened his mouth to say something, but nothing came out. He pressed his lips together and looked off to the side, avoiding further eye contact with his father.

Remy's eyes bore into Latimer, then his eyes softened. "No matter, come quickly! Their king has graciously agreed to arrange your gift this morning before you begin your journey. He awaits us now."

Latimer followed his father down the path in the forest and they approached their fort that was located by the beach, near the area where the ships embarked. As they continued to walk, the green foliage started to thin out and they were surrounded by sand, rocks and the forts that he had helped build for the French colony residing there. The King of Senegal was standing with his queen by his side and behind them was their princess, Adaeze. Latimer's heart fluttered as he made eye contact with her, but she quickly looked away from him. Behind Adaeze and the king and queen were a line of servants. Remy and Latimer stood in front of the king while their own men lined up behind them.

"Their king is gifting you a servant. You may take any of your choosing back home to France," Remy announced as he motioned his hands towards the male and female servants lined in a row.

Latimer leaned and whispered into his father's ear. "Father, I cannot accept."

Remy jerked back in shock and then leaned back to Latimer and whispered in response, "You must! This man is of great importance. We have many treaties between his people and ours. We do not want to upset him. Now, make your choice!"

Latimer stepped away from his father and took a deep breath. His heart pounded within his chest while he stepped towards the king. "Sir, I kindly decline your offer. However," he said as he bowed down to the king, "I have a request of you. It would bring great pleasure to me if I were able to show Adaeze my home, in France."

Remy stiffened like a board and nudged his son. "Their princess?! She is not an option, Latimer!" he whispered harshly to him.

Latimer did not budge and paid no mind to his father.

The blood below the surface of his skin seemed to have caught fire as the nerves overwhelmed him; he began to speak to the king again, "I hold no wish to treat her as a servant...but," he gulped, unsure of what would follow after he said this, "as my wife, your majesty."

There was an eruption of gasps and confused banter around them from both the French and the African people.

"Latimer...what have you done?" Remy cried in anguish.

Adaeze's eyes widened, and she trembled where she stood, her skin dewy as she had broken out into a simple sweat. Remy rushed up to Latimer and tried to grab him, but Latimer dodged his grasp, keeping his eyes on the king who began to laugh. His laugh echoed across the compound and everyone immediately stopped talking amongst themselves.

The king and his guards stepped toward Latimer. All of the French guards, including Remy, stepped forward as well in defense.

"I kindly offer you a slave," the king spoke in a booming voice full of power, "yet, you disrespect my family and my village by uttering the name of my *daughter* in the same context?!"

The guards behind the king lifted their spears and arrows, and the French guards lifted their rifles in response. Adaeze gasped in horror and her eyes filled with tears. Latimer threw his hands up in surrender.

"S-sir. With your daughter, I am greatly smitten. The love I have for her amounts to no other. I will assure her a sound treatment in my care, this I hold as a promise to you," Latimer pleaded, his voice dry and taut from the nerves.

"To grant you such a thing would be a betrayal to my own people. You shall *never* take her hand. It is best for you to leave, IMMEDIATELY!" the king raged.

The French men behind Latimer roughly grabbed onto him and began to drag him away. Latimer fought against them and broke free briefly before more men grabbed onto him; he was overpowered.

"ADAEZE! ADDAAEEZZEE!" Latimer yelled for her as he was yanked further away.

The king turned to look at his daughter who stood with her mouth shut tightly, her eyes were closed and her mouth trembled. Sweat beaded on her forehead and slowly dripped down the side of her face. Adaeze quickly wiped it away and then turned around, leaving the compound silently.

"Adaeze..." Latimer said one last time in defeat, so quietly that only his father next to him could hear.

Remy turned towards Latimer, then he grabbed him by the shoulders and shook him. "LATIMER! Enough! You look a fool! The ship departs shortly. Gather your belongings promptly. You must board as soon as possible!"

"But, Father!" Latimer pleaded.

Remy loosened his grip on Latimer and his eyes softened again. "Latimer, I love you...however, what you have done was a foolish risk. Carelessness and selfishness run rampant in you, my son! This you brought upon yourself!"

Latimer stretched to peek over the foliage and rocks to the area the king and queen were still standing. He desperately looked around them; Adaeze was nowhere in sight. His shoulders slumped in depression and he walked away on his own, no longer putting up a fight. Some of the men snickered and spat at Latimer's feet as he walked by them. Latimer continued on, paying them no mind.

***

A few hours passed. Latimer stood on the shore facing his father while a team of men carried his belongings onto the ship.

"My duties here will continue for some time," Remy said sadly. "I will miss you, my son."

Latimer was staring at the ground and had not shown any response to his father. Though he did not agree with Latimer's actions, it hurt him to see his son so heartbroken. Remy leaned closer to Latimer, grabbing his shoulders, he helped straighten him up in posture.

"Plenty of women await you back in France," he said while patting him on the shoulders in efforts to comfort him. "Have you forgotten Beatrice? If it is a wife you desire, she has been patiently waiting for such an invitation from you."

Latimer took a deep breath and breathed back out slowly, still refusing to look up. For a moment, he thought to confess that Adaeze was already his wife, but he did not see how telling Remy that would change anything.

"Yes, Father..." He hugged him reluctantly at first, but as

they embraced, he pulled him in even stronger.

Latimer embarked without speaking to any of the other men on board and went directly to his chamber on the ship. He opened the door to the room; this is where he would spend the next few months in the voyage. The room looked so empty and barren. He immediately fell to his knees and prayed intently that one day, somehow, he would be able to see his wife again.

After the ship set sail and they had been at sea for a few hours, night had fallen. The ship was being tossed to and fro in a heavy storm. His shipmates were boisterous, and Latimer heard some of the men cheering as they chugged down wine to dull their fear of the rough waters. The wind whirred and howled against the ship as lightning flashed across the sky, lighting up Latimer's room through the small window that he had.

Latimer was still on the floor with his head in his hands, pondering about his love. He never anticipated that this would happen when he accepted the offer to come to Africa. Adaeze had blindsided him and he was completely enamored from the first conversation they had. She was beautiful, but also very smart and strong. It was not like her to be silent, but Latimer knew that she only did so to protect him.

Latimer smiled, reminiscing of just before they got married. They spent the entire day together and he suddenly asked her to be his wife. They ran as fast as they could and woke up a mutual friend that had the power to marry and brought a few witnesses they could trust that already knew of their love. They married before God and a few friends under the stars while standing in the shallow pool that the waterfall in the clearing poured into.

There was a small cave just behind the wall of water, and they stayed there. Their first night together was something wondrous as they believed in the sanctity of marriage and waited to be physically intimate in a way they knew should be saved for only husband and wife. That night they belonged to one another in a new way, where two became one flesh.

After reminiscing, he continued to pray fervently. Many hours passed, and Latimer's knees became bruised. He bowed his head even further, filled with anguish.

"Let no one split apart what God has joined together," Latimer whispered under his breath as his soul ached for that truth.

Shortly after, as the waves continued to crash to the side of the boat, Latimer heard the sound of the door to his chamber opening slightly. He got up promptly, expecting the wind to have blown open his door. When he turned around, his heart leapt in excitement, for a moment believing that his eyes were deceiving him.

His heart's cry, his answered prayer stood but only a few feet away. Adaeze's clothes were plastered to her body, soaking wet as she stood in his doorway, tears streaming down her face. She ran towards him and jumped into his arms.

"Adaeze!" he shouted in relief as they embraced. He kissed her frantically on her cheeks and then all over. "H-how did you—"

"I'm so foolish!" she wailed. "I must not think of what I have done! I—"

"Shhh, shhh…" Latimer shushed Adaeze gently.

Both of their faces streamed with tears. They embraced even tighter; he lifted her from the floor and took her to the bed where he laid her down. He removed his shirt and wiped away the tears on her face with it, kissing her gently on the lips. Through the tears and puffy eyes, a smile spread across Adaeze's face, blissfully realizing that there was no going back.

Latimer removed her soaking wet clothes from her then covered her with the thick woolen blanket on his bed. He hurried back to the chamber door, making sure that it was firmly locked before he joined his wife beneath the blanket. With breath drawn, they stared each other in the eyes, seeing their future together in the gleam of the others. He held onto her firmly, his body warming hers. Kissing passionately, they knew each other once more, just as sweet and astounding as their first time on their wedding night. They then peacefully fell asleep while the storm no longer raged and the waters began to calm.

**

Five months passed, and Latimer and Adaeze arrived in France. The voyage had been extended, as the ship made multiple stops on the way back for trade as it typically did. Latimer managed to keep Adaeze hidden during the duration of the trip, sneaking food back into the room for her and taking care of her when she fell ill.

They waited until the last of the men disembarked

the ship before they exited the boat themselves. Latimer and Adaeze spent the majority of the morning in town near the port to purchase a wardrobe and other needs for Adaeze, as she had come along with just the clothes on her back.

A horse-drawn carriage was waiting for Latimer. Latimer's house servant, Bernard, sent them to the dock to retrieve Latimer upon his return. Latimer helped Adaeze into the carriage and they sat closely and cuddled, completely smitten and excited for their new adventure. Latimer's home was in the town adjacent to where they docked; their trip was merely an hour.

"How are you? Are you feeling ill?" Latimer asked Adaeze in concern, but his eyes beamed in excitement.

Adaeze giggled, "For the first in some time, I feel quite delightful!"

Latimer grinned from ear to ear. "Wonderful! How is our little one?"

Adaeze looked down and rubbed her growing belly. "He, or she, is great!"

They both laughed in excitement, he pulled her in closer and kissed her tenderly on the cheek.

"Good!" With his arm still around her, he leaned back and looked out the window. "At last! We are home!"

Adaeze looked outside the window of the carriage and saw the grand château they were pulling up to, it glistened in the sun. There were colorful trees and blooming, fragrant flowers that she began to smell as they drew closer. There was an enormous stone fence surrounding the château and large fountains within an elaborate garden decorating the front of it. Birds were chirping, and not a cloud was present in the sky.

The carriage stopped in front of the gates and the men started grabbing their bags and journeyed towards the house. At the front door, there was a small group of people gathered anxiously waiting for Latimer's return.

"Come on! I must introduce you!" Latimer exclaimed.

He was overcome with excitement as he took Adaeze's hand and led her towards the people once they entered the gates. There were two males and one female who were talking amongst themselves. One of the males saw Latimer walking up.

"Latimer! My friend!" he ran up to Latimer and greeted him, hugging him and excitingly patting him on the back. "It's such a pleasure to see you! It has been quite some time!"

"Pleasure to see you as well, Gaetan!" Latimer exclaimed.

The other male stepped forward, his eyebrows lifted. "Monsieur Belmont, your return is far earlier than expected! I received word at daybreak of your ship arriving, and your friends hurried over as soon as I announced the news!" He clasped his hands, his eyes radiant.

The female, who had been coldly eyeing Adaeze since they walked up to them stepped forward, her eyes still on Adaeze as she approached Latimer. She finally turned her gaze to Latimer just before she hugged him.

"You are as handsome as ever, Latimer! I am delighted to see you after such a time!" she said joyously.

Latimer smiled at her and nodded, then he turned to Adaeze. Grabbing her hand, he pulled her closer to everyone. Adaeze looked to the ground, then back up to them shyly.

"Adaeze, I introduce you to my closest friend, Monsieur Gaetan," he motioned towards the first male to speak to him. "This is my servant, Bernard." He motioned to the second male, then motioned to the female. "And this is Mademoiselle Beatrice Dubois. The Dubois family is closely acquainted to the Belmont family. I have known Beatrice since I was merely a boy."

"I am pleased to meet you all," Adaeze replied bashfully, making eye contact with each one of them.

Adaeze could tell that they all were confused by her presence, but were mostly not bothered by her. Well, at least the men were not bothered.

"So, this was part of your payment?" Beatrice said in a harsh tone. Beatrice walked up to Adaeze and picked at her clothing as if inspecting her. She then looked at her hair and then directly into her eyes. "She is far prettier than I would expect. Especially for a slave. She speaks our language fairly well also... how peculiar."

Latimer angrily stepped between Beatrice and Adaeze, forcing Beatrice to back up a couple of steps.

"Adaeze is not a slave. In fact, she is the daughter of the King of Senegal. A princess. She comes from an extensive lineage of royalty in her province," Latimer boasted. "Perhaps, you should avoid jumping to such rash and offensive conclusions, Beatrice," he said angrily.

Beatrice scoffed, "What purpose could she possibly have here, if not a servant?"

"Well," Gaetan quickly interjected, deeming the tension unbearable, "I came to welcome you as soon as you arrived. I have duties to attend to, so I must bid you adieu, Latimer." He hugged Latimer before he left and then nodded at Adaeze. "My goodbyes to you as well, Adaeze."

Adaeze and Bernard watched Gaetan walk away, but Beatrice and Latimer continued to stare at one another. Latimer's eyes flashed disdain and anger towards her. He stepped around her in a way that forced her to back off the porch.

"She is my *wife*, Beatrice. Treat her with respect while you visit our home. Especially seeing as she is now also carrying my child," he said in agitation.

Beatrice's mouth fell open in disbelief, her eyes watering slightly. She glared at Adaeze and laid eyes on her belly before huffing. She whipped her dress around as she turned and stormed off, grumbling under her breath.

Latimer reached for Adaeze's hand that was slightly trembling and he squeezed it to comfort her. He then turned towards her fully and brought her hand to his mouth, tenderly kissing the back of it.

He playfully bowed, sweeping his right arm to the front door. "My darling! Are you ready?" he said to her, his eyes ablaze and his white teeth flashed brightly.

Chapter 13

Adaeze giggled and nodded excitedly. Latimer walked up to the door and turned to Bernard who walked up next to him as well.

"Shall we?" Latimer asked jubilantly.

Latimer and Bernard simultaneously swung open the two large front doors to the château for Adaeze to enter. Latimer held out his hand and she walked up to place hers back within his.

"Welcome home, my love," he beamed.

***

Four more months quickly passed. Latimer and Adaeze had proudly welcomed their first child into the world, a son that they had named Alexander. The boy was merely a few weeks old but already took mostly after his father.

Adaeze sat in the nursery with their baby boy cuddled in her arms as she sang to him. He cooed gently as he stared into her face. His eyesight was still developing, but he still managed to smile. Adaeze was overcome with love and excitedly looked over to Latimer who was also in the room, sitting in the chair next to them. He smiled at her and then moved closer. Latimer joined Adaeze and started to sing along with her. Alexander looked at both of them and giggled. Latimer and Adaeze erupted in laughter and then showered their baby with kisses.

Bernard walked into the room. "Monsieur, Madame, it is almost time for supper. What meal shall I prepare?" he asked softly.

"Oh, Bernard!" Adaeze gently handed Alexander over

to Latimer and walked up to him. "Please, rest. Tonight I will prepare our supper."

Bernard smiled and sighed, "Thank you, Madame." He turned and left the room promptly.

Adaeze felt Latimer gently touch her arm, she turned around to face him.

"That was kind of you," he said.

"I've spent my entire life around servants, slaves and hard workers—people who work tirelessly to no end. Even though Bernard tries to conceal it, I can see that he is quite exhausted."

Latimer caressed Adaeze's face with his free hand; Alexander was still in his other arm. "Another of the many reasons I have fallen madly for you," Latimer gushed, kissing her and then Alexander. He then continued to speak, "Well...the time has come. I shall be home for supper." He handed Alexander back over to her. "I will long for you while I am gone!" he declared to her as he left the room.

"And I will patiently await your return!" Adaeze called out after him.

Latimer heard news of a ship that would be returning to France from West Africa. He didn't know if Remy would be on that ship, but he planned to take a trip down to the docks in hopes to welcome his father home.

Adaeze fed Alexander and then put him to sleep in his crib. She journeyed downstairs to the kitchen and began to take out all the supplies she needed to prepare supper. Adaeze took a sharp knife and began to chop vegetables on the counter.

Beatrice, who had come to visit a few times over the past few months, and oftentimes joined them for dinner, walked into the kitchen.

"Oh!" Adaeze looked up to her briefly then continued to chop away. "I was unaware that you were visiting tonight. How are you?"

Beatrice huffed, then looked down at her hands. "I could be better. Are you preparing supper?" she asked.

"Yes, I am. Would you like to help me, Beatrice?" Adaeze motioned towards the counter where the vegetables and meat were laid out in preparation.

"On how many occasions must I have to tell you to *not* call me by my forename?" Beatrice said coldly, she crossed her arms firmly across her chest and turned her chin up.

"Oh…" Adaeze's shoulders drooped. "I-I am sorry…"

"And no, I would not like to help you. Where is Latimer?"

"He is absent, but shall be returning home soon."

"Bernard?"

"Um…he is asleep in his room on the upper floor," Adaeze said reluctantly.

Adaeze placed some of the vegetables in a pot with some water and moved across to the other side of the kitchen to place it on the fire.

"So…we are alone…" Beatrice asked.

Adaeze felt hesitant and overwhelmed by this bad feeling that had suddenly dropped in her gut. "Yes..." Adaeze swung around to face Beatrice. "Beatrice, what do you—"

Adaeze gasped as she saw Beatrice with the knife, that was on the counter, now in her hand. Beatrice peered at her darkly.

"W-What are you doing Beatr-M-Mademoiselle Dubois?!" Adaeze stuttered in fear.

She began to walk towards Adaeze slowly, her eyes grew darker with every step.

"Oh, how I have longed for Latimer. I have known him *far* longer than you! I cannot just stand by and let you ruin everything I had hoped for once he finally returned!"

Adaeze backed up a few steps as Beatrice continued closer to her.

"Now that you have given birth, I am finally able to do what I have longed to do since you brought your filth into my country," she snarled.

Adaeze eyed the counter beside her and she hurriedly swiped its contents onto the floor. She ran as quickly as she could the other direction. Beatrice screamed in frustration and chased after her. Adaeze passed by the pot she placed on the fire and also tipped it over to slow Beatrice down—Beatrice shrieked in agony.

Adaeze ran out of the kitchen, through the dining room and down the hall. She kept running until she reached the nursery. She ran into the room, turning around to slam the door shut. Her hands trembled as she fumbled with the latch that was stuck in place. She yanked desperately on the latch until it finally closed, locking herself within the nursery with the baby.

***

Latimer walked around, staring at the moon in the sky. He came late, as the ship had already disembarked. Yet there was no sign of his father. He sighed, disappointed about his absence. Latimer was excited for his father to meet his first grandson. He squared his shoulders and began to return home.

"Latimer!" a voice called out abruptly.

Latimer turned to see that his father was running towards him. "Father! I have been looking for you, how was your—"

"We have no time for useless babble, son!" Remy proclaimed frantically.

"Father, what's wrong?!"

"The Princess of Senegal disappeared not long after you departed. *Please* tell me you had nothing to do with it!" his father pleaded.

"Well...yes, she snuck onto the ship before we departed. She is here with me," he disclosed with apprehension.

Remy grabbed onto Latimer's collar and looked him intensely in the eyes. "Your departure with the princess has incited a war, our treaty now shattered between our people and theirs. We had to defend the forts from attacks as their king recruited allies to strengthen his forces. It is a miracle that I am alive—that I am here! Considering I am 'the father of the man who took their princess!'"

"Father, what do we—"

"You must leave; leave as soon as you can! There were men on that ship that are out for revenge. A mob will come for you at any time!" Remy warned.

Latimer was shocked, desperate to get home to his family and take them to safety. "Where am I supposed to go, Father?!"

"There is a ship leaving to New England tonight. I can get you onto the ship before it departs. We must go! Now!" Remy tried to grab Latimer's arm but Latimer pulled back.

"No! I must first go home. I need to retrieve Adaeze and...Alexander." Latimer turned and ran to his horse.

"Alexander?" Remy asked aloud, confused.

Latimer hopped onto his horse and galloped back to his house. The trip was cut to about half an hour as he hurried back as quickly as he could. His jaw was clenched so tightly in anxiousness, nervous about what he would find when he returned home.

After reaching the house, he ran in and called out for Adaeze and Bernard, but no one responded. Hearing his son crying, he ran to the nursery. He slowed to a halt just outside the door as it was wide open and splintered at the hinges. It looked as if the door was broken down. Latimer ran in and took Alexander out of his crib.

He embraced his baby and whispered in his ear, "Where is your mother?"

Bernard then ran into the room, breathing heavily. "Sir! They took Adaeze!" Bernard reported to him.

"Who took her?!"

"Adaeze has been accused! Beatrice was bleeding out on the floor, stabbed by the knife from the kitchen. She insisted that Adaeze be put away, that she was responsible for this wrongdoing. Adaeze was taken to the town jail," Bernard explained.

"Adaeze would never do such a thing! Quick! I need you to take me to her!" he yelled at Bernard desperately.

Loud bangs suddenly rumbled the front door as a group of vengeful men, the angry mob his father spoke of, had arrived at the château. Latimer peeked through the curtains in the window of the nursery and saw a large group wielding torches and demanding that he show his face. Latimer took a blanket and quickly formed a swaddle to wrap Alexander in and strapped him to his body.

"Let's go!" he demanded of Bernard.

They snuck out of the secret escape in the château and came out the other side that was lit solely by moonlight. They ran through the forests and made their way towards the small town not far off in the distance. The jail was visible; Latimer picked up his speed, making sure that Alexander was firmly attached to him as they ran.

Latimer reached the jail and burst through the front door. His friend Gaetan was sitting at the table with his arms resting behind his head and his leg swung over the other. Gaetan jumped up, startled by his brute force entry.

"Release her, Gaetan!" Latimer demanded.

"It was claimed that she attacked Beatrice. She must be confined," he reasoned.

"It is a lie! Never would my wife hurt another in such a way!" Latimer argued as he ran over to her cell and grabbed tightly on the bars.

Adaeze was laying within the cell; she had exhausted herself from tears. Alexander began to cry and Adaeze's eyes opened. She rushed to the bars and pushed up against them, reaching out for Latimer and Alexander.

"Latimer!" she cried out.

Latimer grabbed onto her hand and looked back over his shoulder to Gaetan, his eyes begging. "Gaetan, *please*...you are my closest friend. Put your trust in me. Release my wife. My son and I need her with us. After this, we will depart from you, peacefully."

Gaetan eyed Latimer up and down and then looked to Bernard. He could tell that they had been running and looked exhausted. Gaetan placed the keys to the cell into Latimer's hands, and Latimer quickly unlocked the door.

"Take my carriage also. You will find that it is out back, tied up with my horses. You need it far more than I," Gaetan said.

Latimer hugged Gaetan. "Thank you. Thank you so much, my brother," Latimer expressed in gratitude.

They ran out to the carriage and piled in, Bernard taking the reins.

"Where to, sir?" he asked.

"To the shore. We have a ship to catch," Latimer said, looking over to Adaeze who was especially confused.

"Why are we leaving?" She looked down at Alexander in his arms.

"We are no longer safe here, my love. Your disappearance has caused trouble back in Senegal for your people and mine. We started a war," Latimer informed her.

Adaeze leaned back and sighed. Her eyes pooled up with tears. "I knew this would happen." She then nuzzled her head into Latimer's shoulder. "However, I hold no regrets. You... Alexander...I could not ask for more."

Latimer took a deep breath and smiled.

"Where are we going?" Adaeze asked.

"New England. My father promised us access to a ship leaving tonight. We should be safe there," he stated in confidence.

Latimer, Adaeze and Alexander rode in the carriage and approached the shore. Just as his father promised, he was able to get them on board and met his grandson all the while saying goodbye to his son. They boarded the ship and began their journey to the new land.

Chapter 14

"Let love and faithfulness never leave you; bind them around your neck, write them on the tablet of your heart."

Proverbs 3:3

Plymouth Colony: 1682

L atimer, Adaeze and Alexander had been living in New England, which is present-day Massachusetts, since their arrival just three years prior. The expedition across the Atlantic was relatively short as it was direct and took about seven weeks. With the French fur trade ships traveling to and from the colonies, Latimer and his father continued to keep in touch through letters. His father generously shipped money over to them and even some of Latimer's architectural tools shortly after they had first arrived in 1679.

The French invented a special tool called the spirit level and Latimer used this knowledge and this tool unheard of to the colonists to gain an upper hand in his craft; he was efficient above any other. Many settlers paid him to design and oversee the building of new homes and common areas for the growing population. Latimer also became heavily involved in the fur trade as well. Through this all, they quickly became one of the wealthiest families in the colony.

After being absent a few weeks on a very large trade expedition, Latimer came home to surprise his family with some news. He had purchased the land that encompassed the entirety of a small island just off the shore of the mainland. On this land, he planned to build them a home, as the one they lived in since their arrival was previously constructed by settlers that came before them.

Latimer had taken Adaeze and Alexander on a trip to show them the land and cast his vision of their future. Latimer piled his family and their supplies into a boat and rowed them to the island in just over fifteen minutes. He had packed enough supplies to camp for a few days to provide an ample amount of time exploring the island with his family. They arrived onshore just a few hours before sunset.

Latimer toted a wheelbarrow full of supplies through the forest as Adaeze walked alongside him with Alexander in her arms. They continued until they reached a clearing where a very small house was located at the top of a hill.

Latimer pointed. "That is where I will build us our own home. Exactly how you want it, darling," Latimer said, glancing over at Adaeze.

Her eyes lit up, but then she furrowed her brow shortly

after.

"Who lives there if the whole island is ours?" she asked curiously.

"The gentleman who sold me the land states there were no signs of inhabitants here when he acquired the land many years ago," he assured her.

Latimer left the wheelbarrow where it stood and started walking towards the house. Adaeze stayed back with Alexander. Halfway up the hill, he stopped to turn to them.

"There is nothing to worry about. I ensured it was safe before I brought you." A grin as wide as the world spread across his face as his eyes ignited from excitement. "Come! You must see the view from atop the hill!"

Latimer sprinted the rest of the way up the hill and stepped onto the porch of the house. Adaeze grabbed Alexander and rushed up the hill behind Latimer. She set the boy back down as she stepped onto the front porch of the small home. She faced the horizon with Latimer; the sky swelled with rich warm colors as the sun quickly began to descend. Latimer wrapped his arms around her and gently moved her in front of him, his chest warming her back.

"I will build you a grand balcony, in this very spot. This will be your daily view. You can sing and read to our boy...look at the sunset, the stars, the treetops..." Latimer whispered into her ear.

"This is marvelous," Adaeze whispered back, almost breathless from the beauty of it.

Adaeze quickly turned around within Latimer's arms, slightly catching him off guard. He waited patiently as it was clear that she had something important to say.

"The timing seems all too perfect. I have been meaning to tell you this..." Adaeze's glossy eyes searched Latimer's as he listened closely.

Adaeze did not speak, but she giggled as she grabbed ahold of his hand and delicately placed it over her womb. Latimer immediately pulled her in for a kiss as his heart raced in thrill. After he kissed her multiple times, he looked her in the eyes and then dropped to his knees to kiss her belly.

"At last! Another!" he called out.

Alexander, though not understanding, saw his father on his knees and ran over to cuddle into his side. Latimer pulled Alexander onto his lap before standing to his feet. He kissed Alexander on the forehead as he looked at Adaeze.

"I love you," he said endearingly.

"I love you too, Latimer." Adaeze smiled bashfully back at him.

They then spent a few more moments staring at the horizon. The sun continued to set and the sky began to darken.

"You need your rest! I will get you and Alexander settled!" Latimer said after noticing the time.

"Wonderful!" Adaeze excitedly took Alexander out of his hands and turned back to look at the view, both her and Alexander looked off in the distance. She pointed to the clouds and the glistening reflection of the colors in the water before the darkness consumed the scenery.

Latimer trekked back down the hill and lugged their supplies up to the house, deciding that they would stay within the abandoned home for the night. The little house was quite odd. It did not seem to have been built by natives or by any colonists as the style did not fit either. Latimer came to this very location months ago before he purchased the land; the home was just as it was found then, untouched.

The interior had just two rooms. The main room had the bed and all of the living area, including the kitchen with seating and a table that had all collected a very thick layer of dust and dirt. The second was a very tiny room void of any furniture; it may have been used as a place for storage. The house had torch-equipped sconces lining the walls, a few were within the main room and one was within the smaller room.

They entered the home and got settled. Adaeze prepared them a meal and they ate. Then after some time of prayer, playing and laughter, Latimer laid out the blankets he brought with them. Every night, Latimer and Adaeze would sing Alexander to sleep. They tucked him in and sang until he fell asleep. Then shortly afterward the parents joined the child, falling asleep also.

It was not long into the night when Latimer was startled awake, having broken out in a cold sweat. Only a few hours had passed. He sat up in the bed and looked to his right to see Adaeze and Alexander still peacefully sleeping.

As sudden as his waking, Latimer felt an unbearable

uneasiness. The sweat on his forehead begat his clammy skin, and he lifted his arm to wipe the dew from it. Quietly getting up from the bed, he walked into the smaller room and closed the door behind him. He let out exasperated breaths while trying not to wake his family. More sweat poured from his pores, so much so that it was useless for him to wipe it away anymore. He did not understand the feeling that overcame him, but it felt as if his body was screaming to be elsewhere.

Latimer paced within the room while trying to catch his breath as anxiety had taken it away from him. He stumbled over a floorboard that was slightly elevated and caught himself before crashing to the floor. He turned towards the door of the room hoping he did not wake his family. A few moments passed; he was relieved as there was no sound or movement from them.

Filled with curiosity now, he quickly grabbed the torch from the sconce near the door and lit it. He knelt down to examine the floor to find the floorboard he stumbled upon. As he found it he tugged, and a few more boards that were attached lifted along with it. It was a hatch to an underground chamber.

Latimer took the torch that was in his hand and shoved it down the hole. To his horror, he saw a pile of human bones and two empty coffins. Dried blood was splattered along the sidewalls of this underground chamber, clear evidence that something terrible had happened there.

Now understanding what must have been the source to his unexplained anxiety, he jumped to his feet. Simultaneously, there was a loud crash, followed by Adaeze and Alexander both screaming on the other side of the door. Latimer's heart dropped and his body filled with adrenaline. Latimer burst through the door into the main room where they were sleeping.

"Adaeze! Alexand—"

Latimer slid along the floor, torch still in hand as he fell to the ground and lost his words. His eyes widened in terror. Alexander was cowering in the corner of the room, his elbows and knees scuffed up and bleeding. The front door to the house was ajar and a dark figure was kneeling on the bed, grasping tightly onto Adaeze, the figure wrapped around her in a way that Latimer could not tell what it was doing to her.

Latimer leapt up from the ground and sprinted towards them. "No! Step away from her!" he yelled.

Before Latimer had the time to comprehend what happened, he was thrown with a mighty force up against one of the walls of the house. The shadowy figure that had just been wrapped around Adaeze was now directly in his face. From the force, Latimer lost his grip on the torch and it was hurled across the room, landing on the floor.

Latimer choked as it felt like his ribs had cracked, it quickly became difficult for him to breathe. Adaeze's limp body fell to the floor just beside the bed, she was drenched in the blood that continued to escape from two puncture wounds in her neck. Latimer's eyes grew wide, his mouth agape with horror from what he saw.

Latimer was seized by the throat, then he was lifted off the ground with great strength as he kicked and flailed his legs.

All Latimer could do was tremble as he looked pure evil straight in the eyes, his neck stinging as sharp nails dug deep into his skin. It was a male with silky black medium-length hair. Fresh blood dripped from his lips, and his eyes were extremely wide and intense: his pupils were slit vertically like that of a snake, and his irises seemed to glow like a holographic red film, the rim around the edges of his irises were a deep maroon—nearly black. His hand around Latimer's neck was ice-cold, adding to the stinging that continued to intensify. A bone-chilling hiss filled the room as another figure invaded the home through the wide-open door.

"Yve, this one is *passionate!*" the male who had seized Latimer spoke in excitement while peering back over his shoulder to the woman who had just entered.

The sound of the man's voice sent frightful chills shooting down Latimer's spine. His voice sounded unsettling—poisonous to the ears, the words flowed off his lips smoothly, his s's drawn out and serpent-like.

The woman stood very elegantly and was in a floor-length black and brown dress. Her hair was also bone-straight and black with part of it pinned up. She had the same intense red eyes as the male. She glanced over at Alexander who was still cowering in the corner before looking back to the male.

"No matter, Evadin. Just have your way with it already… it is irritating me," she hissed.

"My-wife! W-what have you done?!" Latimer managed to speak within the Evadin's grasp.

Evadin's eyes intensified, a smirk spread across his face.

He chuckled. "You see...my mate and I have just returned from an extended voyage. I would sincerely like to thank you! What a pleasant welcoming gift! Delivered straight to us...on a silver platter."

"Mmmmm," Yve inhaled deeply and leaned closer to Alexander. "Can I have the boy? He smells lovely."

There was a sudden upsurge of warmth in the room as the wooden floorboards caught fire and the flames were starting to spread from the dropped torch. Latimer's heart pounded even faster, longing to protect Alexander from these beasts and the fire.

"Why, of course darling, but save me just a trace." Evadin leaned into Latimer, speaking into his ear tauntingly, "The young humans...such fragile necks. So *sweet*."

Latimer squirmed and fought within Evadin's grasp, hardly making him budge, his strength was nowhere near apt. "N-No! Please! Spare him! KILL ME! I beseech you...spare my little boy!" Latimer's throat burned as he forced out his pleas.

Evadin winced. "Oh, how pathetic. Showing so much passion for something that is merely supper. I shall kill your little boy..." Evadin's eyes flashed fervently as he spoke, "...and force you to drink with me! Ah! Now...now that would be delightful, would it not? Feeling your son grow weaker with every sip? I imagine you would enjoy it far more than you think..."

"Go to Hell!" Latimer shouted. He kicked and flailed even more violently to break free.

Adaeze suddenly coughed, spitting up blood onto the

floor beside her. Her head tilted and she looked in his direction, her eyes were filled with despair. "L-Latimer..." she mumbled nearly inaudibly.

Latimer stretched his neck in an attempt to see her, as Evadin had blocked a clear view of her. Alexander finally got up from the corner and ran over to Adaeze, throwing himself on top of her and crying. Yve then traveled across the room to stand over them both.

"Hm...she smells even more delightful than the boy..." Yve said as she looked at Adaeze curiously and heard the extra heartbeat within her. "And...no wonder. There is yet another here; I can hear it clearly." She looked back towards Latimer and Evadin.

"Please! Please...let them live!" Latimer cried out, tears streamed down his face.

Yve sighed. "Come on...put that *thing* out of its misery..." she enticed Evadin.

Evadin's grip on Latimer's throat tightened, Latimer gasped for air and felt the warmth of his blood flowing from his own neck due to the nails that cut even deeper into his skin. Smoke began to billow within the room and flames slowly crawled across the ground to the left of them. Evadin lunged for Latimer and plunged his fangs into his flesh. Latimer screamed in agony.

After a few short moments, Evadin released Latimer from his grasp and he fell facedown to the floor. Determined, he pushed past the pain and immediately attempted to run to his family, however, he did not have enough strength to rise to his feet. He dragged himself along the floor towards them.

"PAPA!" Alexander screamed for him, his little face was red from tears and distress.

"Adaeze...A-Alexander..." Latimer groaned as he crawled.

The flames began to climb up the walls and the thick smoke grew denser. Evadin spectated greedily as Latimer struggled to drag himself across the floor. He pondered a moment, then gave Yve a hand signal; she hissed again just before shoving Alexander to the side and biting Adaeze.

Latimer's hands bled as he clawed at the ground harder in an attempt to pull himself along to reach them. He grunted, wailing as he saw Adaeze, who had a little fight left in her, go completely still. Yve then grabbed Alexander and paused to smile at Latimer. She held tightly onto the collar of his shirt, her eyes then flickered up to Evadin.

"N-n-" Latimer groaned, as he no longer had any strength to keep on.

Evadin stood over him and reached down, pulling Latimer up to himself from the floor by his shirt. Latimer, still with his eyes on his son, reached for Alexander with all of his might. Evadin bit Latimer one last time. With his son still in Latimer's sight, his vision faded to black.

***

"The next thing I knew...I woke up in the underground chamber with an immense hunger I didn't fully understand at the time. Atop of me were the charred remains of the home that had burned to the ground." Latimer explained, his head and shoulders were slumped.

Adrien stood stiffly, his hand rested on his mouth. He sighed heavily in empathy. "My God. Latimer, I..." Adrien expressed, his heart burdensome, not sure exactly what to say. "I'm so sorry about your family."

"No one knows about them. I never told the others," Latimer said while walking a few feet to his right.

There was a line of opaque white curtains along one side of the room that Adrien had overlooked when he first entered. Latimer walked over to them and with two fingers, he gently pulled the curtain back to reveal a nook that extended the size of the room. Adrien stared at Latimer without moving, unsure of what to do. Latimer gestured for him to enter, and without any more hesitation, Adrien approached him. He then stepped through to the other side of the curtains.

There were a few more portraits on the wall. One of them was a bust of a woman who was finely dressed and lavished with jewelry. Her hair was in an updo and her eyes were big, bright and full of life. Adrien assumed that it must have been Adaeze as she had the bronzed brown skin that Latimer previously described. In the middle was a portrait of Adaeze along with a handsome man with tanned skin and light freckles.

Upon examining it further, Adrien recognized Latimer's features. Adrien was surprised to see how normal Latimer once looked, odd to see him in any way other than what he was accustomed to. In the lap of Adaeze was a small child that couldn't be seen clearly in that particular portrait. The next portrait was a close up of a toddler with a head adorned with bouncy ringlets of light brown, reddish hair. Alexander.

"Is that...Adaeze and Alexander, Latimer?" Adrien said while he stepped closer and mulled over all of the portraits. "She was gorgeous. They were both *so* beautiful," Adrien said in astonishment.

"Yes," Latimer responded morosely. "Yes, they were..."

Adrien scratched his head, confused. "Forgive me, but that still doesn't explain what is going on in this room." Adrien stepped back to the center of the room and turned around in a circle. "Why are all of these portraits hanging on the wall?" Adrien walked to the end of the line of portraits and pointed to the one directly before his. "This guy, I look a lot like him!"

Latimer walked up to Adrien slowly. "That is because... that portrait is of Gabriel. He is your father, Adrien."

Adrien was immediately overcome with so many emotions: fear, shock, joy and bewilderment. His heart mainly leapt above all else and he drew a sharp breath. His father. His *father!* There he was, the portrait so realistic that it felt as if he was in the flesh, staring straight back at him. A face that he had longed to recall for as long as he could remember, right before his very eyes. Adrien trembled, dropping to his knees before the portrait. He grasped at the fabric of his shirt on his chest. He stared at the portrait and began to sob, and through his tears, he gazed in awe.

"My f-father?" Adrien managed to mumble. He died when I was young. *How* do you..." Adrien's words trailed off, terrified of what could be the answer to the question he was about to ask.

"Your father and I never spoke, but...I knew him very well," Latimer said. Crossing his arms, he began to pace. "Twenty years after I turned I was still a Hunter. I had gotten into an altercation with Harvesters from present-day New York when I tried to hunt in their territory. From my lack of feeding that night I was desperate, heading back to Massachusetts. I did not know why but I felt as if I was drawn to the area, as if I had lost a small sliver of the little self-control I had left."

Adrien wiped his tears and stood up; he turned to look at Latimer while he spoke.

"It was a few hours before dawn and I needed to kill. There was a lone male walking the street towards a line of homes a mile or so down the road. There was an enduring connection I felt with the young man, but in my pit of thirst, I was compelled to ignore it. I attacked him from behind, tearing at his throat. The blood," Latimer paused shortly but then continued angrily, "was *sweeter* than any I had ever experienced."

A tear ran down the side of Latimer's face. Adrien raised his brows in response, shocked to see him that way.

"It was only after I had drained the body completely of blood did I come back to my senses. I rolled over his body, curious to the strong connection I felt before. My heart, which had hardly a beat in two decades seemed to race. I recognized this face. It was...my son's..." Latimer's voice trembled.

Adrien stiffened even more-so than before, his eyes grew wide and he immediately understood Latimer's pain, his soul-shattering remorse.

"I then remembered quite clearly what Evadin said the night my family was attacked. He forespoke that I would enjoy the feeling of my son growing weaker as I drank from him... and...I *did*." Latimer continued to speak through a clenched jaw, "Just as he said..."

"Latimer..." Adrien said empathetically.

"He was carrying a bouquet of white roses when I killed him," Latimer continued, "smashed into the dirt, the white roses were also now speckled with his blood. After I buried my son I picked the flowers up, knowing he must have been taking them to someone." Latimer paused for a moment and turned his back to Adrien. Though it had been hundreds of years, the wounds were still fresh, still unbearable. "I found his home. Within it was a young mother with her newborn. I felt the same connection to that child...just as I did my son. I knew for sure that was my son's son. I watched from the window as his wife cooed their baby, ensuring him that his father would return soon. I placed the roses on that doorstep, delivering them as my son was supposed to do. As he would have...if it weren't for me."

Latimer turned to face Adrien again and stared him directly in the eyes. Adrien understood the pain that was seeping from Latimer as he spoke.

"From then on, I was attached to Massachusetts. I could not leave. I came back to the island to fulfill the promise I made for my family. Atop the hill, atop the place our life together was cut short, I built the very house I planned to build for them."

Latimer pointed downwards. "The grand balcony we first came face-to-face once you turned, that is the balcony my wife dreamt of. The room you are in now was going to belong to our second child."

Adrien looked down to the floor, speechless.

"I have stayed here since, I have watched over my son's son and all the generations born after him. There was no other purpose in my existence than to do so," Latimer explained further.

Adrien's eyes jumped up and then followed along the long line of portraits on the wall. The first portrait he now recognized as a twenty-three-year-old Alexander. There were about fourteen total generations displayed on the wall chronologically, with the last portrait being his own. Adrien's eyes widened, he jerked his head back towards Latimer as he finally got it.

Adrien thought back to a few months ago, the night he and Latimer played music in front of the others for the first time. The new odd memory that flooded to him from the night of his father's death: the touch of a cold hand to his forehead in his crib. The hand belonged to Latimer, and he must have been comforting him, knowing that his life would change drastically, very soon.

"Adrien, I have watched all my descendants from birth, including you. Nineteen years ago, when Gabriel, your father, passed...you were the only one remaining. *You* are the last of everything and all that I have left in this world. I could not, I would *not* let you die in the street that night!" Latimer declared.

Chapter 15

"Even when their paths wind through the dark valley of tears, they dig deep
to find a pleasant pool where others find only pain. He gives them a brook of
blessing filled from the rain of an outpouring."

Psalm 84:6 TPT

The Harvesters traveled further north in the nights after discovering that Hunters had infiltrated their territory. After many failed attempts to contact their allies in the north, Latimer and Cade visited the homes of their allies. They found their houses destroyed and their corpses burned. By the tracks they discovered, the Hunters seemed to have retreated further away in the opposite direction of Massachusetts. They deduced that the Hunters traveled in a pack of five. When Latimer and Cade returned, they formulated a coordinated plan with Coran and the others in the event the Hunters stepped back into their territory.

December 27th: Voyage Nightclub

Cade sat on a red leather couch, his elbow resting on

the back of it. He waited in anticipation for a call from Coran as his family had increased their patrols of the border. Cade normally frequented this spot, coming mainly to observe and to sometimes scout, but this night, he was waiting for his next planned reaping. He needed to ensure his strength for a possible battle. The others reaped within the last couple of nights, to guarantee their greatest strength as well.

Cade was there alone, but the club was teeming with people. A man walked up to the couch next to Cade and sat down. He propped his leg across the other and also rested his arm along the back of the couch. Cade looked over to him from the corner of his eye and saw that the man was already peering back at him. When Cade's eyes met his, Cade immediately jumped to his feet. This man was not one he recognized, for he had never seen him there before. The man mimicked Cade's movements, jumping to his feet as well.

He was dressed in a brown suit and his hands were encased within brown-leather driving gloves. His blonde hair was tousled and an eyepatch was strapped around his head, covering his left eye. He had two golden ring piercings, one in his brow, and the other in the center of his bottom lip. His eye reflected red, clearly a vampire. The vampire smirked at Cade, then softened his posture. As Cade scrutinized him suspiciously, the vampire's eye morphed into grey: he was not a Hunter.

Cade walked over to the vampire, but then he faced the crowd while he began to speak, "Now is not the proper time for a new face to show in town," he advised.

The vampire sighed. "As you can see, I mean you no harm, my friend. I am merely just passing through," he said as he adjusted the leather around his wrists. "Ransom. In case you need to know my name."

"Ah, Kiana briefly mentioned you. We just came from Vermont. There is nothing up there for you. I suggest you turn back. Return to wherever you came from." Cade turned to face Ransom fully. "The Harvesters north of here have been wiped out. Hunters are the cause. Coup d'état."

"So I heard—Kiana mentioned this to me. I am fairly close to Lazaro. I won't believe he is dead until I see his corpse myself. If he is, he will surely be avenged," he expressed angrily.

Ransom backed up slightly then suspiciously looked to his left and then to his right across the crowd of people as if looking for someone.

"The Hunters are clearly working in ways that are not typical for their kind." Cade looked down at his watch. "Now, if you'll excuse me, I have other important matters to attend to," Cade disclosed as he turned to leave.

Ransom watched as Cade left the building. He exited from the side door and entered into a quiet alleyway just outside of the club. A man was digging through the dumpster behind the building at the very end of the long alleyway, the sound of the metal clanging broke the silence.

"Just in time," Cade said to himself as he watched the man from afar.

The man who was digging through the dumpster stopped

and turned around abruptly, having heard something behind him. He saw nothing but darkness down the alleyway, no clues as to anyone else being near. He continued in the trash just as Cade snatched him up and fed on him while he leapt into the air. Cade had the man's mouth covered tightly so no one heard his screams as they ascended. Cade landed on the roof of the club and finished him off, sighing in content as he dropped the body near his feet.

Terrified screams echoed between the buildings, and a deafening noise filled the streets of the city from a sudden uproar. Cade ran to the edge of the roof and peered over it. A crowd of people was stampeding out of Voyage. Cade knew that there was a skylight on the second level of the roof, so he rushed to the very top and peeked down through the glass. He saw the sudden carnage below.

The nightclub was littered with bodies and spilled blood. A group of iron-masked Hunters, four in total, had Ransom backed into a corner. At once, they attacked. Ransom initially put up a good fight but was quickly overpowered by their numbers. Ransom looked upwards, focusing on the skylight; he locked eyes with Cade. Ransom leapt up three stories and crashed through the glass, Cade fell backward from the force of it. Ransom reached out a hand and pulled Cade back up to his feet.

"Your Hunters are here," Ransom affirmed. He held onto his side where he had been wounded. "You best go tell your people," he said as he ran to the edge of the roof.

Ransom looked over the ledge to see the stampede of

humans running down the street. He turned back around to Cade and gave him a look of disdain before he flew off and disappeared into the sky.

Cade quickly shuffled back over to the skylight. One of the Hunters, Kyle, was already staring through the gaping hole in the ceiling as Cade peeked in. Cade noted Kyle's appearance matching the description of one of the Hunters Adrien encountered days ago. Kyle's eyebrows lifted, grinning beneath his mask as he held eye contact with Cade. He then flicked something out of his hand. The couches near him burst into flames. The other Hunters doused the place and the corpses in gasoline, fueling a raging fire.

Cade retreated from the skylight and rushed to pull out his cellphone. Still no call from Coran. Cade was concerned about the lack of signals from Coran, Xylia and Kiana. Cade attempted to call Latimer, but the phone continued to ring, also with no answer. Any plan they concocted had quickly fallen apart. He wasted no more time, leaving the scene to get to Latimer's as soon as possible.

***

Adrien was trying to wrap his mind around what Latimer had just shared with him as he paced the room. He stopped in front of Latimer and started to laugh.

"So...*you're* my ancestor?!" Adrien exclaimed. "I thought that was impossible?"

"It is," Latimer said. "I have done something that should have been impossible. I assume this is what makes you more powerful: sharing both my mortal blood and my immortal venom. Your strength and the rate in which you heal is *abnormal*... even for a vampire."

"I have so many questions I—I don't even know where to begin!" Adrien had both of his hands on his head in disbelief, grasping onto his hair. He drew in a short breath. "The money, my inheritance...that was from you?"

Latimer nodded. Adrien chuckled and then took his hands out of his hair to point at him.

"The instruments donated to the group home?"

Latimer nodded.

Adrien laughed again, but this time even louder, "The cello that I learned on...that was yours. This explains so much!"

Latimer managed to crack a genuine smile, something that Adrien had rarely seen. Adrien rushed over to Latimer and pulled him into a tight embrace. Latimer patted him endearingly on the back.

"This means so much to me!" Adrien exclaimed. "I thought I had no family my entire life...but you? You've *always* been there."

"I am so sorry...this is not how your life was supposed to be," Latimer said softly. "I wanted to keep you safe, far away from this curse."

Adrien released Latimer and stepped back. "I agree...my life was not supposed to be like this. But now I at least understand why I am here." Adrien brought his hand to his mouth, then looked back up to his father's portrait. "So...my father. What happened to him?"

Latimer's fists clenched, anger brewed within him. His jaw muscles visibly twitched as he ground his teeth together. He let out a sharp sigh and closed his eyes tightly.

"Latimer..." Adrien said uneasily. "What happened?"

The room was silent, so silent that Adrien could hear cars and sirens from the city. His eyes darted around Latimer's face.

Adrien started to assume, "Latimer...did you—"

"I was watching over your father the night he died. Everything happened so quickly, I..." Latimer paused for a bit, racking through his thoughts. "It was *him*. I hadn't seen him since that horrendous night in the small house on the hill, I believed I was hallucinating, that my eyes were deceiving me. Evadin killed your father and he made me watch while he did it. I couldn't move; he rendered me powerless with his control over me. After it was all over, he vanished and left your father's body with me. It was at that moment that I knew I felt that strange feeling before. That loss of control. That very feeling is what led me to Massachusetts the night I murdered my son. I realized that all those years ago, he led me to my son...like a puppet. Just like I had to bury my own son, I had to bury your father also."

Adrien turned and punched through the wall. Concrete and small tiles shattered, crashing to the tile floor. "Where is he?!" Adrien yelled.

Adrien stormed towards the door to exit the room, then he froze suddenly as a thought came to his mind. He remembered a few nights ago when he approached Latimer about the unknown guest in their home. Adrien had never seen Latimer so fearful before, so spooked. He turned back around to face Latimer.

"Wait—the night that I...killed Jenna. You left the house to see the others. Before then, I asked you who visited you earlier. The voice I heard must have come from *this* very room. You said that it was no one of importance, but...it was him. It was Evadin...wasn't it?" Adrien hypothesized.

***

December 24ᵗʰ: Three nights prior

Adrien was still laying within his coffin while Latimer was in the portrait gallery. His arms were crossed as he faced the wall, staring at a few of the portraits he had painted of his descendants. A nervous chill ran down Latimer's spine as he suddenly felt a presence behind him. A figure leaned within the doorway, his back against one side of the frame. Latimer did not need to turn around to know who it was.

"What do you want?" Latimer asked dryly, turning around to face him.

"Ahhh, you are emitting severe emotions at the sight of me. As your creator, I can feel them as nearly as my own," Evadin said as he straightened his stance and stepped into the room, starting to walk towards Latimer. "All this rage and revulsion... it's so...*intoxicating*." Evadin chuckled. "Maybe I should come visit more often."

Latimer crouched in a defensive stance and hissed. In a

split second, Evadin had turned him around as he seized him by the neck.

Evadin leaned into his ear. "Does this bring back memories...Latimer?" he taunted.

"W-what do...you want?" Latimer mumbled.

"Hmph." Evadin shoved him, walking to the nook that was hidden behind the white opaque curtains, and through to the other side.

"My family and I...we did not deserve this!" Latimer said in anguish through his clenched teeth.

Evadin walked the length of the three portraits on the wall, observing them in amusement. He stopped in front of the one with all three of them together. "The extent of *love* you had for those creatures..." He laughed menacingly. "Amusing... but if there is a true answer you yearn for, you see...love is an emotion that has long since been extracted from my being. It's a heavy corpse rotting in the cold, hard earth. In its place sits a vampire. I'm clothed with the unruly need to infect and eradicate this sickening emotion, exchanging it with sorrow... hatred...seclusion." Evadin swung back around, his eyes were fiercely ablaze. "That glorious night when you murdered your son. Your remorse, your misery...mmm...was nothing short of transcendent." His voice then quieted to a whisper, "I long to feel that again."

Latimer's hands balled into fists, wanting more than anything to tear him apart to atone for what he had done.

Evadin slithered around the room and turned his

attention to Adrien's portrait on the wall. "The redhead. You turned him...I'm surprised you didn't slaughter the mutt as well..."

"If you touch him, I will—"

"MY touching him is the slightest of your concern. Need I remind you what happened with his father? You have no power if I chose to take it. Your treasured little redhead is sound asleep just one story below. It only takes one thought, ONE impulse induced by me...and *you* will rip that futile pest to pieces."

"Please..." Latimer's eyes grew large as he pleaded.

"I am very old, Latimer," Evadin sighed in annoyance. "Every century that passes forevermore renders this existence dull. You fail to grasp the only reason you remain to exist is to entertain me. You serve no purpose other than that."

"It was hundreds of years before you showed your face, decades since the last. Why leave me alone all these years, and then—"

Latimer felt as though an unseen cloud had wrapped itself around him. His brain function shifted as he could no longer speak, he was suddenly rendered powerless and all he could do was gasp for air.

Evadin's head tilted to the side, his eyes squinted in indignation while a smirk smugly spread across his lips. "You know...you should try it sometime. With your redhead. This control. To have it over another...there is *nothing* like it."

Latimer continued to grunt and gasp as he tried to speak. He stumbled backward, grabbing at his own throat, his eyes filled with terror.

"Well, now that you've quieted down, let's get to the point of my little excursion. There are a few of my...*friends*...tracking me with the intention to own my head. One, in particular, you know awfully well."

Through his fright-filled eyes, Latimer's brows furrowed in confusion.

"I could care less. This world is no longer among my interests. Nevertheless, I've graced you with my presence because they will not hesitate in tearing through your pathetic group of Harvesters...just to get to me. Why not make this all the more... pleasurable, right?"

Just as quickly as he appeared, Evadin vanished from the room. Latimer dropped to the floor, continuing to gasp for air.

***

"What a sick freak! The way he controls you is the reason you refuse to use that ability on me...isn't it?" Adrien growled. "Oh, I'm gonna—"

"Out of the question," Latimer interjected. He walked around Adrien to exit the room, and he continued to speak as he moved towards the staircase, "I didn't tell you of him for you to do anything rash." Latimer stopped at the top of the stairs and sighed, lowering his head.

Adrien rushed up to Latimer and stood just inches behind him. "Come on, Latimer! That guy needs to pay for what he's done to you and your family! To OUR family!" he shouted.

There were a few moments of silence as Adrien pondered some more. "The Hunters. *They* want him dead. Having a common enemy makes us allies!" he insisted.

Latimer shook his head in disagreement. "The history between Harvesters and Hunters has never failed to leave casualties. The Hunters want Evadin and he has now entered our territory. Tactically, they will want to take us out first, eliminating any possible divergence we will be to their objective. They expect us to be hostile; there will be no discussion, no agreements."

"Let's just leave. We have nothing here anymore. Your last tie here was me and mine was Jenna," Adrien concluded in desperation.

"Evadin is still able to control me as well as know my location at all times. No matter where we go—if he were to let me leave in the first place—he would be aware. However, Adrien, I will not let anyone significant to me die by my hands again. You must leave, even if I cannot accompany you," Latimer urged him.

Adrien scoffed. "I would rather die by your side than let you die on your own. No...I am not leaving you." He groaned and grabbed onto the back of his neck, rubbing it as he thought some more. "Uh...who was it that Evadin mentioned you knew as well? Maybe they could be our chance to survive this! If they are a friend, that is."

Latimer squinted. "I have never made associations with any Hunters; all the ones I have met, I have also killed."

Both Latimer and Adrien turned back towards the staircase simultaneously as they heard someone enter the house downstairs.

"Latimer!" Cade called out.

Within moments, both Latimer and Adrien descended to the first floor and met Cade face-to-face.

"Cade?" Latimer asked, concerned.

"The Hunters. They are here. There were more than just the two Adrien mentioned from days ago." He paused, breathing heavily with fear in his eyes. "They attacked Voyage. I have *never* seen Hunters attack such a public location."

"Coran...you have not heard from him?" Latimer asked.

"No...I cannot get ahold of any of them. I am going up there." Cade turned around and headed towards the door.

"I'm coming, too!" Adrien called after Cade and caught up with him.

Cade snickered and turned to face Adrien. "Of course, given your track record, I have the utmost confidence in your ability to fight. Hope there aren't any Hunters at hand, though—they won't let you live like I chose to," he mocked.

"Does my survival *really* concern you?" Adrien responded snarkily.

Cade scoffed, then continued towards the front door. As he grabbed the handle, Latimer rushed towards him.

"Wait!" Latimer called out as he sensed that someone was near.

It was too late, the door swung open. Standing right

there in the front doorway of the stone home was the homicide detective, Michelle, who was prepared and positioned. The barrel of her pistol was pointing into the house. Startled to see more than just one, she shifted her pistol's point between the three of them.

"Hands on your head! Don't move!" she ordered them. "I am here for Adrien."

Chapter 16

"There is a way that appears to be right, but in the end it leads to death."

Proverbs 16:25

I t was a silent night near the northern state border at Coran and Xylia's mansion. This silence was interrupted abruptly by what sounded like that of an army approaching. One by one, bodies fell from the sky. Some of them landed in the surrounding trees, causing the sound of snapping wood to resound, while others planted firmly in the snow-covered grounds. Those that appeared were all equipped with the same iron masks that were worn by the Hunters Adrien and Cade had encountered before.

Maniacal laughter echoed in the courtyard as they advanced towards the house in formation. With their bare hands, they broke through the brick walls and smashed through the windows, hurling themselves into the house that had been swiftly breached. Vampires continued to fall from the sky until their numbers reached over thirty in total. They wreaked havoc, destroying whatever stood in their path.

One of the Hunters, a woman, stood isolated on the rooftop while the others ravaged the home. She tilted her head backward and closed her eyes as she listened to the sweet sounds of destruction. Inhaling deeply through the grates in her mask, she searched for a familiar scent, the very scent that governed her deep-seated motive. Using her vantage point from the highest point of the house, she turned to look at the glowing lights of the city in the distance.

Squinting her eyes in a glare, she leapt from the rooftop. Though her feet were strapped into black stilettos with golden accents, she landed gracefully on the ground below. Prowling through the courtyard, she made her way to the front entrance, then walked through one of the gashes that were formed in the brick wall before her. Stepping over the rubble, she entered into the home where the group of Hunters were gathered, waiting for her.

At the forefront of the faction of Hunters stood Gina and Kyle. They patiently waited as their leader approached them. The leader's eyes darted around the room, searching for something, her eyes unsatisfied. The sound of her heels on the tile flooring echoed eerily throughout the foyer. She wore a forest green V-neck pencil dress with a collar. Her golden belt was tautly wrapped around her waist. She stopped just a few feet in front of them before removing her mask and firmly planting her hands on her hips.

"Bring their bodies to me..." she hissed.

The room fell silent as the vampires looked amongst one another in uncertainty.

"BRING THEM!" her voice boomed, her patience worn thin.

"Their scent is still fresh," Gina piped up. "They just left. No longer than a quarter of an hour ago…they must have fled."

"Cowards!" Kyle shouts. "We can still seize 'em before they get too far away. I say we go after 'em! Let none get away. We'll give meanin' ta the name *Hunter*…let's tear 'em apart!"

The leader looked around the room, peeved with her arms crossed, then her eyes landed on Kyle. Lurching forward, she flipped him to the ground and his neck was met by the sharp heel of her stiletto. The heel sunk into the surface of his skin.

"You and three others disappeared from our ranks earlier tonight. You've tried to wash the scent of the humans from you but I can *smell* them." Her eyes raked around the room. "Keep your masks in place. Do not stray from our true intent!" she spat out venomously. "Do so…" her eyes drifted back to Kyle and scanned him from head to toe, "…and you will be the one lacking *your* filthy limbs."

She yanked her heel from him and walked away. Kyle leaned up on one elbow as he watched her place her mask back on her face. She then lifted her hand and snapped her fingers, marching back through the hole in the wall as the horde of vampires followed suit.

***

Michelle's eyes jumped between the three standing in

front of her, her heart racing. She squared her shoulders in efforts to hide her fear, as she was taken aback by their appearances. Her gaze was then drawn specifically to Adrien. She stared him straight in his eyes, wincing from the intensity of them. Adrien recognized Michelle as the woman who was snooping around his home just hours prior.

"You?!" Adrien breathed in bewilderment.

She began to shout, "I said hands on your h—"

Adrien yanked her into the house and spun her around, pinning her onto one of the stone pillars in the foyer. Michelle grunted from the impact and a shot was fired, the bullet pierced through the ceiling and caused dust to rain down onto Adrien. Adrien annoyingly shook the dust off his head and pried the gun from her hand, tossing it to the ground. It slid across the stone floor until the wall forced it to stop. His forearm went up to her throat. He hissed, showing his fangs fully. Michelle's eyes grew in horror.

"What the—" She grasped onto his arm and tried to pull it off her. "Let me go!" she shouted.

Michelle normally knew how to escape from this sort of chokehold, but Adrien was far too strong. She struggled and quickly became breathless from her attempts to force him off her.

"How did you find me?! Why are you here?!" Adrien yelled.

Michelle grasped at Adrien again, trying to break free.

Cade sighed exasperatedly. "We don't have time for this. I

am leaving for Coran and Xylia's. *Now*," Cade announced quickly as he approached the front door. He looked over his shoulder. "Are you coming, Latimer?"

Adrien looked over to Latimer and they made eye contact. Normally, the Harvesters would stay away from any involvement with someone like Michelle, but at this point, discretion was out of the window because of the Hunters.

"Take care of this," Latimer said to Adrien before glancing at Michelle briefly, with sorrow in his eyes.

"Go ahead, I'll catch up. I won't be long," Adrien said over his shoulder.

"Let's go," Latimer ordered Cade as he passed him up and led the way out of the house.

Just as they stepped foot outside, they both leapt into the air and disappeared. Michelle was peering over Adrien's shoulder and saw them vanish.

She gasped, then focused her glaring eyes back on Adrien. "You killed her! You killed the others too, didn't you?!" Michelle screamed while grasping even more tightly onto his arm. She tried to dig her nails into his skin but even that did not work.

Adrien ripped open her jacket to expose her neck, then he lunged forward to sink his fangs into her flesh. He felt an intense burning similar to what he felt from the sun, and it stopped him before his teeth touched her skin. The sensation came from necklace draped around her neck, a delicate silver cross dangled on the end of it.

"Ahhhh!" Adrien yelled and released her from his grasp. He bent over, his head throbbing and burning as he held onto it.

As soon as she was free, she darted over to the pistol and picked it up to wield it towards him.

"Admit it! You did this!" she accused again, this time with tears in her eyes.

Adrien grunted as the pain wore off. He straightened his stance and looked down at the pistol in her hand. "That will do no good on me," he boasted as he took a few steps towards her.

"Don't move. I will shoot," she warned.

Adrien took another step and she squeezed the trigger, shooting him in his right shoulder. The bullet caused the right side of his body to jerk backward from the force, but this barely hurt him. He held eye contact with her as he grimaced, pulling the bullet out of his arm with his fingers. The small flesh wound was quickly filled with fresh tissue as the wound closed up right before Michelle's eyes. She stumbled backward, unable to comprehend what she just saw. Flicking the bullet off to the side, he bolted to her and grabbed for the necklace to tear from around her neck.

"Jenna!" Michelle cried out abruptly.

Adrien stopped and looked at Michelle angrily. *"What?"* he asked through a clenched jaw.

"She loved you!" Though Michelle feared for her life, she didn't look away from him; she continued to stare courageously into his crimson eyes with intent. "Why she chose to speak so highly of her murderer is beyond me!"

"You spoke with her?" he asked desperately.

"I was the only one she confided in. I...tried to help her."

Adrien noticed the tears in Michelle's eyes and was confused. It was obvious to him that this woman was involved with Jenna in a way he was unaware of. Noticing the badge on her from when she was in his house earlier that night, he knew that she was some sort of law enforcement. It was evident that she also cared for Jenna beyond just merely doing her job.

"She kept asking if we found you. Jenna was more concerned about you than anything else. We were searching for your corpse...but, you are *clearly* not dead," she said, perplexed.

Adrien released her and stepped back, her necklace still intact. Michelle lifted her arms, they trembled as she pointed her pistol at him again. Adrien stood silent, placing his hand up to his lips; he stared at her as his eyes squinted inquisitively.

"You know...I met you before," Michelle said wearily. "Many months back. At a park. My brother and I spoke with you briefly."

Adrien suddenly remembered Michelle. The woman who nearly knocked him out with a soccer ball the very day his life changed forever. His heart ached to think back to the few hours he spent out at that park, dreaming of a future he thought he would soon obtain. A dream that he would be living out now if the circumstances were different.

"You've...*changed*. What in the world happened to you?"

"You see a monster." He took a deep breath. "That's what I am. I don't like what you see any more than you do."

Michelle continued to stare at Adrien; she tightened her grasp on her gun, prepared for any sudden movement.

"Hurting Jenna..." He stumbled backward until his back pressed up against one of the walls, reliving the anguish from her death. "That was the last thing I ever wanted to do. I would do *anything* to get her back," he quavered.

"You didn't just hurt her...you *killed* her," Michelle asserted coldly.

He slumped over as he leaned with his back against the wall, his head hanging low as he gazed at the floor. Michelle was unable to prevent the sudden flood of empathy that had rushed to her, and this shocked her to the core. She could feel the level of pain and guilt radiating from him. She cleared her throat, trying to focus on all the terrible things evidence suggested that he had done. Michelle scoffed, and the corners of her lips drew in disgust.

"Tell me more. What did she say about me? I need to know." Adrien looked up to Michelle through his hair that was partially covering his face.

"I don't need to tell you anything." Michelle reholstered her gun and then reached into her pocket. "But, I do have an obligation to take you in." She pulled out a pair of handcuffs. "You are coming with me."

Adrien laughed. "Are you serious? Killing me is about all you can do." He crossed his arms while still pressed up against the wall. "Good luck figuring out how to do that." His lips folded in as he waited for her to make a move.

Michelle pursed her lips, then grabbed a hold of her necklace, handcuffs still in hand. She held onto the cross gently with her fingers and closed her eyes; she took a deep breath before opening them again. When she opened her eyes, she suddenly saw Adrien differently. She saw a man who was tormented by a darkness that he didn't initially choose, someone who was lost and needed direction. In that short moment, she knew that there was a greater purpose behind this all. Adrien, in particular, had a specific purpose, an importance that she could not comprehend. She squinted her eyes at him, plagued by this sudden download of information. Placing her hands on her hips, she shook her head in frustration; she did not want to help this man.

In the corner of her eye, she then spotted her brown leather case laying on the floor in the other room. Adrien followed her eyes to it, and he scoffed as he realized how she found him.

"This..." She jogged over to the case and picked it up off the ground and dusted it off, walking back towards Adrien with it. "This is how I found you. Wasn't easy getting over here. Take it." She held out her hand, offering it to him.

Adrien looked down at it then back at her, he took it reluctantly. He opened it to see the electronic tablet that she used to track his location.

"My case notes have everything I documented about her: our conversations, the trouble she was in, all instances of contact and evidence I found pertaining to anything related. On the tablet, there are emails back and forth between us."

Adrien brought the case closer to him. "That night...that man...he found something he wasn't supposed to find. He hurt her. I entered the house to protect her but..." He rubbed his chin while looking to the ground. "I killed her myself. I didn't want to, I couldn't stop. I was supposed to save her. I couldn't. I tried with all that was within me. I tried."

Michelle stared silently at him, the heaviness in the room so thick that she could feel it. "I thought I was going to save her too." She rubbed onto her neck and looked in the opposite direction awkwardly. "Look," she said, looking back towards him. "She sent me an email the night she died, but it had a letter within it directed to you. I didn't see the email until days later. It's a tough read, but it is there...in case you want to take a look." She pointed at the tablet.

He looked at her eagerly. "She...she wrote me a letter?" he said in disbelief.

"Yeah...she did." Michelle gestured towards the tablet again.

Adrien promptly turned on the tablet. Her email was already open and he saw a subject line titled with his name. His hands began to tremble as he lightly pressed on the email thread. It filled the screen and his eyes eagerly started to read the words displayed.

Michelle,

Brock and I are going to a Christmas party tonight. This is my only opportunity. As you know, this will be the first time I get to leave this house since we ran into each other at the café months ago. I have finally gathered enough hard evidence against him, and it is all on this phone you gave me. I plan on leaving this phone with a note in the women's restroom at the venue. Hopefully, whoever finds it will bring this in and I will finally be free from this. Once he is taken to prison, I would then like to take you up on your offer to help me relocate to another state…if your offer is still open, of course. Thanks again for all of your help. You are truly a saint.

Please print the next part of this email out if you can? I know Adrien's body was never found, so I still have this hope…that maybe he is still out there somewhere. If you ever find Adrien, could you give this to him?

Dear Adrien,

I thought I saw you a few months ago. Standing outside my window. I soon realized that it was only my imagination, me dreaming so strongly just to see your face again. It made me think of all the times you opened up to me about what you've seen. The man with the black scarf. I am sorry I didn't take you more seriously with that when you were here. I should have listened better, been more appreciative of you expressing your fears to me. I wish I could hear your sweet voice again. Adrien…I miss you so much.

You may never read this letter…but there is something I need to get off my chest somehow. You are an amazing man—very caring, talented, intelligent and good-hearted. I never deserved you. I deceived you and lied to you constantly.

When we first met I already knew about you. The "poor orphaned boy who mysteriously turned into a mega-rich man" is how people spoke *of you. You didn't ask for that title, and I knew there was more to you than that. Your time volunteering with the homeless and using your wealth to make a difference in the world really inspired me. Despite all you did, I saw that you were still lonely, that you did not choose to be; like your title, it seemed to choose you. I figured that if you saw me similar to you in this way, you would accept me even more. I was so intrigued by you, so I lied to you about being abandoned by my own family.*

We connected, mainly, through this. Adrien, our relationship was built on the foundation of my lies. The truth is, I was the one who abandoned them. You always spoke about how you would kill to have a family of your own, and if you knew what I had done you would have lost respect for me and wouldn't have understood.

Upon leaving my family, I believed I could do better for myself on my own, but it didn't work out as I had hoped. I was embarrassed about my living situation, so I never shared it with you. The place I used to live in was a dump. Once it became condemned, a businessman named Brock purchased the area with plans to demolish and build new housing there. He already knew about my situation, so he offered me a place to stay. I accepted. I told him about you from the start and his intentions seemed pure. I was naïve; it turned into something more.

The night before you proposed to me, my heart shifted. I finally realized that you had something in your eyes that Brock never did: a fire, true passion, a love that was real. After I worked up the courage, I tried to leave him, but he did not accept that well. I never could have imagined what would happen to you because of the mess I created.

Please forgive me. I am sorry I messed up, I am sorry I was too late. My selfishness not only got you hurt but also created a monster

within another man. You fell in love with a girl named Jenna...but...that
wasn't me. I'm so sorry...you deserved much better.

-J.M.

Adrien's grip on the tablet loosened, and he dropped the device. He exhaled heavily and staggered in a daze. Michelle watched him as he sank, sliding down the wall, his shirt pulled up as he placed all of his weight against the hard stone. He slid, eyes fixed in the distance in a blank stare until he sat on the floor.

Michelle stood awkwardly for a few moments, then walked over to him. She knelt down in front of him and spoke to him on his level, "I am sorry that this happened to you. What you have done cannot be undone, but I truly believe that there is a possibility for redemption, there is forgiveness for anyone who asks for it."

Adrien looked up at her. "Not for me. I don't deserve that."

Michelle chuckled. "None of us do. But that doesn't change the truth. That's the beauty of it."

Adrien's eyes wandered as he thought, pondering her words. "I would like to believe that," he sighed. He gazed back at the tablet in his hand. "I wish she knew I would have loved her even if she told me the entire, ugly truth," he sighed again. "Thanks for letting me read that."

Michelle smirked, and at first reluctant, reached forward and patted him on the shoulder.

"Uhh...d-don't do that," Adrien said, flustered by her unexpected touch.

"Oh!" Michelle yanked her hand away. "I'm sorry. Don't want you to eat me," she joked, trying to lighten the mood.

"Well, I was planning on it!" Adrien laughed.

Michelle laughed awkwardly as she reached into her holster and pulled out her pistol again.

***

Cade and Latimer arrived at the ruins of Coran and Xylia's home. Most of the house had been torn down brick by brick. Everything was overturned and a fire had begun to envelop one half of the building.

"They've been here already! Coran!" Cade shouted as he darted around the home in search for them.

"They are fine. I can tell they were not here when the Hunters arrived," Latimer said while examining the wreckage. He knelt down, running his hands along the bricks. "How many of them did you say were at the club tonight?" Latimer asked.

"There were four of them. Two males, two females."

"Over thirty Hunters were in this room not long ago."

Cade turned to face Latimer, his mouth agape. "I have never heard of that many Hunters gathered together!" he exclaimed.

Latimer leaned up against the dining room table that was miraculously still in one piece. He sighed. "This is far worse than we initially believed. They must have multiplied their numbers when they retreated after overthrowing the others in Vermont. This may explain why Coran and his family have vanished. They may have fled in the face of this enormous threat." Latimer looked Cade in the eyes. "You still have the opportunity to leave. There is no need for you to risk your life here."

"I couldn't do that. We need to figure out our next move. What are we going to do?" Cade wondered.

"Die!" a voice shouted from behind them.

Cade turned around to see a male Hunter within the room, ready to attack. The Hunter charged for Latimer who quickly knocked him down. Then the two of them pinned the Hunter to the ground, restraining him from moving any further. The Hunter growled and hissed at them.

"Where are the rest of you Hunters?!" Cade interrogated him.

The Hunter snickered mischievously. "Just missed them!"

"Tell me where they are!" Latimer demanded.

The Hunter squirmed under them as Latimer began to pull on his arm, the bones within them starting to snap.

"Ahhhhh!" the Hunter screeched.

"Tell me!" Latimer demanded again.

"To…the next location!" the Hunter responded, laughing in between grunts.

Cade and Latimer looked at one another.

"That's why just the two came days ago!" Cade exclaimed. "To scope out our territory…mark out specific locations to attack. Which means…"

"They are probably closing in on my home. We must go! NOW!" Latimer shouted.

Latimer looked above him to see a hole that was in the ceiling from the Hunter breach. He leapt up and flew out of the house as Cade wrestled with the Hunter. Cade grabbed a sharp piece of rubble from the ground and stabbed him through the heart with it. He took the body and tossed it into the raging fire before he followed behind Latimer.

Chapter 17

"We are hard pressed on every side, but not crushed; perplexed, but not in despair; persecuted, but not abandoned; struck down, but not destroyed."

2 Corinthians 4:8-9

Adrien jumped to his feet, startling Michelle in the process. He thought he heard something in the distance. Rotating around in a circle with his hand to his chin, he listened closely. His eyes squinted in suspicion.

"Quick! Get up!" he told Michelle.

"W-what?" Michelle stood to her feet.

"Something's wrong," he responded. He walked up to one of the very small glass windows and pressed his ear against it.

"What is it?" she asked.

She stood on her tiptoes in an attempt to see over him and through the window also. He shushed her and continued to listen. Turning back around to her, he motioned for her to follow him.

"Follow me," he whispered.

He started to move towards the staircase, but Michelle stayed where she was. He turned to look at her and raised an eyebrow as she stood back with her arms crossed, planted firmly in place.

"No way," she said sternly.

Adrien scoffed and rolled his eyes; he ran over to her and grabbed her quickly. He carried her up to the second story with enhanced speed. He then dropped her off in his room, right next to his coffin.

"Whoa! What the—" She swayed, dizzy from the quick trip. "Don't you dare put your hands on me again!" she fumed as she angrily jumped away from him.

Adrien rolled his eyes again. He walked over to the coffin, the lid creaking as he lifted it. "Get in," he advised.

"Are you kidding me?!"

"It's way too quiet outside. We are not alone. Get in!" he tried to persuade her.

"Over my dead body!" she retorted, her eyebrows raised at her own choice of words. She backed away from him, looking for a way to escape from the room.

"Your stubbornness will get you killed! GET. IN." Adrien pulled on her arm and then pushed her towards the coffin.

BOOM!

A loud noise resonated from the story below, startling both of them. Michelle jumped into the coffin and Adrien closed her within it. He left the room and locked the door before rushing back downstairs. When he arrived, he saw that the front door was wide open, flurries of snow were flying into the house as the wind outside had picked up.

"Adrien!" a voice called out from behind him.

He swiveled around. It was Coran.

"Where's Latimer? Cade?" Coran asked.

"They went to look for you!" Adrien responded, confused by his sudden appearance.

"My family is safe. Out of state. But I came back to help tear up some Hunters with you guys!" he hooted.

The raucous sound of glass shattering and stone crumbling came from the floor above them and on their level, surrounding them. The house quickly filled with violent hisses and the sound of boots thumping along the floor as vampires ran towards Adrien and Coran's scent.

An avalanche of dust, books and papers erupted to their right as a vampire crashed through one of the sidewalls of the house with brute force. The Hunter immediately spotted them and attacked without hesitation. Coran took him on, using speed to his advantage.

Adrien got jumped from behind. Adrien flipped the vampire over his shoulders and onto the ground. He stomped as the vampire rolled to dodge his foot, and Adrien swung again, this time kicking the vampire straight in the face. The force lifted the vampire off the ground and across the room, knocking others down that were approaching.

Coran shoved his fist through the vampire's chest in front of him and he removed his hand, with their heart within it. The vampire collapsed to the floor.

Adrien wrestled with the next vampire as they tore at his shirt. He managed to break loose, but not before they took a chunk of flesh from his arm just below his shoulder.

"ARGH!" Adrien hollered.

The gash was so deep that the bone was visible. Adrien yelled, grabbing the vampire by the throat with his other arm. Adrien tightened his grip on the Hunter, and Coran leapt over to them and swipe kicked the vampire's legs from under him as Adrien pulled up and twisted the opposite direction. The vampire fell headless to his knees, then the body toppled to the side.

Two more vampires emerged from the second floor and caught both Adrien and Coran from behind. They were both successfully restrained but tried to break loose from the grip of their Hunter opponents.

A louder crash of glass and debris came from the side of the house, then suddenly, the two vampires that had overpowered Adrien and Coran were yanked away and tossed into the air. Stone buckled at the force of the vampires as their backs met the wall, and they vanished into the cloud of dust it formed.

Adrien fell to the ground, but a helping hand darted into his vision. He looked up to see Latimer, who had just arrived with Cade. Adrien grabbed onto Latimer's hand, and Latimer yanked him up to his feet.

"Are you alright?" Latimer asked, his eyes scanning Adrien for injuries.

Adrien looked at his arm where the chunk of flesh was torn from his shoulder. His shirt was badly tattered, but his skin and muscle were restored, the wound completely healed.

"I'm good, let's do this," Adrien said as he raised his fists.

All four of them arranged themselves in a circle, ready to defend themselves further, standing back to back. Vampires continued to pour into the house and surrounded them. Cade spotted fragments of sharp rubble at his feet. He kicked them into the air and caught them in his hand, tossing a steel bar and some wood to the others.

Coran whirled the steel around in his hands, his mouth set widely in a grin. "Show us what you got!" Coran challenged the Hunters that approached, he was full of adrenaline.

Just outside of the house, there were even more vampires swarming around, finding more areas to break in. They scaled the building like ants on a hill and hissed as they broke down the stone statues, pillars and walls.

The Hunter leader stood in the distance, observing the invasion. Alongside her were the four Hunters who ravaged the city earlier in the night.

"They are stronger than we thought they would be," Gina huffed.

"I didn't sign up for all this standin' round," Kyle said. "I came here ta feel their bones crush beneath my boot, I came ta hear 'em beg for mercy." He turned towards their leader. "Please… release ya trustful executioner."

The leader stared off, void of emotion. She caught a whiff of something intriguing, her head lifted in the air before she closed her eyes and breathed in deeply. She then opened her eyes, focused on the third floor of the stone home. She slowly nodded at Kyle in permission of their release. The group of four walked towards the home.

The Hunters, though great in numbers were being picked off quickly as they swarmed the Harvesters. The Harvesters worked well in a team and used strategy to their advantage. Six vampires charged towards the group at once, one of them sliding low to the ground and finally breaking up their strong formation. Latimer grabbed onto a chair and swung it around, striking one of the Hunters into the other. The chair shattered into pieces. Coran jumped into the air and caught a scrap in each hand, as he came down onto two vampires, killing them both simultaneously by piercing their hearts.

Cade caught another one of the Hunters by the wrist as he blocked their blows. He twisted the vampire around and flipped her to the ground, then pinned her down with a knee to the chest. Adrien ran up and stomped the vampire into the stone floor. The floor cracked and broke open from the force. Cade then staked the vampire in the heart.

Latimer held yet another two vampires at bay. They hissed ravenously, then they suddenly stopped and no longer fought against him. Latimer looked confused as Coran, who had broken down one of the pillars, swung it in their direction, swiping the same two vampires into the wall and crushing them with the stone.

"Did you see that?" Latimer asked.

"See what?!" Coran asked as he twisted to face the next vampire that was approaching him quickly.

This vampire leapt at Coran and then crossed his own arms to his chest so he could not defend himself. Coran killed the vampire instantly, then tossed his body to the side. Coran and Latimer both looked at one another in bewilderment. Coran pursed his lips, and his eyes squinted in suspicion. Then they both turned to even more Hunters as they came up to attack. The Harvesters kept working as a team while the corpses of the Hunters piled up around the house. There seemed to be no more.

Coran laughed heartily. "Don't tell me that was it! I have barely even warmed up!" He jerked his body to snap a few of his bones back in place.

Cade, Coran and Latimer were covered in minor wounds. Adrien did not have a single scratch remaining on his body, though the tears in his clothes suggested he had been injured the most out of them all. They all look around cautiously, waiting, as the room had fallen silent.

Rubble and stone shifted around at the front. They all turned to face the four Hunters who casually stepped in. They walked over all of the corpses strewn across the floor, unbothered by the carnage that surrounded them. The four of them lined up on the opposite side of the room and faced them directly. These

Hunters didn't immediately attack like the others, they stood patiently...sizing them up as their opponents, marking their targets.

"Time ta end this once an' for all," Kyle spoke tauntingly, and then he made eye contact with Latimer. "YOU! The one with the purty hair...wanna be the first ta die?" He lifted his arm, the tip of his pointer finger as a crosshair.

The house fell silent again, silent enough to hear the sudden thump from above and the sound of high heels as they walked across the rooftop of the house. Adrien glanced upwards, but the others kept their eyes fixed on the Hunters. In this moment of distraction, Kyle made the first move and the rest of the Hunters lunged forwards as well. Latimer, Cade, Coran and Adrien ran towards them. Latimer took on Kyle, Cade took Gina, Coran targeted one of the male Hunters and Adrien challenged the last, another female Hunter.

Cade was overpowered immediately by Gina as she grasped him and lifted him up, tossing him over her shoulders into one of the walls. Slightly dazed, he quickly got up to his feet and dodged her as she came at him again, slashing her claws at him. He continued to move around, dodging her, but she was very fast. Eventually, they scaled the staircase to the second story. Gina caught a part of his torso with her sharp nails.

"Gaaahhh!" Cade yelled as jerked away from her.

Blood poured from his wound. Grabbing onto her hair he yanked her, forcing her body to twist in the air before she hit the floor and slid up to a closed door. When she stood to her feet,

Cade charged her and tackled her into Adrien's room, shattering his door to pieces.

Coran somersaulted in the air as he jumped over the Hunter after him. Planting his feet, he quickly threw a punch, and the Hunter adjusted too quickly to his maneuver and grabbed Coran's fist. The Hunter jabbed him in the gut multiple times before Coran was able to retaliate with an uppercut to his jaw. The Hunter tumbled and used the momentum from his fall to the floor to roll back up to his feet.

Adrien did not have much experience in hand-to-hand combat aside from the occasional fight he would get into while growing up in the group homes. His advantage in speed and strength proved no use against this Hunter. She gracefully dodged every punch and kick he sent her way as she anticipated each one, his face was easy to read. She swung her arm around and struck him with her elbow in the back of his neck. As he keeled over, she kneed him in the chest.

Latimer administered a throat punch to Kyle, causing him to gag. Quickly twisting his body in foresight, Latimer dodged Kyle's roundhouse kick retaliation. Latimer then swept his feet from under him and Kyle fell on his back. As Kyle lay on the floor, Latimer jumped on top of him and punched him repeatedly in the face, his teeth chipping under the force. Kyle swished around his mouth before spitting blood into Latimer's eyes, which temporarily blinded him. With both legs, Kyle kicked Latimer with such force that he was propelled into the ceiling.

***

As the battle raged on, the scent was overwhelming. The leader of the Hunters punched through the roof and dropped down into a room that was secluded from the others. Dust swirled as she landed on the once spotless white tile floor. She could smell Evadin stronger than she had before, and she eagerly burst through the door in front of her to enter into another dark room. She heard the faint trickle of a water fountain as she walked further into the room. Her eyes scanned the walls as she passed by the portraits displayed in a line along the wall. From the corner of her eye, she spotted an opaque curtain and approached it, peeling the curtain back before stepping to the other side.

***

Gina wrapped her legs around Cade's neck while they were on the floor. Cade attempted to break free from her grasp, but he only managed to stand to his feet with her still attached to him at the neck. Using her upper body strength, she flipped backward and used her legs to fling him across the room. Cade crashed into Adrien's coffin and it toppled over. Michelle rolled out of it and onto the floor.

Michelle covered her head, screaming in terror. Gina spun around and hissed at Michelle, and in this moment Cade took the opportunity to gain the upper hand. He grabbed onto Gina's head while she was distracted and he quickly snapped her neck; she fell face-first to the floor.

Adrien had the female Hunter that he was fighting on top of him. She attempted to gouge out his eyes by pressing her thumbs in his sockets. He grabbed onto her wrists and flipped her to where he was then on top. Slapping away her hands, he wrapped both hands around her neck and began to choke her. In the process, her mask was ripped off her face. She hissed, then her eyes grew dark as her pupils dilated. Adrien looked towards the staircase, as did she. She pushed Adrien off her with such a great force that he was suddenly airborne.

The Hunter had smelled Michelle and scaled the stairs to enter Adrien's room. Cade had just grabbed something to stake Gina, to finish the job, when the other female Hunter entered the room. When she entered the door, he turned around and staked the unsuspecting Hunter, instead.

The toss from the hungry Hunter had catapulted Adrien across the room. He landed on a piece of stone with steel jutting out from it. The bar impaled him through the stomach and he released a blood-curdling scream.

Latimer spun around, breaking away from his grapple with Kyle. "ADRIEN!" Latimer called out.

Adrien's hands fumbled around the blood-soaked bar piercing through him, but he was unable to get a good grip to yank it out. Latimer entered the room and quickly lifted Adrien to prop him against the wall. Adrien's wound had already healed around the steel that was impaling him, and he screamed in agony. Latimer grabbed onto the bar and began to yank it from his abdomen. Adrien groaned and gurgled as the wound was made fresh again; he felt the elevated ridges on the metal of the bar grinding against his spine on the way out.

The stone on the other side of him was preventing Latimer from fully pulling out the bar. Latimer felt around his back for it and quickly chopped the block off with his hand.

Kyle quickly approached the both of them.

"Aahhhhhh! L-La-" Adrien tried to speak, unable to do so coherently.

Latimer finally yanked the steel bar from him.

"L-Latimer!" Adrien yelled.

Latimer turned around, but Kyle caught his hand that still held onto the bar, and Kyle twisted it around. He forced the metal into Latimer's chest and through to his heart. Latimer grunted, a sharp pain shooting through his body.

Suddenly, the sound of a rushing wind filled the room.

"Stop! STOP!" The leader of the Hunters cried out desperately.

"Straight through the heart," Kyle said proudly. He yanked the bar out of Latimer's chest and stepped aside.

Latimer was still conscious, and he looked up, seeing the leader standing in front of him. Her eyes, though they were crimson, were ones he would never forget. Adaeze stood a few yards away with her feet set wide apart, her chest moving rapidly, as she was breathing frantically. She had the same design of face paint on her skin, but instead of the soft rouge it used to be, the designs were now red and black. She ripped the iron mask from her face and tossed it aside as she ran to Latimer.

His knees buckled as he began to collapse. Adaeze slid along the floor, scraping her knees on the stone. She caught him before his body would have hit the floor. Blood streamed from her eyes as she desperately grabbed onto him and pulled him into her. They made eye contact. Through the grimace on Latimer's face, a smile cracked across his dry lips, just before he closed his eyes.

Chapter 18

"The eye is the lamp of the body. If your eyes are healthy, your whole body will be full of light. But if your eyes are unhealthy, your whole body will be full of darkness. If then the light within you is darkness, how great is that darkness!"

Matthew 6:22-23

West Africa: August 1678

*G*listening waters that glowed from the light of the moon sloshed around their shins as the lovers tread knee-deep in saltwater. To their left, the lower half of the horizon was blanketed by a shimmery black surface of soft waves and current. The Atlantic Ocean, vast in its entirety, seemed to go on for an eternity.

Latimer laughed, starting to run horizontally to the shore, approaching a large, rocky structure. Adaeze followed suit, scrunching her waterlogged skirt to her upper thighs so she could run after him. They both rounded the corner of the rocky structure and Adaeze gasped as she saw what Latimer led her to on the other side.

It was a shallow cave that opened towards the sea. It was shallow enough to where the moon was able to fully illuminate it. Beautiful fragrant flowers grew on the edges of the rocks as well as throughout the cave. Tiny tide pools glistened in the moonlight and patches of land were elevated out of the water, providing a dry walking path for them. Latimer stood at the entrance, then bowed, offering his hand for her to take. Adaeze slipped her hand within his and they walked into the cave together.

"The other night, I was restless in my chamber," Latimer said. "So, I wandered around and happened to discover this cave. I waited until the moon was full to bring you. It is more beautiful than I could have ever imagined, especially now that you are here with me," he said to her affectionately.

"Latimer..." Adaeze responded shyly, feeling the heat rush to her cheeks as she blushed.

Latimer chuckled and stopped walking. "Something about this place makes me realize what it is I truly long for." He turned towards her and grabbed both of her hands now into his, staring deep into her eyes. "Every day...every night...you are the only thing I can think about. You matter more to me than I can ever begin to explain. I want to be with you...forever."

Adaeze gasped, her eyes glistening with tears. She quickly buried her head into his chest. "What have we gotten ourselves into? I never expected our feelings would grow so strong. I love you more than anything, Latimer...but...this will all end eventually, it has to." She leaned back and looked up to him.

"Does it not?"

"Who says it has to? I love you beyond words, Adaeze. We are meant to be. What we have is absolute. No matter where this life's journey takes us...there is nothing more I would want than for you to still be by my side."

He kissed her tenderly on the lips. Adaeze smiled.

She nodded at him eagerly. "I will be...as long as I can. Until the end...I promise you."

***

Firmly cradled in Adaeze's lap, Latimer lay still. The wound on his chest ceased to bleed as he had fully succumbed to death. Adaeze mourned while she squeezed his shoulders, staring into his face. She blinked rapidly, still trying to grasp who she was holding.

Adrien dropped to his knees. Without paying mind to Adaeze, he grabbed onto Latimer's collar with both hands and balled the cloth into his fists.

"Latimer! LATIMER!" Adrien lowered his head into Latimer's shoulder and cried into the cloth.

Coran's arms were held behind his back tightly by his Hunter opponent. He stared in disbelief, speechless at the sight of Latimer.

Cade ran down the stairs and immediately stopped as soon as he saw what was before him.

"Behold!" Kyle hollered, throwing his hands in the air as if showcasing a prize. "The world's most beautiful corpse!" he laughed menacingly while he looked directly at Adrien. "He ain't comin' back ta ya now, boy."

Adrien lifted his head, his lips curled as he snarled ferociously, his eyes furiously set on Kyle.

"AHHHHHHH!" Cade snapped and charged Kyle.

"Cade, no!" Coran called out from across the room.

As soon as Cade reached him, Kyle grabbed him by the throat and lifted him off the ground.

"Nice try, but ya gon' have to do worse than that!" Kyle hooted.

Kyle body slammed him onto the floor. The impact shook the entire house. Cade grabbed on to Kyle's arms, attempting to pull his hands from around his neck.

"The itsy-bitsy vampire came up ta fight the best. Down came my reign, then I broke 'em and the rest!" Kyle sang tauntingly as he pushed down with greater strength, slowly snapping the bones in his neck.

"Cade!" Coran called out. He yanked free from the Hunter restraining him but was quickly grabbed and restrained once more.

Adrien jumped up and sprinted over to Kyle, swinging his leg, he planted his foot into his side, sending him soaring across the room. Kyle crashed to the ground and Adrien ran up to Kyle as he leapt back up to his feet.

"Come on, try me!" Kyle grumbled deeply as they faced off.

Adrien lunged forward and grabbed ahold of Kyle's arm. Adrien tugged back towards himself, yanking Kyle's arm out of its socket. Kyle yelled and jerked back from him, holding onto his shoulder in pain. Kyle's eyes narrowed as he growled beneath his mask.

Kyle stepped forward but suddenly stopped, he trembled as if he was fighting against something unseen. He began to sweat. Bending over, he grabbed onto his head. "Come on, let me hurt 'em! Only a graze!" Kyle pleaded to something, or someone, unknown.

Adrien observed, slack-jawed, then realized he must have been under his creator's control. Kyle stumbled onto one knee as if he had been released. He snarled viciously as he leapt towards Adrien. As the gap between Kyle and Adrien closed, his fist stopped abruptly.

Adaeze now stood between them, her eyes glaring at Adrien. Adaeze shoved Kyle to the side and then forced Adrien against the wall. Adrien's eyes frantically searched her face, then they grew wide as he realized who she was.

"Adaeze?" Adrien guessed in awe.

"I've seen your face—on that wall. Who are you?" she prodded.

Adrien began to gripe, "He loved you! How could you—"

Adaeze grabbed Adrien by his chin, her fingers digging into his cheeks and forcing them upwards. She forced his head side to side and examined him.

"Your face. It's so familiar. You...you have his eyes," she whispered. "Who are you?!" she then screamed desperately.

Adrien growled, then yanked his chin from her hands. He spat in her face. Adaeze recoiled, turning her head away to wipe her face with the sleeve of her dress. She looked back to Adrien, her eyes ablaze. Grabbing onto his shirt, she lifted him and slammed him into the wall again. The wall rumbled as dust showered onto them.

"Who are you?! Why was he here?! How...*how* was he here?!" she cried out, her veins raised by her temples.

Adrien looked at her, dumbfounded. "You didn't know? You didn't know who you ordered these Hunters to tear through? To kill?!"

Adrien watched as her expression changed, she was clearly at a loss.

Adrien continued, "He thought you were gone...spending centuries mourning over you. He was still as in love with you as he ever was."

Adaeze exhaled sharply, then she released Adrien. She ran back over to Latimer and sat on the floor next to him, pulling him into her lap again. "No, no...*mon amour*," her voice quivered as she mourned over him.

"What the hell?" Cade said, standing to his feet. "Who is this woman?"

Adrien sighed. "Latimer's wife."

Cade and Coran both turned to look at one another, they

were both stunned.

"*What?* I don't understand." Coran turned to look in Adaeze's direction. "Why would she want us dead?"

Adrien started to pace with his fingers up to his lips. He stopped abruptly and spun around to face them. "He's...far more behind this than Latimer and I realized."

Cade stepped closer. "Who?"

Adrien breathed in deeply then clenched his jaw, grinding his teeth. "*Evadin*," he claimed.

"Who?" Coran asked as he struggled within the Hunter's grasp.

"Release him," Adaeze demanded. Her head was slightly turned to where she could see Coran and the Hunter that restrained him in her peripheral.

The Hunter immediately released Coran. Adaeze cleared her throat as she used the cloth on her shoulders to gently wipe off her tears. She slowly lifted a hand, then motioned with her fingers for the Harvesters to come closer. Cade and Coran looked at each other hesitantly, then approached her slowly. Adrien also approached, joining them as they surrounded Adaeze.

"I suppose...you were all close to him," her voice trembled as she spoke.

Adrien sat down and placed his hand on Latimer's chest, and he looked up at Adaeze through his hair. "Yes..."

"I-I" she stuttered. "I...didn't know. I believed that he died, long ago..."

Adrien's eyes dried to sandpaper as he stared blankly at Latimer's face. It seemed so serene. Adrien's heart ached so much that he had to look away. His eyes jumped around the room to the carnage that surrounded them. He felt a fiery rage within him that consumed the sadness; an overwhelming anger grew in its place.

Standing to his feet steadily with both of his hands in fists, he then stormed towards the front of the house without saying a word. As he drew closer to the front, his pace continued to rise until he broke out in a full sprint through the fragmented walls and into the forest.

As he ran, he lifted his voice. His throat stung as he screamed at the top of his lungs, running at a speed he had yet to reach. With no plan, he didn't know where he was going. As he zipped through the forest, he couldn't help but recall pieces of the last full conversation he had with Latimer: *You are the last of everything, and all I have left in the world—I have practically had no family my entire life, but you…you've always been there.*

Somehow, though he did not think it was possible, what he felt now was worse than losing Jenna. Abruptly stopping in the middle of the forest, he knelt to the ground in the snow.

***

Adaeze gently picked up Latimer. Looking to her right she saw a room that had been untouched. Carrying him over into the music room, she gently set him down on one of the couches. She kissed him on the forehead before swiftly turning to fly out of the house herself. Cade and Coran watched her leave. They followed in pursuit.

Adrien felt a hand gently touch his shoulder. Looking up, he saw Adaeze who was now standing over him and looking down.

"Anyone who shows this much love for my Latimer deserves to be followed. We shall fight together, finally bring the subject of all of our affliction down to his knees," she said.

Adrien stood up and faced her just as Cade and Coran caught up to them.

Coran chuckled. "Count us in. I'm down for a little more action! We can get the job done...just us."

"Who are we going up against here? Tell us more," Cade requested.

"He's thousands of years old, the only ancient vampire still in existence," she stated.

"Evadin is also Latimer's creator...he's the cause for Adaeze and the Hunters coming here," Adrien added on.

"An ancient?" Cade asked concerned. "Do you know what he wants?"

"He finds all of this...entertaining. Something tells me there may be more to it than he was letting on," Adrien responded pensively.

"How do we find him?" Coran asked as he lifted his hands and cracked his knuckles.

Adaeze gritted her teeth. "He's here...somewhere in the city. The last of his scent I picked up was at Latimer's home.

We were picking up his scent everywhere. The house had the strongest scent we've come across so far."

"We must split up then, so we can cover more ground," Cade insisted.

"Yes. If either of us discovers his location...hold back— no one makes a move until we are regrouped," Adrien added, "Adaeze and I will go together. Coran...you and Cade go back to the house. Latimer kept a secret room on the top floor; the entrance is behind the largest bookcase on the second floor. You'll be able to pick up Evadin's scent there...knowing it will help you."

Cade and Coran left, leaving Adrien and Adaeze alone again. The forest fell silent; Adrien looked over to Adaeze, who was already staring back at him.

"Again, I ask. Who are you?" she asked quietly.

Adrien looked at her uncomfortably, then he took a deep breath. "I...I am your family. The last of it."

Adaeze's face twitched in response, she squinted her eyes in confusion. "No...my son, he—"

"Your son...didn't die that night. He lived on...he had a family."

Adaeze moved closer to Adrien. "He did?!" she blurted out with a joyful cry.

"Yes...he did," Adrien said back to her. His mouth was slightly agape, hoping that he would not need to explain in detail what ended up happening to him. "Hundreds of years later...you got me."

Adaeze sighed as if a huge pressure was relieved from her. She then started to laugh joyfully. A smile looked awkward on her, as it was an expression that had grown foreign to her. "Latimer was able to create you? You have my blood within you... his blood. That's...*impossible*. Latimer should have killed you when he attempted to turn you," she expressed in astonishment.

Adrien thought back to Latimer telling his recount of the night he killed his son, he spoke about the blood being sweeter than any he had ever tasted.

"So I have heard. I guess, somehow, Latimer has been the only vampire to be able to do so," Adrien responded.

Adaeze stepped closer and lifted her hand to his face, lightly caressing his cheek with the back of her hand. "Looking at you now, I can only begin to understand the amount of love Latimer must have had for you. You are like the son we never had a fair chance to raise," she said gently.

Adrien laughed now, oddly feeling as if a warmth was emanating from her skin. He suddenly felt a deeper level of comfort with her; he felt safe. Adaeze's maternal presence made him long all the more that Latimer was still with them. He smiled from ear to ear as she removed her hand from his cheek.

Adaeze felt the cells in her body begin to vibrate. She turned her back to Adrien as she fought the feeling she was suddenly overcome with.

"Uh...Adaeze?" Adrien asked, sensing something was wrong.

Adaeze crouched down before she pushed off powerfully

into the air. She ascended quickly and disappeared through the clouds. Adrien watched her vanish.

"W-what the?" Adrien said, then he pursued after her.

***

Coran and Cade arrived back at Latimer's house. Coran began to climb up the staircase, but Cade stopped and looked around, confused. Coran reached the top of the stairs and turned around.

"What's the hold-up?" Coran asked.

"All of the bodies...they're gone," Cade claimed.

"*What?*" Coran leapt down the stairs to rejoin him on the first floor.

From where they stood, Coran could see that he was right. They split up and investigated the rooms that were littered with corpses just less than half an hour prior. Every single corpse was nowhere to be found. Cade entered the music room and hastily approached the couch where Adaeze placed Latimer. Coran stood in the doorway.

"Latimer's body...it's gone as well," Cade said in concern.

"What is going on here?" Coran asked uneasily.

"I don't know," Cade said as he ran past Coran. "We must stick to our task."

Coran followed Cade upstairs and they searched around the second floor for the largest bookcase as Adrien suggested. Cade then remembered that he never finished Gina off with the stake. He walked over to Adrien's door and peeked in to see that the room was empty. Cade saw the toppled coffin also and remembered the human that spilled out of the coffin during the battle as well.

Cade left the room and looked around suspiciously. Just outside of Adrien's room there was a gash in the wall that was formed by the Hunters' initial breach. The hole led to a section of the roof. Cade walked to the hole in the wall, then he peered out to see a relatively fresh set of footprints on the snow-covered shingles.

"Over here!" Coran called out.

Cade lingered as he examined the footprints. They belonged to the human. He peered out into the trees and then stepped out onto the roof. Walking across the shingles, he made his way to the opposite side of the house. His aerial view gave him clear visuals of the tracks that were left behind. Cade deduced that the three Hunters they left unattended must have taken the corpses with them. The human had also managed to escape, unscathed, on her own.

"Cade!" Coran yelled again.

Cade rushed back over to the hole in the wall and re-entered the house. He ran over to Coran who was down the hallway, standing in front of an ordinary-looking bookcase. Coran slid the case to the side. Sure enough, Adrien was right. There was a hidden door behind it. They glanced at one another briefly, then they quickly entered, following the spiral stairs up to the next floor.

Fresh air and snow steadily flowed into the room from

the hole Adaeze formed in the ceiling. They stepped over the debris and walked to the portrait room. They both examined the walls, looking at all of the portraits of Latimer's past that were kept as a secret for so long. Coran cleared his throat, looking away from the wall once he saw Adrien's portrait.

"You got it?" Coran asked him.

Cade stood staring at the portraits of Latimer and his family on the other wall.

"Cade?"

Cade snapped out of his trance and eyed Coran from the side. "I wonder why he kept so much from us," he said.

"Who knows, but now's not the time to try and figure that out," Coran reckoned.

Cade shook his head quickly, readjusting his focus. "Yes, of course." Cade paused, suddenly realizing that something was familiar. "Coran...I've caught this scent before. Earlier tonight."

Coran stepped forward eagerly. "Where?"

**

Adaeze landed behind a charred building in an alleyway, falling to her knees. She was breathing heavily and sweating profusely. The building was covered in signs that warned others from entering. She quickly stood back up and looked around her. She heard a large crowd of people in the distance but the immediate area was vacant. Adrien landed behind her shortly after.

"What was that?! Why did you lead us here?" Adrien

asked, looking around cautiously. He recognized where they were: Voyage Nightclub.

"I don't know. I-I lost control. I have no idea how I got here," she stammered as she was still breathing heavily.

Adrien looked at her uneasily, knowing what the loss of her free will entailed. There was a metal door to the building near them, and both of them turned towards it. Just a few moments afterward, the door swung open. Yve stood in the doorway, glaring intensely. When she saw Adaeze, she smirked.

"Thank you, my dear Yve," a voice called out from within the building.

Yve stepped to the side and revealed Evadin standing in the middle of the club, his back to the open door. The room was mostly dark. Some of the laser lights were still working as they swept around the room, flickering on and off due to the damage from the fire. Every so often, the colored lights illuminated Evadin as the smoke continued to softly drift around him. Evadin placed one foot behind the other and pivoted to face them both.

"My apologies for cutting your conversation short." He smiled at them maliciously. "I was beginning to tire from biding your arrival."

"Evadin!" Adrien yelled, charging into the building.

The smoke wafted around Adrien's legs and arms as he ran towards him. He leapt to tackle Evadin, but Evadin vanished quickly, causing Adrien to fall to his face and slide across the wooden floor. Adrien then quickly got back up to his feet. Evadin was now behind him.

"There is something unique about you, Adrien. Different. Now tell me…what makes you so?" Evadin inquired.

Adrien slowly turned around, but Evadin had disappeared once again, he was not where his voice clued him to be.

"It's such a pleasure to finally meet you…face-to-face," Evadin's voice had changed in location again.

Adrien jerked around in the direction he heard Evadin's voice and was startled with how close he suddenly was. Evadin sliced into his cheek with one of his nails.

"Mmmm." Evadin looked to the blood on his fingers, then back up to Adrien as he licked it off them.

Adrien's wound healed instantaneously and Evadin's eyes burned in excitement. "Now would you look at *that*."

Adaeze charged for Evadin next, but he quickly vanished once more, his speed was greater than them both. He appeared on the second story and leaned over the railing, looking down on them from the story above.

"I'm going to kill you for what you've done!" Adaeze shouted up to him, both of her fists clenched as she trembled in enmity.

Evadin erupted in laughter. "What a shame to see this mountain of pain in such a beauteous face…I wish I could *feel* it." Evadin glanced over to Yve. "But you have all brought this upon yourselves—falling victim to your emotions. It is your weakness, your flaw. Indubitably, it is my fuel. Fuel to get you to do what I desire."

"Latimer is dead because of you! He's not around for you to play around with anymore, to feed off! For that reason alone, I am actually happy for him. Kill me...now, as you threatened him. I challenge you to try!" Adrien demanded boldly.

Evadin scoffed then he stood up straight, releasing the railing. "Ahhh, that is where you have mistaken me, Adrien. If I truly wanted you dead, you would be...ashes, and well before Latimer's demise. Even if you did not have something I yearned for, to eradicate you now would prove to be without purpose."

"You're not getting anything from me!" Adrien declared.

Evadin walked casually towards the staircase and over the glass floor that overlaid the large aquarium. The aquarium was filled with dead fish that had floated to the top, the sharks within the tank were still alive but moved along sluggishly, as they were dying also.

Evadin reached the staircase and descended it; his arms were crossed over his chest. "Fortunately, your presence...is all I required." He looked over to Adaeze. "The both of yours."

The metal door behind them swung open suddenly. Both Adrien and Adaeze quickly spun around to see Kyle, Gina and the other male Hunter standing in the doorway.

Adrien turned back towards Evadin and smirked. "Looks like we've got some back-up," he said in confidence as he squared his shoulders to him.

The Hunters stood completely still without making a sound or saying a word. Adaeze signaled to them and their eyes didn't even focus on her, but instead turned towards Evadin.

Adaeze looked back over to Evadin, confused. He was already staring at her, his mouth smugly set in a grin.

"Tell me, Adaeze. These vampires...the ones you gathered for the sole purpose of seeking me out, to aid in my destruction... were they derived from you?"

Adaeze's eyes grew, looking back over to the Hunters.

Evadin chuckled. "Now...that would have been *far* more tactical, don't you agree? Without doing so, there is no telling where their true allegiance lies."

Evadin nodded at the Hunters, then they began to drag the corpses of all of the dead vampires from the battle into the building. They continued to pile them in one by one, bringing them to the center of the floor. Latimer was the very last one to be tossed inside.

"Latimer..." Adrien whispered in anguish.

Evadin looked at Adaeze. "Their orders: to follow your lead, to attack, maim, injure...but to avoid exterminating the..." Evadin's eyes shifted to Adrien, "*asset*."

Adaeze was perplexed. "What is truly going on here?!"

Evadin walked a few steps closer towards them. "Why, darling, I am glad you asked." Evadin's hand darted in Adrien's direction, snatching him up by his neck again. Evadin's nails dug into his neck and caused him to bleed.

"Let him go!" Adaeze hissed. She tried to attack Evadin, but her control was relinquished from her once again.

Evadin dropped Adrien and in turn, Adaeze restrained

Adrien from behind. Yve stood off the side as she controlled Adaeze against her will. Adrien struggled, trying to break free from her grasp.

"A vampire's appeal to his mortal blood is substantially impeccable. Not even their creator holds the ability to control them into restraint, if one were to attempt to turn a family member." Evadin was staring at the blood running down Adrien's neck. "His venom is like pure...*liquid diamond*. Latimer was driven by guilt, entitlement and love. This was all amplified by the passing of each generation. When I killed Adrien's father, Gabriel, it made Latimer all the more desperate to protect Adrien...this love surpassed all odds as he was now the last left of his lineage. Latimer—unlike I—had no idea what he truly created when he successfully transformed Adrien to our kind...the *possibilities* that would arise from it. He has fulfilled his purpose, the impossible. The time has come, Adaeze, for you to fulfill yours."

Adaeze hissed, then she bit into Adrien's neck. He screamed, twisting and contorting, his blood feeling like liquid magma burning through his veins. The pain managed to be unlike any he had felt thus far, and soon enough, his vision blurred. He strained to see Evadin through his blurred vision. Evadin's face slowly filled with a vile sneer. Adrien fought against it, but his screams of agony became muffled as he slipped out of consciousness.

Chapter 19

"The life of mortals is like grass, they flourish like a flower of the field; the wind
blows over it and it is gone, and its place remembers it no more."

Psalm 103:15-16

A family sat together on the couch in their living room. A father and a mother, with their two teenage boys, shared a bowl of buttered popcorn amongst themselves. They excitedly watched their weekly sitcom. Suddenly, the phone rang. Exasperatedly rolling his eyes, the father shimmied himself off of the couch and walked over to the phone. He put the receiver to his ear, his face of content immediately shifting to fear as he heard the person on the other line. Dropping the phone, he ran back into the living room and yanked the silver controller off the coffee table to change the channel.

"Heyyyy! Dad!" one of the boys yelled with a mouth full of

half-chewed popcorn. "Change it back!"

Both boys and the mother turned towards the Dad who was speechless as he stared at the screen. The mother, equipped with a glare, got up from the couch and yanked the controller out of his hand to change the channel back, but the voice coming from the screen stopped her from doing so. They all turned towards the television and listened intently.

"I am here at the scene of tonight's massacre." A reporter stood in front of the camera with a mic held firmly in his hand for a live broadcast. "There are many casualties as first responders rush to tend to any remaining survivors. Deputies are—"

"You guys have to leave, NOW!" Michelle barged into the shot, now on the live broadcast herself.

"Ma'am, are you a witness?" The reporter shoved the mic into her face. "We are live! Tell us what you saw!"

"Did you hear me?! It's not safe here!" she yelled back, she then turned to speak directly into the camera, "Leave the city! Everyone! Leave before it's too late!"

A hand then landed onto her shoulder and she jumped, startled by it. She turned to see her father, the Chief of Police. He led her away from the camera and she followed along reluctantly.

He leaned over into her ear. "We do not want to cause panic. This is not like you. You are not following protocol."

"Sir, we must evacuate as soon as possible," Michelle insisted.

"Now, tell me why you believe we should *evacuate* the city.

This is not a natural disaster," he demanded for an explanation.

In the moments of terror Michelle spent at Latimer's home, she managed to sneak out through a gash in the wall onto the roof of the house. There she patiently waited as she witnessed the Hunter vampires gathering up the corpses and overheard them speaking of their plans, including where they were headed. Michelle rushed over as quickly as she could once the coast was clear.

"Not just the city. We need to get them as far away as possible. I have no time to explain. More people are going to die if we don't!" Michelle informed him desperately.

Something caught the corner of Michelle's eye as she spoke to her father; she looked upwards, seeing Cade and Coran as they leapt across the rooftops of the buildings. She followed the path of their direction down the street, towards the destroyed nightclub that was quarantined.

***

Only a few minutes had passed and Adrien awoke, now on the floor, to even more excruciating pain. He continued to writhe. Laid out on his back, he examined his arms as he felt a crawling sensation beneath his skin. Red veins began to surface. He watched in terror as the pain that shot through his body aligned with the growth of this new vein pattern; it ascended up his arms and to his shoulders. The veins then began to quickly change color, morphing into a bright yellow hue. He dug his fingertips into the fabric across his chest, ripping his shirt in two to see the veins also covering that portion of his body.

Adaeze stood off to the right of him, her arms planted by her sides as she gazed at him helplessly, shaking as she attempted to move. Evadin walked over to Adrien and grabbed him by his hair, yanking him across the floor towards the pile of vampire corpses. Adrien grasped onto Evadin's hands that were firmly wrapped into his locks; he was still too weak to fight back as the pain continued to ravage him.

Evadin stopped atop one vampire, pried open its mouth, then inflicted a wound to Adrien's neck. He shoved Adrien above the vampire as the bright yellow liquid dripped into the vampire's mouth.

"Fascinating!" Evadin exclaimed. "Your veins now course with *pure* venom."

He moved on to the next vampire, continuing to re-inflict the wound as he went along since Adrien healed far too quickly.

"Of the thousands of years I have walked this earth, all I have known is pathetic excuses of life: the creation of humans, the fall of man and then the curse of our kind. Even vampires are a failure. We came about to end that in which God loves. You see, I was one of the first...I know what *our* curse purposed us for," Evadin explained.

Evadin had finished with all the vampires except for one, Latimer. He began to drag Adrien towards him.

CRASH!

Shards of sharp glass rained down from the ceiling. Cade and Coran plummeted to the ground through the skylight that was still partially intact. They landed a few yards behind them with their fists raised, prepared to fight.

"Let him go!" Coran commanded.

***

Michelle's father swiveled around to the loud shatter from the skylight down the street. "No one is supposed to be in that building." The chief grabbed his walkie-talkie and beeped in. "Officer Miller, please detain any trespassers on the quarantined property."

"Dad!" Michelle grabbed his shoulders and attempted to turn him back around to face her, but he continued to bark orders into the walkie. "Dad! DAD!"

He lowered the walkie and finally turned around to face her, his face filled with fury.

"If I'm wrong, the worst that could happen would be a few hours wasted...if I am right, people will die that could have easily been saved!" she pleaded.

Her father was taken aback by her fervor. He had also never seen Michelle so frightened before. He turned to the officer beside him, seeing also that the people who overheard Michelle's warnings were starting to flee.

"Andrews, gather your troops. Get these civilians out of here safely. I am issuing an accordance of an emergency evacuation of the city," he ordered.

"No, not just the civilians. Our people, too—*everyone*," Michelle insisted.

***

Evadin walked towards Cade and Coran. The two Harvesters backed up hesitantly, their eyes focused on what was behind him. They were looking past Evadin and over at the pile of corpses.

The same vein pattern Adrien was exhibiting began to cover the corpses, except their veins were black in hue. After a few seconds, the corpses began to stir. One by one, they began to twitch as their muscles fired back up. A few of them began to slowly rise.

Evadin turned around and looked at the bodies gradually rising. Adrien gasped, then rushed over, crawling to Latimer. He looked down at him and then back to the risen vampires. Without a second thought, Adrien cut himself and fed Latimer the venom from his veins.

Cade and Coran were frozen, staring at the re-animated vampires.

"What...the..." Coran gasped in disbelief.

"How...is this possible?" Cade whispered back to him.

Evadin grinned at them, then turned back around to Adrien. "Self-preservation has kept us from fulfilling our true duty: complete extermination. Vampires—risen from the grave—will have no sense of such values."

"No..." Adrien breathed out slowly, still holding onto Latimer. He looked down at him in dismay.

The vampires were all standing, but none of them had opened their eyes. Their chests rose up and down marginally as they began to breathe, then their chests sped up as their shallow breathing became rapid. At once, their eyes all opened, revealing their eyeballs in their entirety: black as space, vacant. Their noses twitched violently as they caught an intriguing scent, slobber dripping from their mouths as they began to snarl.

The vampires suddenly burst past Cade and Coran and through the brick wall behind them. The entire building rumbled from the impact. Cade was knocked to the ground and Coran was thrown into the rubble and trampled. The vampires were wild and ravenous beasts, snarling, snapping and hissing as they ran. Both Cade and Coran jumped up to their feet.

"We have to stop them!" Cade yelled, knowing exactly where the vampires were headed.

Cade and Coran both turned towards Adrien. Adrien looked up at them and nodded.

"Go," he whispered.

Cade and Coran swiftly turned around and jumped through the hole in the wall in pursuit of them.

"Now, this is my kinda party!" Kyle hooted.

Kyle, Gina and the third remaining Hunter chased after Cade and Coran.

Adrien, enraged with anger, pounded his fist into the floor. He then cautiously looked at Latimer, who remained still. Adrien stood to his feet and growled as he faced Evadin. The pain had fully subsided for him and he felt that he fully regained his strength—and more.

Adrien lunged at Evadin and attempted to strike, but Evadin leapt out of the way. Adrien continued to fight, but every swing missed as Evadin casually moved out of his range. Adrien grew even more enraged and began to move quicker. Balling his fist firmly, he jabbed his arm forward and struck Evadin in the chest. Evadin reacted immediately, the sole of his shoe met Adrien's abdomen, kicking him over the couches behind him. He landed on the floor next to Latimer's corpse, and Evadin jumped over the couch to continue their brawl.

Adrien quickly turned his head in Latimer's direction. Latimer was now covered in the same black veins as the other risen vampires, and his limbs started to move. His body began to slowly rise. When he finished rising to his feet his eyes opened, and like all of the others, they were also as black as night.

***

Groups of people out in the streets of the city were being led to their vehicles quickly by the cops. Michelle was standing next to her father as she helped one of the families get into their car. She reiterated to leave the state if possible. As the car drove off, Michelle looked down to see that the mother had dropped her necklace. It was a cross pendant similar to the one that she owned. She picked it up and ran after them.

"Hey! Wait!" she called out after the vehicle that quickly zoomed off and turned onto the next road.

Michelle kept chasing the car until she rounded the corner. The car was too far gone as the taillights quickly faded into the distance. There was a steady stream of cars now vacating the area.

SCREECH!

CRASH!

Screams and chaos suddenly echoed around the corner as the sound of vehicles crashing into one another increased. Loud popping followed as law enforcement began to open fire. Michelle, startled, sprinted back around the corner to see what was going on. Once she reached the road and rounded the corner building, she lost her footing on the ice, in horror of what she saw before her.

The horde of risen vampires had reached them. The creatures were tearing through crowds of people, jumping into the ambulances, throwing out the drivers and attacking them on the ground. People were running in a panic and were getting caught and devoured. The cops were shooting relentlessly, but the bullets had little effect on the vampires.

Michelle shuffled behind a parked car on the road and peeked around as she stayed low. Her heart raced as she fumbled around for her gun strapped in her holster. She then heard a family screaming not far from her position. She spotted them about twenty yards away. Michelle's father was with the family, shooting at a fast-approaching vampire. She got up and sprinted towards them. She slipped on the ice again but regained her footing to press on even quicker. The bullets from the chief's pistol barely slowed the vampire as it tackled him to the ground.

"DAD!" Michelle screamed. She tried to shoot, but she had no clear shot of the vampire.

The vampire then moved from Michelle's father and proceeded to attack the rest of the family. Tears streamed down Michelle's face as she yelled. She was closing in, and now that she had a clear shot, she fired at the vampire. The bullets did not stop it. Michelle threw herself on top to protect the little girl, now the only survivor of that small family, just before the vampire turned to attack her. Michelle pointed her semi-automatic pistol at the vampire and wrapped her other arm around the girl's head to cover her ears.

She opened fire, emptying the rest of the clip into the vampire as it was just inches away. It stumbled backward slightly but then snarled, crouching in preparation to attack. The vampire lunged forward just as a car with screaming people zoomed by, grazing the vampire on its arm. The vampire whipped around and jumped on top of the moving vehicle, shoving its hand into the roof of the vehicle and peeling it back like the top of a tin can. Reaching in, the vampire started yanking the people out and eating them on top of the moving car.

Michelle now had the child's eyes covered to protect her from the horrific display around them. Michelle spotted her Dad a few feet away and called after him, rushing over with the girl still in her arms. She set the child down briefly so she could quickly roll her father onto his back. He was still barely alive.

"Dad! We have to get you to—"

He held up his hand to silence her, and then he began to cough weakly. "Get...the girl...save her," he grunted. He winced before he closed his eyes.

Michelle desperately felt for her father's pulse and did not find it. She had no time to grieve as the commotion behind her continued to intensify. Michelle turned around and saw more vampires traveling their way. She hurriedly reached into her pocket and draped the cross that she had just found around the girl's neck, then she desperately searched around for refuge. She spotted a body bag only a few yards away. Michelle swept the child up into her arms and ran towards the body bag. She unzipped the bag as soon as they reached it.

"Alright, get in!" Michelle ordered.

The girl looked back at Michelle in fear and then grasped onto her tightly. Michelle tried to pry her from her torso but was unable to do so without hurting the little girl. Thinking quickly, Michelle climbed into the bag first. She then beckoned the girl again to come with her. They both squeezed into the bag and Michelle covered their faces with the black rubberized material, zipping themselves in.

***

Coran and Cade caught up to the horde of vampires. Coran jumped on top of the car where the vampire had torn into the vehicle, and it turned around to attack him. Coran wrestled with it as it tried to bite him. The vampire was snapping at him like a wild beast. Cade joined, grabbing the vampire from behind and quickly twisting its neck. The vampire slid down through the hole in the roof of the car that was now heading straight towards a building.

One last person was in the car, now pinned beneath the

fallen vampire. Cade reached in and pulled her out from under the creature. The fallen vampire started moving again, having already healed from the injury Cade inflicted on it.

"Jump!" Cade yelled to Coran.

Cade and Coran jumped off the car just before it crashed into the side of a building, causing an immediate explosion. Cade set the person in his hands down, and she quickly thanked him before she turned to run down the street. Hundreds of people were continuing to flee.

One car skid down the road, having lost traction on the icy pavement and hit a light post. That car, now blocking a lane, caused a pileup. Some of the risen vampires scaled buildings, breached apartments and yanked people out to devour them right on their balconies. The reporter who had been streaming live just a few moments before was sprawled out on the ground, the mic still loosely held in his hand. The cameraman was also dead, but the film was still rolling as bits and pieces of the attack were broadcast on live television.

In the chaos, Cade and Coran were outnumbered and overpowered.

"There's...there's just too many of them," Coran said in defeat as he looked around them.

Coran was suddenly tackled from behind, and so was Cade. Gina, Kyle and the other Hunter had caught up to them. Gina and Kyle had them both pinned down as the third Hunter approached with a piece of metal debris.

"Don't worry, we'll bring y'all back once y'all die," Kyle

hissed menacingly into their ears.

Just as the third Hunter wound up to strike Cade and Coran, the Hunter was thrown across the street. Cade and Coran looked up, seeing that help had arrived. Xylia, Kiana and Ransom appeared with another Harvester: Lazaro. Ransom tore Gina off Cade and threw her into Lazaro; she screeched as he beheaded her in a split second. Coran used the opportunity of distraction to gain the upper hand, kicking Kyle off him.

The risen vampire that crashed into the building in the fiery car explosion emerged from the wreckage, fully engulfed in flames. It saw the Harvesters and attacked. Xylia, Kiana, Lazaro and Ransom fought off the risen vampire and those passing by. They quickly realized that these new vampires were more difficult to kill.

Kyle landed in the middle of the street as people and risen vampires were stampeding along either side of him. The third Hunter that was also thrown across the street rose to his feet as one of the resurrected vampires grazed his shoulder. The risen vampire turned back around angrily and bit into the Hunter's arm, shaking him around in his mouth like a chew toy.

The Hunter fell to the ground when the risen vampire released him to continue down the road. The Hunter tossed back and forth, foaming at the mouth, then his skin was quickly consumed by the black veins as well. The once Hunter got back up, eyes pitch-black, and joined the other risen vampires in their rampage. All of them witnessed this and were stunned, including Kyle.

"Do not, under any circumstances, let those *things* bite you!" Cade called out as all the Harvesters fought to defend one another, and any human they could, from the risen ones.

The crowd of humans were thinning out at an alarming rate as the streets started to pile up with bodies. After Kyle had another look at the number of Harvester vampires that appeared and the increasing chaos, he flew off.

***

The sound of destruction and screams from out in the streets traveled all the way back into the abandoned nightclub. Latimer stood slightly hunched over but calmly breathing. It seemed as though he had no focus as he stared into vacant space. His nose began to instinctively twitch as he shifted his head to the right, his chin touching his shoulder. After looking over his shoulder through the hole in the wall behind him, he turned towards the large gash in the bricks and ran towards it.

Adrien, who was still on the floor, had been holding his breath. He exhaled sharply. "Latimer?!" he called out desperately.

Latimer immediately shifted his direction and headed for Adrien instead. The sound of Adrien's voice was a trigger, inciting a violent eruption from Latimer as he grew vicious. He jumped on top of Adrien, pinning him to the ground while he snapped at him, attempting to tear into his flesh.

"Latimer...Latimer! STOP! It's me!" Adrien yelled as he held him at bay. "It's me...Adrien!" Adrien cried out desperately, staring into his black, empty eyes.

Evadin stood not far off, watching with a smirk plastered

across his face. "That's no longer Latimer," Evadin said snidely.

Latimer turned his head in Evadin's direction and leapt off Adrien; Evadin was now his target. Evadin grinned as he tried to exercise his ability to control Latimer, but then his expression quickly changed as Latimer continued to approach him without hesitation. Latimer slashed into his abdomen. Evadin recoiled, and then grabbed Latimer, slamming him against a pillar.

"Haha, wonderful! This I did not foresee!" Evadin exclaimed as he covered his wound with his other hand.

Latimer broke free from Evadin's grasp, but then Evadin quickly grabbed him again and threw him further away. Latimer crashed through the aquarium glass lining the back wall, water gushing from the impact and forcing out shards of glass and dead marine animals onto the floor.

Having witnessed Evadin's loss of control over Latimer, Adrien planned quickly. He dashed over to Yve and grabbed her, forcing her directly in Latimer's line of sight as he emerged from the aquarium. Latimer then targeted Yve and tackled both her and Adrien to the ground. With Yve on top of Adrien, Latimer tore into her throat. Yve screamed as she attempted to force Latimer off of her with no success. Her blood started to trickle onto Adrien, who was pinned beneath her.

It was not long until Yve met her demise, and Adaeze instantly regained her free will.

"LATIMER!" Adaeze yelled. Adaeze ran towards Latimer as he stood to his feet.

"Adaeze, no!" Adrien grunted, still stuck between Yve and

the floor.

Latimer turned towards Adaeze, hissing as he lunged for her next. Adrien tossed Yve's body to the side and got up as fast as he could. He noticed that his speed had increased, as he caught up to Latimer and was able to restrain him just mere inches from Adaeze. Frozen where she stood, Adaeze gazed into his black, vacant eyes. Slobber dripped from the corners of Latimer's mouth as he continued to snarl.

"Latimer," Adaeze whispered.

She lifted her hands and placed them on either side of his head, steadying his face. The hissing stopped, but his upper lip was still slightly lifted in the corner.

"Do you recognize me?" Adaeze asked gently as she examined his face.

Adrien felt that Latimer was no longer fighting against him, so he slowly started to let go as he continued to watch him suspiciously. Just as Adrien's grip was almost released, Latimer snarled even louder than before and snapped at Adaeze, almost biting her cheek. Adrien grabbed onto him tighter and attempted to pull him back into his chest, but Latimer violently swung his elbow and dislodged himself from Adrien's grasp.

Latimer's weight shifted onto Adrien and they both fell onto the ground again. Adrien then wrapped his arms around Latimer's head and twisted abruptly, snapping his neck to knock him out. Latimer's body went limp as he stopped moving completely. Adrien sighed as he pushed Latimer off to the side.

"He's gone!" Adaeze yelled to Adrien.

Adrien started to assure her, "No, he will—"

"No, Evadin. He is gone!" Adaeze announced in panic.

Adrien twisted around to look for Evadin. There was a substantial trail of blood leading out the back door of the club into the alleyway. The ancient had disappeared.

Yve's body then started to move as she rose to her feet, now covered in black veins also. Adaeze and Adrien stood by silently as she followed the loud sounds and scents through the gaping hole in the wall. The club was now vacant, aside from the stunned duo and an unconscious Latimer.

Chapter 20

"Hope deferred makes the heart sick, but a longing fulfilled is a tree of life."

Proverbs 13:12

*I*t was just a quarter of an hour before sunrise. The streets that once resonated with the sounds of all the destruction and slaughter had fallen silent. The silence was deafening—contrary to any level the heart of a busy city should ever reach. There was the very faint crackle of embers as they slowly simmered out in the remains of a fire.

The silence was interrupted as the zipper to a body bag was ripped open. Michelle sat upright, gasping desperately for air. She turned quickly to the child who was sound asleep beside her, tears were dried onto her cheeks.

"Come on," Michelle coaxed gently as she peered around at their surroundings. She looked back down to the girl. "It's time to go," she whispered.

The child did not move. Michelle's heart dropped. She seemed to be asleep, but the lack of oxygen in the bag must have been too much for her tiny body to withstand. Michelle frantically repositioned herself as she hurriedly began to perform CPR on the child. With no response, Michelle looked around them in desperation, the streets seemingly vacant.

"Please! Someone!" she cried out, as her eyes landed on the abandoned ambulance in the distance. The lights still whirled silently with no evidence of anyone able-bodied near it. "Someone help us!" Michelle yelled as she continued to labor in her efforts to revive the child.

She blew air into the girl's mouth again and pressed her hands onto her chest, pumping firmly but gently to avoid cracking her delicate sternum. Suddenly the little girl began to cough, stilted breathing following steadily after.

"Oh...thank God!" Michelle sighed in relief.

Michelle continued to kneel next to her as she watched the child wake and slowly sit up. As the child began to look around, Michelle quickly blocked her view.

"My name is Michelle, what is yours?" she asked in an effort to distract her.

The girl blinked a few times and roughly rubbed her face before looking back at Michelle. Her eyes were big and glossy. Her dirty hands left muck on her cheeks.

"A-Ariel," her little voice whispered.

Michelle smiled, then brushed the girl's hair out of her

face and wiped off her cheeks with her sleeve. "That is a beautiful name! I am your friend, and I need you to come with me so I can make sure you stay safe, okay?" she asked.

The girl nodded hesitantly in response.

Michelle then stood to her feet and offered both of her hands out to her. "Are you ready, Ariel? We need to get you out of here." Michelle looked over both shoulders before facing the girl again. "You cannot look around you though…okay? I will need you to close your eyes and keep them shut tight. Can you do that for me?"

The little girl's eyes welled up with tears as she pursed her lips and puffed out her cheeks and chest. She nodded and moved closer to Michelle for her to pick her up. Propping the child onto her hip and firmly within her arms, she turned around and walked the roads, being careful to step over the bodies strewn across the pavement, including her father's.

She paused over him and held back her tears. "I'll come back for you," she whispered weakly.

Michelle withheld her full reaction, not wanting to alert the little girl in her arms. Gritting her teeth, it took all that she had within her to not scream in agony at what lay before her. Michelle's eyes scanned the area nervously, as she expected to also find her friend Anna among the ill-fated souls who tragically lost their lives. Fortunately, she did not see her body in the mass gravesite.

There were entire families who had died together. Within the rubble from the buildings where some of the vampires scaled and tore into apartments, there were even more bodies. Michelle glanced at the girl slung with her arms over her shoulder and her face digging into her neck. Her eyes were still shut tightly.

The road was blocked by rubble, but she remembered her car was just the next street over parked in an alleyway. Michelle made a beeline for the adjacent street. She spotted her car at the end of the alley parked right off to the side of one of the streets. With her vehicle in sight seemingly untouched, she ran to it. She yanked the back door open to her car and carefully buckled the child in the seat then sat down in the driver seat of the car, locking themselves inside of the vehicle.

Whipping out her cell phone, she felt a short-lived burst of relief, shattered when she realized her phone was unresponsive, having lost all battery power. No longer able to hold her emotions in, she broke down in tears in the car. She threw her phone down to the floor of the passenger seat and huffed, banging her head onto the steering wheel in defeat.

Abruptly, a loud noise filled the air as helicopters flew above the city skyline, shortly after a blast of sirens startled her. To her right, emergency vehicles and police started to funnel down one of the main roads. Michelle lifted her head and eyed the patrol cars as they passed; they were out of their jurisdiction, clearly there since the local forces were overpowered.

Michelle jumped out of the car and unbuckled the girl out of the back seat to run to the side of the road. One of the ambulances stopped for them.

***

Adrien sat and stared at the screen in front of him with his hand covering his mouth. The television was flashing images on the local news from just hours prior. He slowly looked around him to view the expressions of the others. Faces of fear, anger and confusion were the consensus.

There was no other place to convene on such short notice for the group of Harvesters. Many of the risen vampires had gotten away, and the Harvesters retreated as the day drew dangerously near. They had gathered now, eight in total: Adrien, Cade, Coran, Adaeze, Xylia, Kiana, Ransom and Lazaro in the music room at Latimer's home as they sought refuge from the sun. They moved the television into the room so they could watch any news stories unfold during the day.

Adrien's eyes fell on the one who was paying no mind to the news. Lazaro's eyes twitched as Adrien's locked onto his, and without hesitation, he got up and walked over. He had been watching Adrien instead of the television. Lazaro was staring at him intensely, his eyes wide like that of an owl stalking its prey. He stood in front of the screen with his arms crossed, looking down at Adrien as if observing an object on display at a museum.

"In the words of a wise man named Solomon, 'There is nothing new under the sun,'" he said. Lazaro dropped to eye level with Adrien and reached out, touching his skin.

Adrien flinched, and then he jumped up from his seat.

"But...*this* is something truly unprecedented," Lazaro said as he continued to stare at Adrien's vein riddled flesh.

Ransom stepped forwards. "The *impossible*...right before

our very eyes. What more could come of this?" Ransom then twisted around and his eye landed on Adaeze who was standing towards the back of the room. "What kind of new malison have you created?"

Lazaro pivoted as well, then aggressively approached Adaeze. "Nothing good, I am most certain. After all, YOU are responsible for the death of my own!" he growled.

The group of Hunters that Adaeze led attacked the Vermont Harvesters, destroyed all of their homes and murdered every single one of them, or so they had thought. After Ransom fled Voyage earlier in the night, he hurried to Vermont and searched the wreckage more thoroughly for Lazaro, who had been badly injured and buried beneath the ground and stories worth of debris. With his injuries and lack of feeding, Lazaro did not have enough strength to escape on his own. Only hours ago, when Ransom came to his aid, did he find out the fate of his friends. He fed and quickly regained his strength in a promise to destroy those responsible for it. They ran into Xylia and Kiana, who were fleeing, on the way. Lazaro and Ransom said they would join ranks in their fight, so they all came back.

Lazaro crossed the room, his stare of vengeance dead set on Adaeze. Adrien rushed over to get between them.

"HEY!" Adrien yelled. "Back off!"

They hissed at one another as a stand-off commenced. Lazaro's eyes kept jumping to Adaeze over Adrien's shoulder. He saw that her face was filled with unmistakable remorse.

"I'm so sorry," she whispered under her breath.

Lazaro blew air from his nose and grit his teeth. "'Sorry' does not even begin to atone for what you've brought upon me..." He paused, then looked around to the others in the room and also the carnage on the television. "To *all* of us!"

Coran, who had watched this interaction closely, also stood up. He took the remote control and paused the television just as a risen vampire was shown snarling into the camera.

"Lazaro, I am sorry for what has happened. But Adrien already explained this to you. Evadin is the one to blame for this all. The blood is on *his* hands, not hers. The way things stand, we cannot afford to be at arms with anyone in this room right now. We're all allies," Coran reasoned with him.

Lazaro's shoulders dropped. "You're right," he agreed half-heartedly. He moved back to the other side of the room and sat on one of the arms of the couch as he crossed his arms over his chest.

"Evadin mentioned that these new vampires," Cade added, "these...*Slayers*...have no sense of self-preservation. The sun must have overtaken all of the ones who got away, it must have finished our defense for us."

"Slayers, eh?" Adrien scoffed. "Is that what we're calling them?"

"I hope your theory is correct," Ransom spoke again. "They were exceedingly strong and unpredictable, far worse than the most feral Hunters I have had the displeasure of crossing."

Xylia, who had been pacing in the room, stopped and stood next to her daughter.

"As soon as the sun sets we must disperse. Search for more Slayers, exterminate them if there are any left," Xylia instructed.

"I cordially disagree," Lazaro stated from the couch. "Without our numbers, I guarantee every one of us would have succumbed to the Slayers last night and joined their ranks. We take one from *her* book," Lazaro said through gritted teeth as he avoided eye contact with Adaeze. "Ransom and I will make some calls before nightfall to warn others we know. We travel together, we gather more of us…we do *not* disperse."

"Sounds like a plan," Coran said in agreement.

Kiana cleared her throat. "What about you? What will you do?" Kiana said as she looked over to Adrien and Adaeze.

Adrien turned his head towards the door that was opened to the hallway. "We…don't know," he said solemnly.

***

Just a few hours before sunset, the others had migrated to the sleeping quarters. They were getting their well-needed rest before leaving upon nightfall. Adrien did not rest, but he instead paced outside of the door that led down to the basement. He paused with his hand over the knob, but then sighed heavily and walked away.

He found himself on the opposite side of the house. He was sitting in the shadows, staring out to the forest through one of the stone walls that was partially knocked down from the battle that originally took Latimer's life. The sunlight reflected off the dead branches and remaining snow while the trees swayed gently in the wind.

Adrien continued to stare, though the indirect light made his eyes sting. He still longed for what he saw. To feel the warmth on his skin again, the way he used to enjoy it. He stood to his feet as he heard someone approaching. He squinted into the light and saw someone come around the corner, peering into the home.

"I figured this would be the safest time for me to return. I am honestly surprised to see you're still in town." Michelle stood directly in the sun while looking into the shadows at Adrien.

"Why did you come back here?" Adrien peeked over her shoulder and scanned the trees around her. "Did you bring others with you?"

Michelle inhaled deeply, then sighed. "I am alone...no one knows about this place but me."

Adrien looked at her silently, then placed his hands on his hips impatiently.

"My father is dead. There was carnage for miles. There is damage that cannot be undone. I have never seen or heard of *anything* like this." Michelle paused as she took a very deep breath. She lifted her hand and shielded her eyes to see into the shadows better. Her eyes jumped at Adrien's new appearance. "What in the world?" she whispered.

Adrien looked down at himself, the yellow veins clearly visible. His skin looked translucent in areas where the veins were able to be seen even more clearly.

"I am sorry about your father. I know what it's like to lose one," Adrien said sympathetically as he stepped forward.

Michelle rubbed her face with one of her hands and looked off to the side. "He was a great man. He was a hero, though—he saved many by starting the evacuation." It was silent for a while as she thought about her next words, then she continued to speak, "Some people survived the attack itself, and those people were only able to get away because of your...*friends*."

Adrien pursed his lips, then he looked down at his feet.

She then added on, "The news was blocked beyond the local channels. They didn't want to incite a nationwide panic. They're in denial—they have chalked it up to be anything but the supernatural. They fabricated an explanation, saying that a contaminated water source made...*people*...become violent and cause mayhem. We have upped our patrols with orders to terminate on sight anyone who resembles anything of what we saw last night."

"Seriously?" Adrien whispered. He put his hand to his chin then squinted as he looked at Michelle. "Why are you telling me this?"

"I give you information hoping for some in return," she said expectedly.

"What do you want to know?" Adrien asked in hesitation.

"I want you to tell me how to kill you, and those like you," she said sternly.

"Are you planning to kill me?" he asked.

"I saw who you used to be, before all of this. I see that what you are now was not your own doing. What happened to you could have happened to anyone," she reasoned.

Adrien sighed, relieved that there was someone else who remembered how he used to be.

Michelle then tapped her fists together and looked at him through her brow. "For some reason, all of this...all that has happened: the park, Jenna, even up until now...I was led to you for a reason. I don't know why, but I am not supposed to kill you. I don't understand it, not one bit."

"And who told you that?" Adrien asked. "That you're not supposed to kill me?" he clarified further.

She looked up to the sky that continued to darken as night approached. "I'm not sure you would believe me," she said.

They stood in silence for a while, neither of them budging an inch from where they were firmly planted.

"A stake to the heart," he sighed. He then looked at her neck with the cross pendant. "The cross is a weakness for us, as well as UV rays and beheading. That's how you kill us."

Michelle turned her back to Adrien. "Thank you," she said as she walked away and slipped back into the woods.

***

Night had fallen, and the Harvesters had geared up and prepared to leave. They all convened in the foyer. As Lazaro and Ransom spoke to Cade, Xylia and Kiana about their plan of action, Coran stepped up to Adrien.

"We will keep in touch," Coran said, then he turned around in search for Adaeze. "Where is she?"

Adrien nudged his head down the hall. "She's with him."

Coran nodded, then looked down to his feet. "I understand why you are doing this." He looked back up to Adrien intensely. "Be careful, though. It may look like him but...it isn't. Not anymore, at least," Coran sadly warned Adrien.

Adrien sighed, then looked off to the side. Coran patted him on the shoulder before he turned around to join the others. With their weapons they fashioned out of remaining debris lying around the stone home, the Harvesters set out to leave after they said their goodbyes.

Adrien stood in silence for a few minutes. He closed his eyes, breathing in deeply. The silence was broken when the door to the basement was slammed. He looked over to see Adaeze now leaned up against the door, her nails digging into the wood as tears streamed down her face. She sensed that Adrien was watching her. She glanced over to him and then turned the opposite direction before disappearing into one of the other rooms.

He sighed again as he focused on the door. Adrien had avoided going down there since they returned. The thought of seeing Latimer in the state that he was in again sent chills down his spine. Guilt weighed him down, as well. Adrien turned to enter the music room, then shortly afterwards he approached the door to the basement. He opened the door slowly and quietly walked down the steps into the dark corridor.

The sound of Latimer banging against the reinforced bars and chains holding the cell doors closed echoed eerily from the end of the hall. Adrien took a deep breath and continued to trek the hall until he reached the cell. Within his hands were a chair and his cello. He tossed the chair down and sat in front of the cell. Adrien held eye contact with Latimer as he snarled and growled, slobber occasionally flying out through the bars and onto the stone floor just outside of the enclosure.

He picked up his bow and began to play. The weighty notes slightly drowned out the monstrous sounds coming from Latimer as they echoed through the narrow, dark hallway. Closing his eyes now, Adrien entered into his memories. Adrien saw his father as he leaned down to hug him and kiss him before he left the house the night that he died. There were no longer any holes in the memory, as now he could clearly see it all. Adrien also remembered seeing Latimer as he reached into his crib that night. Not only did Latimer touch him, but he sang Adrien a song to comfort him. The same song that was the first song he learned on his cello, the same song that played as he proposed to Jenna, the same song he had decided to play now. Adrien had never realized, until that moment, where he had first heard it.

Adrien chuckled, then he opened his eyes. To his surprise, Latimer, though eyes still black, was no longer ravenous, but was slowly swaying in the cell. Adrien's adrenaline spiked, and he continued to play the song even louder.

A hand gently touched Adrien on the shoulder, and he turned to see that Adaeze had joined him down there.

"We used to sing this song to our son..." she whispered, with a slight grin across her lips, though her eyes still expressed melancholy.

Adrien smiled and leaned into her hand as he continued to play. Soon after, she lifted her voice and began to gently sing the words to the song. Minutes turned into hours that they spent down there, singing and playing the same tune.

"Adrien..." a faint voice suddenly murmured.

The cello dropped to the stone floor as Adrien leapt up and pressed against the cell bars, peering in at Latimer.

"Latimer!" he called out in excitement.

Latimer was on his knees at the cell door with one of his hands grasping onto the bars. Adaeze dropped to her knees also and shuffled up to the metal. She placed her hand onto his and he slowly looked up, squinting at her.

"Adaeze?" he whispered weakly. "My bride...have I made it to Heaven?"

He reached between the bars to touch her chin, and she allowed him to pull her in closer. They gently kissed.

Adaeze began to speak, "*Mon amour! Je suis désolé*...I did not kno—"

"My darling, do not apologize," he responded softly.

"It is like music to my ears to hear your voice after all of these years," Adaeze said longingly.

Latimer sighed as they both leaned into the bars until their foreheads touched. "As is yours to mine," he whispered back.

They had several intimate moments, then Latimer looked over to Adrien, who was patiently waiting. Adrien saw that the dark veins remained on Latimer's skin, but the blackness faded from his eyes partially. Latimer's eyes, aside from that, looked extremely different than before. There was a sense of hope, and yet, a vast fear and despair in them.

Adrien jumped to his feet and began to rustle with the chains on the cell door. "Let's get you out of there," he said quickly.

"No!" Latimer yelled.

Adrien dropped the chains immediately. "Why? You're fine...there's no use for you to be in there now," he reasoned with him.

Latimer stood to his feet, his eyes quivering as they continued to fill with even more fear and despair. Adrien could not grasp why he was so fearful. What did he remember? What did he see?

"Latimer...what did you see? When you died?" Adrien said, his eyes flickered to Adaeze as he asked the question.

She stood up also and looked at Latimer quietly, curious of his answer. Latimer's eyes grew large, his face wincing and his jaw cracking as his teeth ground against each other. Adrien recognized this as a response to something he did not want to speak about.

Latimer squinted his eyes. "How am I here?" he asked, filled with confusion.

"I will explain. I promise. Tell me...if you saw anything at all...what did you see?" Adrien asked in deep concern.

Latimer slowly backed up and shuffled to the far right side of the cell. He looked the other way in silence for a few moments, then closed his eyes. "Though we are immortal in this world," he began to speak, "*this* world is only temporary," he said.

"What do you mean?" Adaeze asked.

"I saw it from afar, and there is only one way." He paused again, racking through his thoughts. "It leads to a paradise of all paradises. No more pain, no more hunger, no more sickness, no more...*darkness*."

"If this is so, then why do you seem so afraid? That sounds like something I would want...don't you?" Adrien asked curiously.

Latimer stared forwards without blinking. "More than you can imagine," he said solemnly.

Adrien gasped. "What have I done? Did I take you from that, Latimer?" he asked, suddenly feeling a flood of guilt rush back to him, yet again.

Latimer's eyes widened, but he still did not blink. "*No...*" he said darkly.

"Then..." Adrien trailed off, unsure of what to say next.

"How deep we allow this darkness to take us is ultimately our choice. It has always been our choice," Latimer said. "But... with what we *are*, I am unsure if this is obtainable to us, this paradise of paradises," his voice began to tremble. "How could it? *How* could it be?"

Adaeze and Adrien looked at one another, and then back

to Latimer bleakly.

"Now, what happened while I was...gone? How am I here?" Latimer asked again. He walked towards the cell door once more and pressed his face against the iron.

Adaeze immediately grabbed onto his hand as it dangled on the other side, holding it firmly within hers. She squeezed his hand, and then looked over to Adrien to nod, encouraging him to explain.

"Evadin pitted us against one another, the body count from the battle here was intentional," Adrien began to explain. "Adaeze's venom is now also in my veins. Having both yours and hers within me created..." he looked down at himself, specifically the bulging veins surfacing his skin, "*this*. Evadin used me to raise you all from the dead. But when they all came back, they were not the same. *You* were not the same. Stronger, faster... empty shells."

"For...what purpose?" Latimer asked hesitantly.

"To create an army. He...said that these new vampires would fulfill our true original purpose: to exterminate the humans."

"Where is he?" Latimer questioned further.

"We don't know. He vanished," Adaeze explained.

"You must go," Latimer demanded. "You cannot stay here or he will find you...*use you* again, Adrien."

"Okay. Let's get you out of the cell first and we can all go together," Adrien said as he grabbed back onto the chains.

"No, something is still wrong. Leave me in here," Latimer said.

"Latimer...come on," Adrien argued.

"Leave me, Adrien!" Latimer demanded.

Adrien was not listening and started to break the chains off with his hands.

"LEAVE ME!" Latimer's voice boomed in the corridor so loudly that both Adrien and Adaeze stumbled back from the cell.

Latimer's eyes blackened and he began to snarl, sounding like the same monster from before. The one they knew was now no longer present with them again.

"Latimer?" Adrien whispered.

Adrien reached down and picked up his cello. Latimer shoved his arm through the bars as he tried to reach for Adrien, but rather grabbed onto the handle of the cello. Adrien pulled against him and Latimer crushed the wood with his hands, breaking off the handle. Adrien was flung back, hitting the wall behind him with the wrecked instrument left in his hands.

Adrien grasped tightly onto the broken pieces, then he rushed out of the basement and into the foyer. He bent over while propping himself up against the wall. He breathed heavily as his adrenaline rushed, but then he managed to crack a smile. He stood up straight and looked over to Adaeze who had followed him out there. Adaeze looked at him, at first confused, but then she smiled back. They had an unspoken understanding. The Latimer that they loved was still within the creature locked up below; no matter what, they would *never* leave him.

Adrien inhaled deeply, then he turned to walk outside with the instrument fragments still in his hands. It was broken, but it was nothing that couldn't be repaired. Once outside, he lifted his head and gazed up at the sky as the thick clouds parted to reveal the moon shining brightly. This was not at all what he had imagined, but he finally had the family he had longed for all his life. He felt a peace within him that he hadn't experienced since the last time he reflected at the moon and stars on his private beach while human.

Though Adrien mostly obtained what he had hoped for, he still felt a substantial hole aside from the loss of Jenna. An unexpected void was still there, an abyss evidently in his soul. He couldn't identify what it was—or how to fill the hole—but he also felt closer to discovering the solution. He was filled with new hope, knowing that he would find his answer one day.

www.ingramcontent.com/pod-product-compliance
Lightning Source LLC
Chambersburg PA
CBHW051607100726
47898CB00001B/267